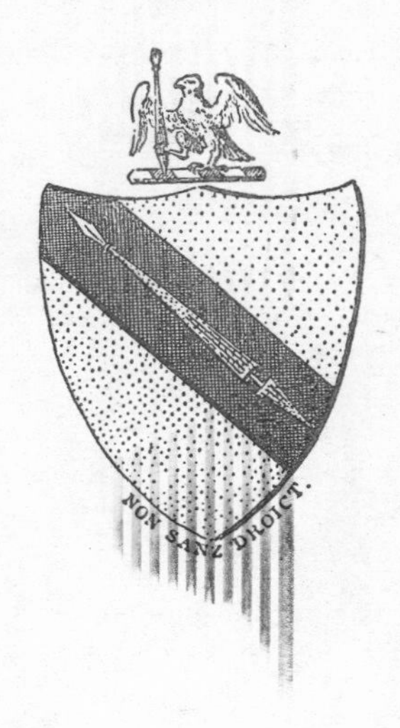
NON SANZ DROICT.

William Shakespeare

and

John Fletcher

THE TWO NOBLE KINSMEN

Edited by Clifford Leech

The Signet Classic Shakespeare
GENERAL EDITOR: SYLVAN BARNET

PUBLISHED BY THE NEW AMERICAN LIBRARY,
NEW YORK AND TORONTO,
THE NEW ENGLISH LIBRARY LIMITED, LONDON

CAREFULLY SELECTED, EDITED, AND PRINTED, SIGNET CLASSICS PROVIDE A TREASURY OF THE WORLD'S GREAT WRITINGS IN HANDSOMELY DESIGNED VOLUMES.

Library of Congress Catalog Card Number: 66–26767

First Printing, September, 1966

SIGNET CLASSICS *are published* in the United States *by The New American Library, Inc., 1301 Avenue of the Americas, New York, New York 10019,* in Canada *by The New American Library of Canada Limited, 295 King Street East, Toronto 2, Ontario,* in the United Kingdom *by The New English Library Limited, Barnard's Inn, Holborn, London, E.C.1, England*

PRINTED IN THE UNITED STATES OF AMERICA

Contents

Shakespeare: Prefatory Remarks

Between the record of his baptism in Stratford on 26 April 1564 and the record of his burial in Stratford on 25 April 1616, some forty documents name Shakespeare, and many others name his parents, his children, and his grandchildren. More facts are known about William Shakespeare than about any other playwright of the period except Ben Jonson. The facts should, however, be distinguished from the legends. The latter, inevitably more engaging and better known, tell us that the Stratford boy killed a calf in high style, poached deer and rabbits, and was forced to flee to London, where he held horses outside a playhouse. These traditions are only traditions; they may be true, but no evidence supports them, and it is well to stick to the facts.

Mary Arden, the dramatist's mother, was the daughter of a substantial landowner; about 1557 she married John Shakespeare, who was a glove-maker and trader in various farm commodities. In 1557 John Shakespeare was a member of the Council (the governing body of Stratford), in 1558 a constable of the borough, in 1561 one of the two town chamberlains, in 1565 an alderman (entitling him to the appellation "Mr."), in 1568 high bailiff—the town's highest political office, equivalent to mayor. After 1577, for an unknown reason he drops out of local politics. The birthday of William Shakespeare, the eldest son of this locally prominent man, is unrecorded; but the Stratford parish register records that the infant was baptized on 26 April 1564. (It is quite possible that he was born on 23 April, but this date has probably been assigned by tradition because it is the date on which, fifty-two years later, he died.) The attendance records of the Stratford grammar school of the period are not extant, but it is reasonable to assume that the son of a local official attended the school and received substantial training in Latin. The masters of the school from Shakespeare's seventh to fifteenth years held Oxford degrees; the Elizabethan curriculum excluded mathematics and the natural sciences but taught a good deal of Latin rhetoric, logic, and literature. On 27 November 1582 a marriage license was issued to Shakespeare and Anne Hathaway, eight years his senior. The couple had a child in May, 1583. Perhaps the marriage was necessary, but perhaps the couple had earlier engaged in a formal "troth plight" which would render their children legitimate even if no further ceremony were performed. In 1585 Anne Hathaway bore Shakespeare twins.

That Shakespeare was born is excellent; that he married and had children is pleasant; but that we know nothing about his departure from Stratford to London, or about the beginning of his theatrical career, is lamentable and must be admitted. We would gladly sacrifice details about his children's baptism for details about his earliest days on the stage. Perhaps the poaching episode is true (but it is first reported almost a century after Shakespeare's death), or perhaps he first left Stratford to be a schoolteacher, as another tradition holds; perhaps he was moved by

> Such winds as scatters young men through the world,
> To seek their fortunes further than at home
> Where small experience grows.

In 1592, thanks to the cantankerousness of Robert Greene, a rival playwright and a pamphleteer, we have our first reference, a snarling one, to Shakespeare as an actor and playwright. Greene warns those of his own educated friends who wrote for the theater against an actor who has presumed to turn playwright:

> There is an upstart crow, beautified with our feathers, that with his *tiger's heart wrapped in a player's hide* sup-

> poses he is as well able to bombast out a blank verse as the best of you, and being an absolute Johannes-factotum is in his own conceit the only Shake-scene in a country.

The reference to the player, as well as the allusion to Aesop's crow (who strutted in borrowed plumage, as an actor struts in fine words not his own), makes it clear that by this date Shakespeare had both acted and written. That Shakespeare is meant is indicated not only by "Shake-scene" but by the parody of a line from one of Shakespeare's plays, *3 Henry VI:* "O, tiger's heart wrapped in a woman's hide." If Shakespeare in 1592 was prominent enough to be attacked by an envious dramatist, he probably had served an apprenticeship in the theater for at least a few years.

In any case, by 1592 Shakespeare had acted and written, and there are a number of subsequent references to him as an actor: documents indicate that in 1598 he is a "principal comedian," in 1603 a "principal tragedian," in 1608 he is one of the "men players." The profession of actor was not for a gentleman, and it occasionally drew the scorn of university men who resented writing speeches for persons less educated than themselves, but it was respectable enough: players, if prosperous, were in effect members of the bourgeoisie, and there is nothing to suggest that Stratford considered William Shakespeare less than a solid citizen. When, in 1596, the Shakespeares were granted a coat of arms, the grant was made to Shakespeare's father, but probably William Shakespeare (who the next year bought the second-largest house in town) had arranged the matter on his own behalf. In subsequent transactions he is occasionally styled a gentleman.

Although in 1593 and 1594 Shakespeare published two narrative poems dedicated to the Earl of Southampton, *Venus and Adonis* and *The Rape of Lucrece,* and may well have written most or all of his sonnets in the middle nineties, Shakespeare's literary activity seems to have been almost entirely devoted to the theater. (It may be significant that the two narrative poems were written in years when the plague closed the theaters for several months.)

In 1594 he was a charter member of a theatrical company called the Chamberlain's Men (which in 1603 changed its name to the King's Men); until he retired to Stratford (about 1611, apparently), he was with this remarkably stable company. From 1599 the company acted primarily at the Globe Theatre, in which Shakespeare held a one-tenth interest. Other Elizabethan dramatists are known to have acted, but no other is known also to have been entitled to a share in the profits of the playhouse.

Shakespeare's first eight published plays did not have his name on them, but this is not remarkable; the most popular play of the sixteenth century, Thomas Kyd's *The Spanish Tragedy,* went through many editions without naming Kyd, and Kyd's authorship is known only because a book on the profession of acting happens to quote (and attribute to Kyd) some lines on the interest of Roman emperors in the drama. What is remarkable is that after 1598 Shakespeare's name commonly appears on printed plays—some of which are not his. Another indication of his popularity comes from Francis Meres, author of *Palladis Tamia: Wit's Treasury* (1598): in this anthology of snippets accompanied by an essay on literature, many playwrights are mentioned, but Shakespeare's name occurs more often than any other, and Shakespeare is the only playwright whose plays are listed.

From his acting, playwriting, and share in a theater, Shakespeare seems to have made considerable money. He put it to work, making substantial investments in Stratford real estate. When he made his will (less than a month before he died), he sought to leave his property intact to his descendants. Of small bequests to relatives and to friends (including three actors, Richard Burbage, John Heminges, and Henry Condell), that to his wife of the second-best bed has provoked the most comment; perhaps it was the bed the couple had slept in, the best being reserved for visitors. In any case, had Shakespeare not excepted it, the bed would have gone (with the rest of his household possessions) to his daughter and her husband. On 25 April 1616 he was buried within the chancel of the church at Stratford. An unattractive monument to his memory, placed on a wall near the grave, says he died on 23 April. Over the grave itself are the lines, perhaps by Shakespeare, that (more than his literary fame) have kept his bones undisturbed in the crowded burial ground where old bones were often dislodged to make way for new:

> Good friend, for Jesus' sake forbear
> To dig the dust enclosèd here.
> Blessed be the man that spares these stones
> And cursed be he that moves my bones.

Thirty-seven plays, as well as some nondramatic poems, are held to constitute the Shakespeare canon. The dates of composition of most of the works are highly uncertain, but there is often evidence of a *terminus a quo* (starting point) and/or a *terminus ad quem* (terminal point) that provides a framework for intelligent guessing. For example, *Richard II* cannot be earlier than 1595, the publication date of some material to which it is indebted; *The Merchant of Venice* cannot be later than 1598, the year Francis Meres mentioned it. Sometimes arguments for a date hang on an alleged topical allusion, such as the lines about the unseasonable weather in *A Midsummer Night's Dream,* II.i.81–117, but such an allusion (if indeed it is an allusion) can be variously interpreted, and in any case there is always the possibility that a topical allusion was inserted during a revision, years after the composition of a play. Dates are often attributed on the basis of style, and although conjectures about style usually rest on other conjectures, sooner or later one must rely on one's literary sense. There is no real proof, for example, that *Othello* is not as early as *Romeo and Juliet,* but one feels *Othello* is later, and because the first record of its performance is 1604, one is glad enough to set its composition at that date and not push it back into Shakespeare's early years. The following chronology, then, is as much indebted to informed guesswork and sensitivity as it is to fact. The dates, necessarily imprecise, indicate something like a scholarly consensus.

PLAYS

1588–93	*The Comedy of Errors*
1588–94	*Love's Labor's Lost*
1590–91	*2 Henry VI*
1590–91	*3 Henry VI*
1591–92	*1 Henry VI*
1592–93	*Richard III*
1592–94	*Titus Andronicus*
1593–94	*The Taming of the Shrew*
1593–95	*The Two Gentlemen of Verona*
1594–96	*Romeo and Juliet*
1595	*Richard II*
1594–96	*A Midsummer Night's Dream*
1596–97	*King John*
1596–97	*The Merchant of Venice*
1597	*1 Henry IV*
1597–98	*2 Henry IV*
1598–1600	*Much Ado About Nothing*
1598–99	*Henry V*
1599	*Julius Caesar*
1599–1600	*As You Like It*
1599–1600	*Twelfth Night*
1600–01	*Hamlet*
1597–1601	*The Merry Wives of Windsor*
1601–02	*Troilus and Cressida*
1602–04	*All's Well That Ends Well*
1603–04	*Othello*
1604	*Measure for Measure*
1605–06	*King Lear*
1605–06	*Macbeth*
1606–07	*Antony and Cleopatra*
1605–08	*Timon of Athens*
1607–09	*Coriolanus*
1608–09	*Pericles*
1609–10	*Cymbeline*
1610–11	*The Winter's Tale*
1611	*The Tempest*
1612–13	*Henry VIII*

POEMS

1592	*Venus and Adonis*
1593–94	*The Rape of Lucrece*
1593–1600	*Sonnets*
1600–01	*The Phoenix and Turtle*

Shakespeare's Theater

In Shakespeare's infancy, Elizabethan actors performed wherever they could—in great halls, at court, in the courtyards of inns. The innyards must have made rather unsatisfactory theaters: on some days they were unavailable because carters bringing goods to London used them as depots; when available, they had to be rented from the innkeeper; perhaps most important, London inns were subject to the Common Council of London, which was not well disposed toward theatricals. In 1574 the Common Council required that plays and playing places in London be licensed. It asserted that

> sundry great disorders and inconveniences have been found to ensue to this city by the inordinate haunting of great multitudes of people, specially youth, to plays, interludes, and shows, namely occasion of frays and quarrels, evil practices of incontinency in great inns having chambers and secret places adjoining to their open stages and galleries,

and ordered that innkeepers who wished licenses to hold performances put up a bond and make contributions to the poor.

The requirement that plays and innyard theaters be licensed, along with the other drawbacks of playing at inns, probably drove James Burbage (a carpenter-turned-actor) to rent in 1576 a plot of land northeast of the city walls and to build here—on property outside the jurisdiction of the city—England's first permanent construction designed for plays. He called it simply the Theatre. About all that is known of its construction is that it was wood. It soon had imitators, the most famous being the Globe (1599), built across the Thames (again outside the city's jurisdiction), out of timbers of the Theatre, which had been dismantled when Burbage's lease ran out.

There are three important sources of information about the structure of Elizabethan playhouses—drawings, a contract, and stage directions in plays. Of drawings, only the so-called De Witt drawing (c. 1596) of the Swan—really a friend's copy of De Witt's drawing—is of much significance. It shows a building of three tiers, with a stage jutting from a wall into the yard or center of the building. The tiers are roofed, and part of the stage is covered by a roof that projects from the rear and is supported at its front on two posts, but the groundlings, who paid a penny to stand in front of the stage, were exposed to the sky. (Performances in such a playhouse were held only in the daytime; artificial illumination was not used.) At the rear of the stage are two doors; above the stage is a gallery. The second major source of information, the contract for the Fortune, specifies that although the Globe is to be the model, the Fortune is to be square, eighty feet outside and fifty-five inside. The stage is to be forty-three feet broad, and is to extend into the middle of the yard (i.e., it is twenty-seven and a half feet deep). For patrons willing to pay more than the general admission charged of the groundlings, there were to be three galleries provided with seats. From the third chief source, stage directions, one learns that entrance to the stage was by doors, presumably spaced widely apart at the rear ("Enter one citizen at one door, and another at the other"), and that in addition to the platform stage there was occasionally some sort of curtained booth or alcove allowing for "discovery" scenes, and some sort of playing space "aloft" or "above" to represent (for example) the top of a city's walls or a room above the street. Doubtless each theater had its own peculiarities, but perhaps we can talk about a "typical" Elizabethan theater if we realize that no theater need exactly have fit the description, just as no father is the typical father with 3.7 children. This hypothetical theater is wooden, round or polygonal (in *Henry V* Shakespeare calls it a "wooden *O*"), capable of holding some eight hundred spectators standing in the yard around the projecting elevated stage and some fifteen hundred additional spectators seated in the three roofed galleries. The stage, protected by a "shadow" or "heavens" or roof, is entered by two doors; behind the doors is the "tiring house" (attiring house, i.e., dressing room), and above the doors is some sort of gallery that may sometimes hold spectators but that can be used (for example) as the bedroom from which Romeo—according to a stage direction in one text —"goeth down." Some evidence suggests that a throne can be lowered onto the platform stage, perhaps from the "shadow"; certainly characters can descend from the stage through a trap or traps into the cellar or "hell." Sometimes this space beneath the platform accommodates a sound-effects man or musician (in *Antony and Cleopatra* "music of the hautboys is under the stage") or an actor (in *Hamlet* the "Ghost cries under the stage"). Most characters simply walk on and off, but because there is no curtain in front of the platform, corpses will have to be carried off (Hamlet must lug Polonius' guts into the neighbor room), or will have to fall at the rear, where the curtain on the alcove or booth can be drawn to conceal them.

Such may have been the so-called "public theater." Another kind of theater, called the "private theater" because its much greater admission charge limited its audience to the wealthy or the prodigal, must be briefly mentioned. The private theater was basically a large room, entirely roofed and therefore artificially illuminated, with a stage at one end. In 1576 one such theater was established in Blackfriars, a Dominican priory in London that had been suppressed in 1538 and confiscated by the Crown and thus was not under the city's jurisdiction. All the actors in the Blackfriars theater were boys about eight to thirteen years old (in the public theaters similar boys played female parts; a boy Lady Macbeth played to a man Macbeth). This private theater had a precarious existence, and ceased operations in 1584. In 1596 James Burbage, who had already made theatrical history by building the Theatre, began to construct a second Blackfriars theater. He died in 1597, and for several years this second Blackfriars theater was used by a troupe of boys, but in 1608 two of Burbage's sons and five other actors (including Shakespeare) became joint operators of the theater, using it in the winter when the open-air Globe was unsuitable. Perhaps such a smaller theater, roofed, artificially illuminated, and with a tradition of a courtly audience, exerted an influence on Shakespeare's late plays.

Performances in the private theaters may well have had intermissions during which music was played, but in the public theaters the action was probably uninterrupted, flowing from scene to scene almost without a break. Actors would enter, speak, exit, and others would immediately enter and establish (if necessary) the new locale by a few properties and by words and gestures. Here are some samples of Shakespeare's scene painting:

> This is Illyria, lady.
>
> Well, this is the Forest of Arden.
>
> This castle hath a pleasant seat; the air
> Nimbly and sweetly recommends itself
> Unto our gentle senses.

On the other hand, it is a mistake to conceive of the Elizabethan stage as bare. Although Shakespeare's Chorus in *Henry V* calls the stage an "unworthy scaffold" and urges the spectators to "eke out our performance with your mind," there was considerable spectacle. The last act of *Macbeth,* for example, has five stage directions calling for "drum and colors," and another sort of appeal to the eye is indicated by the stage direction "Enter Macduff, with Macbeth's head." Some scenery and properties may have been substantial; doubtless a throne was used, and in one play of the period we encounter this direction: "Hector takes up a great piece of rock and casts at Ajax, who tears up a young tree by the roots and assails Hector."

The matter is of some importance, and will be glanced at again in the next section.

The Texts of Shakespeare

Though eighteen of his plays were published during his lifetime, Shakespeare seems never to have supervised their publication. There is nothing unusual here; when a playwright sold a play to a theatrical company he surrendered his ownership of it. Normally a company would not publish the play, because to publish it meant to allow competitors to acquire the piece. Some plays, however, did get published: apparently treacherous actors sometimes pieced together a play for a publisher, sometimes a company in need of money sold a play, and sometimes a company allowed a play to be published that no longer drew audiences. That Shakespeare did not concern himself with publication, then, is scarcely remarkable; of his contemporaries only Ben Jonson carefully supervised the publication of his own plays. In 1623, seven years after Shakespeare's death, John Heminges and Henry Condell (two senior members of Shakespeare's company, who had performed with him for about twenty years) collected his plays—published and unpublished—into a large volume, commonly called the First Folio. (A folio is a volume consisting of sheets that have been folded once, each sheet thus making two leaves, or four pages. The eighteen plays published during Shakespeare's lifetime had been issued one play per volume in small books called quartos. Each sheet in a quarto has been folded twice, making four leaves, or eight pages.) The First Folio contains thirty-six plays; a thirty-seventh, *Pericles,* though not in the Folio is regarded as canonical. Heminges and Condell suggest in an address "To the great variety of readers" that the republished plays are presented in better form than in the quartos: "Before you were abused with diverse stolen and surreptitious copies, maimed and deformed by the frauds and stealths of injurious impostors that exposed them; even those, are now offered to your view cured and perfect of their limbs, and all the rest absolute in their numbers, as he [i.e., Shakespeare] conceived them."

Whoever was assigned to prepare the texts for publication in the First Folio seems to have taken his job seriously and yet not to have performed it with uniform care. The sources of the texts seem to have been, in general, good unpublished copies or the best published copies. The first play in the collection, *The Tempest,* is divided into acts and scenes, has unusually full stage directions and descriptions of spectacle, and concludes with a list of the characters, but the editor was not able (or willing) to present all of the succeeding texts so fully dressed. Later texts occasionally show signs of carelessness: in one scene of *Much Ado About Nothing* the names of actors, instead of characters, appear as speech prefixes, as they had in the quarto, which the Folio reprints; proofreading throughout the Folio is spotty and apparently was done without reference to the printer's copy; the pagination of *Hamlet* jumps from 156 to 257.

A modern editor of Shakespeare must first select his copy; no problem if the play exists only in the Folio, but a considerable problem if the relationship between a quarto and the Folio—or an early quarto and a later one—is unclear. When an editor has chosen what seems to him to be the most authoritative text or texts for his copy, he has not done with making decisions. First of all, he must reckon with Elizabethan spelling. If he is not producing a facsimile, he probably modernizes it, but ought he to preserve the old form of words that apparently were pronounced quite unlike their modern forms—"lanthorn," "alablaster"? If he preserves these forms, is he really preserving Shakespeare's forms or perhaps those of a compositor in the printing house? What is one to do when one finds "lanthorn" and "lantern" in adjacent lines? (The editors of this series in general, but not invariably, assume that words should be spelled in their modern form.) Elizabethan punctuation, too, presents problems. For example in the First Folio, the only text for the play, Macbeth rejects his wife's idea that he can wash the blood from his hand:

> no: this my Hand will rather
> The multitudinous Seas incarnardine,
> Making the Greene one, Red.

Obviously an editor will remove the superfluous capitals, and he will probably alter the spelling to "incarnadine," but will he leave the comma before "red," letting Macbeth speak of the sea as "the green one," or will he (like most modern editors) remove the comma and thus have Macbeth say that his hand will make the ocean *uniformly* red?

An editor will sometimes have to change more than spelling or punctuation. Macbeth says to his wife:

> I dare do all that may become a man,
> Who dares no more, is none.

For two centuries editors have agreed that the second line is unsatisfactory, and have emended "no" to "do": "Who dares do more is none." But when in the same play Ross says that fearful persons

> floate vpon a wilde and violent Sea
> Each way, and moue,

need "move" be emended to "none," as it often is, on the hunch that the compositor misread the manuscript? The editors of the Signet Classic Shakespeare have restrained themselves from making abundant emendations. In their minds they hear Dr. Johnson on the dangers of emending: "I have adopted the Roman sentiment, that it is more honorable to save a citizen than to kill an enemy." Some departures (in addition to spelling, punctuation, and lineation) from the copy text have of course been made, but the original readings are listed in a note following the play, so that the reader can evaluate them for himself.

The editors of the Signet Classic Shakespeare, following tradition, have added line numbers and in many cases act and scene divisions as well as indications of locale at the beginning of scenes. The Folio divided most of the plays into acts and some into scenes. Early eighteenth-century editors increased the divisions. These divisions, which provide a convenient way of referring to passages in the plays, have been retained, but when not in the text chosen as the basis for the Signet Classic text they are enclosed in square brackets [ ] to indicate that they are editorial additions. Similarly, although no play of Shakespeare's published during his lifetime was equipped with indications of locale at the heads of scene divisions, locales have here been added in square brackets for the convenience of the reader, who lacks the information afforded to spectators by costumes, properties, and gestures. The spectator can tell at a glance he is in the throne room, but without an editorial indication the reader may be puzzled for a while. It should be mentioned, incidentally, that there are a few authentic stage directions—perhaps Shakespeare's, perhaps a prompter's—that suggest locales: for example, "Enter Brutus in his orchard," and "They go up into the Senate house." It is hoped that the bracketed additions provide the reader with the sort of help provided in these two authentic directions, but it is equally hoped that the reader will remember that the stage was not loaded with scenery.

No editor during the course of his work can fail to recollect some words Heminges and Condell prefixed to the Folio:

> It had been a thing, we confess, worthy to have been wished, that the author himself had lived to have set forth and overseen his own writings. But since it hath been ordained otherwise, and he by death departed from that right, we pray you do not envy his friends the office of their care and pain to have collected and published them.

Nor can an editor, after he has done his best, forget Heminges and Condell's final words: "And so we leave you to other of his friends, whom if you need can be your guides. If you need them not, you can lead yourselves, and others. And such readers we wish him."

SYLVAN BARNET
Tufts University

Introduction

The Two Noble Kinsmen was first published in a quarto edition of 1634, with statements on its title page that it had been "Presented at the Blackfriers by the Kings Maiesties servants, with great applause" and that it was "Written by the memorable Worthies of their time; Mr. *John Fletcher,* and Mr. *William Shakespeare,* Gent." The publisher was John Waterson, a reputable figure who brought out other plays belonging to the King's Men, the company with which Shakespeare and Fletcher had been intimately associated. Although in 1646, when Waterson assigned to Humphrey Moseley his rights in the play, it was included with two others as simply the work of "Mr. Flesher," there is an immediately strong case for accepting the title page's statement of authorship. If Waterson were looking for a way of attracting custom, it would have been at least as effective in 1634 to attribute the play to Beaumont and Fletcher. Moreover, it appears that the manuscript from which he printed had been used in the theater itself[1] and that Waterson had bought it from the players in the normal way of business. And we shall see that the probable date of composition and first performance was 1613, when we have other evidence that Shakespeare and Fletcher were working in close association.

It is true, on the other hand, that Heminges and Condell did not include *The Two Noble Kinsmen* in the Shakespeare Folio of 1623, where in the preliminary address *"To the great Variety of Readers"* there is an implication that all of Shakespeare's plays were being published in the collection. But it appears that *Timon of Athens* was not origi-

[1] See Textual Note, pp. 177–80.

nally included in their plans for the volume, and we know that *Troilus and Cressida,* probably through difficulties over copyright, was almost left out. And they did omit *Pericles*. That *The Two Noble Kinsmen* was included in the 1679 Folio of "Beaumont and Fletcher" plays is also not substantial evidence against Shakespeare's part-authorship, for that volume brought together many plays in which Fletcher collaborated with various dramatists of his time, the linking of his name with Beaumont's on the title page (as in the earlier Beaumont and Fletcher Folio of 1647) being merely a tribute to the brief association of the two men which laid the basis for Fletcher's fame and established a mode of dramatic writing which was long influential in the English theater.

Nevertheless, the publishing history of the play belongs far more with Beaumont and Fletcher than with Shakespeare. It has been regularly included in collected editions of Beaumont and Fletcher since their Folio of 1679, from Tonson's edition of 1711 to the Cambridge edition of Arnold Glover and A. R. Waller of 1905–12. It did not appear in a collected Shakespeare until 1841, when Charles Knight (who believed that Fletcher's collaborator here was George Chapman) yielded to the extent of including it in a volume of "Doubtful Plays" appended to his Pictorial Shakespeare. By then, though dissentient voices were not infrequently raised, the case for Shakespeare's part-authorship had become more than formidable. Pope, in his Shakespeare of 1725, thought the play contained "more of our author than some of those which have been received as genuine," and Lamb and Coleridge and De Quincey were all convinced of Shakespeare's presence, though Hazlitt and Shelley could find nothing of it. William Spalding, however, in his *Letter on Shakspere's Authorship of The Two Noble Kinsmen* (Edinburgh, 1833; reprinted in the *Transactions of the New Shakspere Society,* 1874), Samuel Hickson in his article "The Shares of Shakspere and Fletcher in The Two Noble Kinsmen'" (*Westminster Review,* 1847; reprinted in the *Transactions of the New Shakspere Society,* 1874), and above all Harold Littledale in the introduction to his edition of the play for the New Shakspere Society (1876–85) brought the techniques of nineteenth-century scholarship to bear on the problem and, though they differed to some extent in assigning to the two dramatists their respective shares, they left little doubt in most readers' minds that here we have a collaboration between the leading dramatist of the King's Men and the writer who succeeded him in that role in 1613.

Yet it is still exceptional to find *The Two Noble Kinsmen* in a collected edition of Shakespeare's plays. Most of its readers during this century have come to know it through its inclusion in C. F. Tucker Brooke's *The Shakespeare Apocrypha* (Oxford, 1908). G. L. Kittredge has it in his *Complete Works of Shakespeare* (Boston, 1936); it is planned for inclusion in the "New Cambridge" edition; and it is now presented as part of the Signet Shakespeare.

The elder dramatist's authorship is commonly recognized most surely in the first and fifth acts, particularly in the first three scenes of Act I and the first, third, and fourth scenes of Act V: that is, the solemn approach of the three Queens to Theseus on his wedding day, the conversation of Palamon and Arcite while they are still in Thebes, the scene where Emilia and Hippolyta talk of friendship, the invocations addressed to Mars and Venus and Diana, and the conclusion of the whole story in Arcite's victory and death. In addition, Shakespeare has been generally found in the opening lines of II.i, where the Jailer's Daughter makes her first appearance, and in III.i, where the escaped Palamon meets the disguised Arcite. In the rest of the play there are frequent echoes of other plays by Shakespeare: the madness of the Jailer's Daughter has obvious associations with Ophelia's, and in the later pages of this Introduction it will be suggested that Fletcher for special purposes was drawing upon his intimate knowledge of his collaborator's work. If we accept the commonly held view of the two writers' shares (and there is little reason to be skeptical about it), it was Shakespeare who wrote the beginning and the ending and introduced all the major characters and strands of action.

But by the time this play was composed he may have been less regularly in attendance at the playhouse than formerly, and it seems likely enough that the final putting together of the manuscript was left to Fletcher. Indeed, more than one scholar has come to the conclusion that he made some insertions in the Shakespeare scenes.

It will be convenient to set out the probable authorship of the play's various scenes thus:

Prologue	Fletcher?
Act I, sc. i–iii	Shakespeare
sc. iv–v	Shakespeare?
Act II, sc. i (lines 1–59)	Shakespeare
sc. i (remainder), ii–v	Fletcher
Act III, sc. i	Shakespeare
sc. ii–vi	Fletcher
Act IV, sc. i–iii	Fletcher
Act V, sc. i	Shakespeare
sc. ii	Fletcher
sc. iii–iv	Shakespeare
Epilogue	Fletcher?

The dividing of the play between Shakespeare and Fletcher has been worked out by scholars primarily on the basis of the stylistic differences between their writing. Certainly even a casual reading of the play will show that certain scenes have a complex, "knotted" verse that is close to Shakespeare's in his later years, while others belong clearly with the open-textured, casual style that Beaumont and Fletcher developed in manifest reaction against the involutions of the earliest Jacobeans. The difference has been brought home forcibly to the present editor through the process of annotation. If one compares the scenes where Palamon and Arcite talk together, putting I.ii and III.i on one side and II.i (from the exit of the Jailer, his Daughter, and her Wooer), III.iii, and III.vi on the other, one sees immediately that the first group requires continuous attention from the reader, and probably frequent recourse to the annotations, while the second group has nearly the familiarity of the English now current. When the editor was preparing the annotations, it was with no thought of giving fuller comment on Shakespeare's portion than on Fletcher's, but in the event it proved that in Shakespeare's the proportion of notes to lines was 51% in the scenes just indicated while in Fletcher's the proportion of notes to lines was 25%. Elsewhere in Fletcher's part of the play the figure is higher, as the terms used in connection with the morris dance of III.v needed comment, and Fletcher can use a more elaborate vocabulary for special purposes (as in the description of the knights in IV.ii and in the account of madness in IV.iii). Nevertheless, the presence of the two hands is obvious almost throughout, and evident at a glance in scenes where the basic material (Palamon and Arcite talking together) is similar.

The time of composition is hardly in dispute. The entertainment which the country Schoolmaster presents to Theseus and his court in III.v is taken over from an antimasque in Francis Beaumont's *Masque of the Inner Temple and Gray's Inn,* presented at Whitehall on 20 February 1613. In the published book of the masque we learn that this part of the entertainment was so well liked by the King that he asked to have it danced again at the end of the whole performance. Such antimasques at court were commonly entrusted to professional players, and it would be an easy matter for Fletcher, with his friend and former collaborator Beaumont's permission, to make further use of what had already proved successful. But clearly this would not be likely except soon after the original performance. The date 1613 for *The Two Noble Kinsmen* is confirmed by the reference in Jonson's *Bartholomew Fair* (1614) to "Palamon" as a character in a play (IV.iii): this is not certain evidence, for the name also occurs in Samuel Daniel's *The Queen's Arcadia* (1605), but Daniel's work was a university play and was already some years old in 1614; Jonson is far more likely to have had a recent and better-known play in mind. Moreover,

1613 was the year in which a lost play called *Cardenio*[2] (which in 1653 was attributed to Fletcher and Shakespeare by the publisher Humphrey Moseley) was twice acted at court, and it was the year too in which *Henry VIII* was almost certainly acted for the first time. Although by no means all Shakespeare scholars are agreed on the double authorship of *Henry VIII,* there is strong cumulative evidence that in 1613, after Shakespeare had come to the end of his series of "romances" and was about to retire from the stage, and when Beaumont on his marriage had broken with the theater and thus terminated the short but highly profitable collaboration that he and Fletcher had known for some five years, a new and brief association was established between Fletcher and Shakespeare, and that *The Two Noble Kinsmen* was one of its fruits.

In these circumstances, and with the assumption that the main planning of the play was, as it has seemed likely, Shakespeare's, we should expect to find a clear enough relationship to the "romances" which Shakespeare had been writing since *Pericles* (c. 1609) and which he had brought to a conclusion in *The Tempest* (1611). And resemblances are hardly to be missed. In *Pericles* he had gone to Gower's *Confessio Amantis* for his story: here he goes to Gower's contemporary, Chaucer. *Pericles* and *The Winter's Tale* have Hellenistic settings: *The Two Noble Kinsmen* takes us to Athens and briefly to Thebes. The "romances" present a world where the gods are freely invoked and where they play a direct part in the action—Diana appearing to Pericles in a dream and sending him to Ephesus so that he may find his lost wife Thaisa, Jupiter appearing to Posthumus Leonatus in prison and offering a riddling promise of good fortune to him and of a happy ending to the strife between Rome and Britain, Apollo being consulted on the question of Hermione's guilt and striking dead Mamillius when his father Leontes rejects the message from the oracle. In *The Tempest* there are, it is true, no gods—they would be out of place in a drama where a human character has unlimited control over events

[2] It may exist in an altered form in Lewis Theobald's version of the story, called *Double Falsehood* and published in 1728.

(though not over the human will)—but there are spirits who represent Juno and Ceres and Iris and who offer divine blessings and admonitions. *The Two Noble Kinsmen* keeps the gods off the stage too, but their altars are there, they are solemnly invoked, and tokens of their favor are given. At the play's end Theseus marvels how the apparently contradictory promises of Mars and Venus have both been fulfilled. More obviously, more disturbingly indeed, than in the previous plays the human characters of *The Two Noble Kinsmen* are subject to divine power. Theseus can devise a plan for finding out Emilia's husband and for ending the strife between the knights, but it is the gods who circuitously determine things, to the wonder and embarrassment of those concerned.

In some striking features this play has a special relationship with *Pericles*. That had a detachable first act (which was omitted at a Stratford-on-Avon revival in 1947), with formal speechmaking in a context of love and death: so has *The Two Noble Kinsmen,* which could easily have been adjusted to begin with Palamon and Arcite already in prison. Then Arcite's encounter in II.ii with the countrymen who will take part in the games for Emilia's birthday resembles Pericles' encounter with the fishermen in II.i, where he learns there are games to be held in Thaisa's honor: both Pericles and Arcite are victors and are received into the lady's favor. But in *Pericles* the games are a formal tournament, which takes place in an atmosphere of high ceremonial, while in *The Two Noble Kinsmen* it is a matter of simple running and wrestling. The tournament, however, is not forgotten and occurs offstage in the final encounter between Palamon and Arcite, each aided by his three knights. The cry of "The mean knight!" which indicates at the end of II.ii that Pericles has been victorious anticipates the cries of "Palamon!" and "Arcite!" and "Victory!" that Emilia hears in V.iii. Here the influence of one of Shakespeare's romances is seen operative on a Fletcher portion of the later play.

But there is a more subtle echo of *The Winter's Tale*. Commentators have sometimes seen there a suggestion that Leontes, believing his wife is being unfaithful to him with his best friend, is unconsciously more deeply outraged by the breach in friendship than by the breach in marriage. Certainly the nostalgic reminiscences of Leontes and Polixenes in I.ii, their sense that an Eden was lost when they grew up and took wives, is to be linked with the passage in *The Two Noble Kinsmen,* I.iii, where Emilia and Hippolyta talk of the friendship between Theseus and Pirithous and the friendship between Emilia and the dead girl Flavina: Hippolyta is not sure that even now she has the first place in Theseus' heart, Emilia has no thought that a husband can be as near to her as Flavina was. In the center of the later play, moreover, there is the friendship of Palamon and Arcite: it is broken when they both love Emilia, but even as they plan to fight to the death (in III.iii) they look back with some longing on their earlier and lighter loves which did not harm their friendship. That is a brief respite, for Palamon is soon asserting his claim again, but the scene where they help to arm each other (III.vi) is strong in its suggestion of enduring affection. They embrace solemnly before the invocation of their respective divine patrons (V.i), and Arcite's words to Emilia when he appears to have won her are heavily charged with a sense of the price he has paid:

> Emily,
> To buy you I have lost what's dearest to me
> Save what is bought, and yet I purchase cheaply
> As I do rate your value.
>
> (V.iii.111–14)

Shakespeare's "romances" are, among other things, love stories, but they are not simple exaltations of the bond which ties most men to women.

This indeed suggests a connection with his earliest plays. *The Two Gentlemen of Verona* was also a play about friendship, and it is difficult not to believe that its very title was echoed in that of *The Two Noble Kinsmen.* There Valentine and Proteus were firm friends until Proteus fell in love with the girl his friend loved. The right and wrong of the matter were simple: Proteus is thoroughly treacherous and gets to the point of attempting rape. When he repents, Valentine has so high a sense of what friendship demands that he is willing to let Proteus have the girl, not thinking even of consulting her. At that time Shakespeare could make discreet fun of the friendship-idea and could quickly make all things come right. Moreover, it was Proteus' villainy and Valentine's simple faith that caused the trouble, while in *The Two Noble Kinsmen* Palamon and Arcite love Emilia because they have to, and Arcite dies because the gods have determined so. That Shakespeare thought back to *The Two Gentlemen* is, I think, indubitable, just as he thought back to *The Comedy of Errors* in the final turn of events in *Pericles,* just as he remembered the rambling romantic plays of the popular theater he first knew when he wrote *Pericles* and *Cymbeline* and *The Winter's Tale*. In going back to beginnings, *The Two Noble Kinsmen* is of a piece with the "romances," though it has a formality of structure, as we shall see, that links it with *The Tempest* more than with the plays that immediately preceded that.

It is, however, another early play that is here most prominently in his mind, and again the resemblance goes along with contrast and deliberate reconsideration. Like *The Two Noble Kinsmen, A Midsummer Night's Dream* begins with preparations for the wedding of Theseus and Hippolyta, it is partly concerned with an amateur performance given before the Duke by his subjects, and it shows the court during a May-morning ceremony coming upon two men who have fallen out through rivalry in love. In the earlier play the wedding is not interrupted, there being merely a planned delay before it takes place; the play-within-the-play occurs at the end, not the middle; the rivals in love have had their quarrel already sorted out by Puck and Oberon before Theseus arrives. And it is not quite the same Theseus in the two plays. The earlier Duke has the authority of the later one, but he is ever sanguine and relaxed: he will not believe the "story of the night," he is patronizing toward play-acting and somewhat ill-mannered during the performance. The Duke of *The Two Noble Kinsmen* may finally attempt to console himself by marveling at the divine legerdemain, but there is an unrelaxed seriousness in him and a continuing puzzlement. The man who at first decrees perpetual imprisonment for Palamon and Arcite, and later death for them both, and after that death for the loser (and his supporters) in the tournament, is a shrewd realist very different from the man who told Hermia he could not bend the law for her sake—her father's authority being supreme—and finally acquiesced in her marriage with Lysander and told Egeus he must accept the situation. We can see a similar change, along with a resemblance, in the later play's echoing of Helena's account of her girlhood friendship with Hermia (III.ii): when Emilia speaks of the relationship between herself and Flavina, Shakespeare is no longer offering a merely gentle picture of two girls together.

Shakespeare, then, using a well-known story that had been prominently in his mind when he wrote *A Midsummer Night's Dream* (c. 1595–96), helped to compose a play that had strong links both with the late "romances" and with early comedies that he had already shown a disposition to recall and to look upon with a changed vision. The reunions at the ends of *The Comedy of Errors* and *Pericles* are as different as we can imagine; the spanning of the years in *Pericles* and *The Winter's Tale* does not make those plays similar in spirit to the romances of the 1570's (and the following decade or so) that Sidney made fun of in *An Apology for Poetry;* magic has a different look in *The Tempest* when we compare that play with *A Midsummer Night's Dream*. There is a certain casualness of manner in *The Two Noble Kinsmen,* such indeed as Lytton Strachey saw in the late "romances" as a whole, but it goes along with a reserving of judgment about human beings and the conditions under which they live.

And in this situation Fletcher was no longer with Beaumont but with an elder dramatist whose plays were always strongly in his mind, to the point where he would deliberately modify an initial Shakespeare-situation and then work out the pattern of event that would result. He and Beaumont had done that with *Philaster* (c. 1609), taking the

Hamlet-situation without the ghost, as later—on his own—he was to write a sequel to *The Taming of the Shrew* in *The Woman's Prize, or The Tamer Tamed* (c. 1611) and, probably along with Massinger, to invert the *Lear*-situation in *Thierry and Theodoret* (c. 1617). With Beaumont he had shared a lodging and had developed a dramatic mode in which their two minds functioned, it seemed, as one: though we may perhaps be able to differentiate his verse from Beaumont's, we do not get the feeling in their joint plays that two diverse attitudes are alternating as each in his turn pushes his pen. Fletcher's later collaboration with Massinger resembles his collaboration with Shakespeare in *The Two Noble Kinsmen* to the extent that we feel the characterization and the march of event are seen through different eyes in different parts of the play. If we are correct, as many people have thought, in assuming that Shakespeare put his scenes into Fletcher's hands and let him do the job of conflating the two shares, this was a situation new to this dramatist. That the story would have attracted him is understandable: the clash between love and friendship in Palamon and Arcite has some similarity to that between friendship and honor in Melantius and Amintor in *The Maid's Tragedy* (c. 1610) and would similarly lend itself to the patterned alternations of conduct that Fletcher delighted in; and there must have been a piquancy in working in association with Shakespeare, to whom he owed much, whose work, however, must have seemed old-fashioned, imperfectly sophisticated. He and Beaumont had pulled Hamlet down to the comic level of Philaster; now Shakespeare's Palamon and Arcite could be irreverently handled in the same play as Shakespeare was presenting them.

It is not that Fletcher makes the kinsmen directly absurd (though coming near it in their exchange of sentiments, followed at once by their quarrel, in II.i), and he clearly has some partiality for Arcite; but he does take a feline pleasure in the way love holds them, in the way they try to live up to the friendship code at the same time as they are protesting their separate devotions to Emilia. And this goes along with a special fluency in his writing (seen, for example, in the prison-and-garden sequence of II.i), and a fondness for setting the story in brakes and flowers. Nature is never ominous for Fletcher, but its presence as a framework for strife is always ironic.

In one place the work of Fletcher's deflating hand reminds us of an effect found in Shakespeare's own *The Winter's Tale,* V.ii, and in scenes frequently ascribed to Fletcher in *Henry VIII* (II.i, IV.i). The Messenger in *The Two Noble Kinsmen,* IV.ii, seems to the present editor's ear to be intentionally comic, with his ecstatic praise of the attendant knights, his overreadiness to speak at line 72, his general extravagance of imagery, and in particular the doting on one knight's freckles and the ludicrous comparison of his sinews to the bodily shape of a pregnant woman (lines 128–29). Here I believe we have Fletcher taking up what he found in *The Winter's Tale,* and pushing it much further both in *Henry VIII* and in *The Two Noble Kinsmen.*

If general opinion is right in assigning the opening of II.i to Shakespeare, it was he who introduced the Jailer's Daughter. But the use made of her is characteristically Fletcher's. First we should note his boldness in giving her so many scenes alone (II.iii, II.v, III.ii, III.iv): the contrast with Emilia's safe establishment in Theseus' court is striking; and while Emilia is always herself, never in love, protesting yet acquiescent, grieved rather than disturbed, the Jailer's Daughter moves from light-hearted romance:

> Out upon't,
> What pushes are we wenches driven to
> When fifteen once has found us!
> (II.iii.5–7)

to fear and hunger, and thence to a sense of exposure:

> I am very cold, and all the stars are out too,
> The little stars and all, that look like aglets.
> The sun has seen my folly.
> (III.iv.1–3)

and thence to madness. The descent is not merely pathetic:

it is comic, as we see in her taking part in the morris dance of III.v, and it is powerfully suggestive of the casual destructiveness of the love-impulse. Aspatia in *The Maid's Tragedy* is too often seen as a merely pathetic figure: there is destructiveness there too, for herself and for Amintor. Fletcher had a strong sense of how disintegration worked, most brilliantly realized in his Maximus in *Valentinian* (c. 1614). And we may, I think, assume that it was Fletcher's idea to have the girl in *The Two Noble Kinsmen* "cured" by making her take her humble Wooer for Palamon, and thus in imagination lie with the man she loved. At the end of the play Emilia is almost on the point of marrying Arcite: the gods intervene, and she is in Palamon's arms. Neither girl has choice, neither girl has, ultimately it seems, the power to differentiate. Moreover, they are linked in that the Jailer's Daughter has to play her part in the morris dance, her madness making her, in the opinion of the Countrymen, the more apt for the grotesque gambols required, while Emilia, trying to preserve neutrality and sobriety, is nevertheless shuttled from one knight's arms to the other's. This gives to the country entertainment of III.v a function in the play: it is a comic counterpart to, and an anticipation of, the final tournament, and their respective roles in the two spectacles bring together the girl who loves Palamon and the girl who weds him. In his development of the subplot, Fletcher seems thus to have continued his work of deflation.

Here, however, it is necessary to distinguish with some care. Shakespeare's handling of Palamon and Arcite and Theseus and Emilia is no simple romancing, as we have seen. They are powerless human beings manipulated by the gods, and in a measure comic in their subjection. But the comedy is wry and serious, nowhere more so than in Palamon's invocation of Venus in V.i.[3] Fletcher's comedy is much more self-conscious, more obviously grotesque, and though it too is wry there is laughter in it.

Not only deflation of the elder dramatist can be seen, but a measure of parody too. The Jailer's Daughter echoes Ophelia; Emilia brooding over the pictures of Palamon

[3] See "A Note on the Source," pp. 188–89.

and Arcite in IV.ii echoes the Gertrude who was made to look on pictures of Claudius and the elder Hamlet; even the Doctor's bed-trick in V.ii (for it is substantially that) may echo Shakespeare's elaborate employments of the device. And again and again there are tricks of wording—e.g., the Doctor's "I think she has a perturbed mind, which I cannot minister to" (IV.iii.60–61)—which take up phrases which Fletcher knew from Shakespeare. The parodying is not hostile or unadmiring. We can remember that in 1613 Shakespeare was forty-nine and Fletcher thirty-four, that we have strong evidence that they worked together on two, perhaps on three, plays: the relationship must have been a complex one. Through the remaining twelve years of Fletcher's career his predecessor's work was never far from his mind, but he enjoyed it without a total reverence. That in writing his share of *The Two Noble Kinsmen* he made the play something of a medley would not deeply disturb him. He did not bring to the writing of any play a sense of full commitment.

A court record suggests that Shakespeare's and Fletcher's play was given there in 1619,[4] and the occurrence in the text of two actors' names[5] enables us to deduce that the play was revived about 1625–26. The title page of 1634 is perhaps deliberately ambiguous in its "Presented at the Blackfriers": this could imply, but need not, that the play was still in the repertory. But after 1642 for a very long time the stage had almost no use for the play.[6]

[4] E. K. Chambers, *William Shakespeare: A Study of Facts and Problems,* Oxford, 1930, II, 346.

[5] See Textual Note, p. 178.

[6] The almost complete disregard of our play in the late seventeenth century is indicated by Dryden's failure to mention it in his Preface to his volume of *Fables* (1700) or to give in his *Palamon and Arcite* included in that volume any clear indication that he had read it. He does, when writing of Emilia at Book I, line 175, use the phrase "To do the observance due to sprightly May," which is a little nearer to "to do observance/To flow'ry May" (*The Two Noble Kinsmen,* II.iv.50–51) than to Chaucer's "to have remembraunce/To don honour to May" (*The Knight's Tale,* lines 188–89), but Chaucer in another context has "to doon his observaunce to May" (line 642). Dryden also makes a little more of the freckled face of one of the kinsmen's supporters (Book III, lines 76, 475) than Chaucer does (lines 1311–12), which could be due to the stress on this feature in *The Two Noble Kinsmen,* IV.ii.120–23. Neither of these points can make us firmly deduce that Dryden gave the play a thought as he adapted Chaucer.

In 1664 Pepys saw at Lincoln's Inn Fields Theatre *The Rivals* (not a new play then), which is a free adaptation of *The Two Noble Kinsmen* and, though it was published anonymously in 1668, can be safely attributed to Sir William Davenant. He was a dramatist of experience and some note in Charles I's reign, he was largely responsible for the restarting of theater performances in London during the Interregnum (his operatic *The Siege of Rhodes* being acted in 1656), and he was one of the two London theater managers in the earliest Restoration years. He made free use of pre-1642 drama, adapting *Macbeth* and (with Dryden) *The Tempest* for current taste. In *The Rivals* he contrived a version of the story he found in Shakespeare and Fletcher, with no Theseus, no petitioning Queens, no invocation of the gods, no tournament, and a happy ending. Though he occasionally keeps to the words he found, he uses none of the old names and changes the place of action to Arcadia. Heraclea, corresponding to Emilia, cannot make up her mind between Theocles and Philander, but finds that Philander is loved by Celania, the daughter of the Provost (no mere jailer): therefore she decides to take Theocles, and Philander consents to love Celania. Davenant wanted to make a refined comedy, and to do it he had to remove most of the action and all the grossness. Celania does go distracted for a while, but only in a polite way. The play is of no importance, but so far as is known it provided the occasion for the only contact with the stage that *The Two Noble Kinsmen* had between the early seventeenth century and the early twentieth century. Not even William Poel is on record as having thought of a revival.

Then in March 1928 the Old Vic staged it, with Ernest Milton as Palamon, Eric Portman as Arcite, Jean Forbes-Robertson as the Jailer's Daughter, and Barbara Everest as Emilia. Writing in *The London Mercury* for April 1928, A. G. MacDonell praised Jean Forbes-Robertson, and noted that Palamon was done comically, in a red wig. This reviewer was much taken with the realistic playing of the mad scenes, and grateful that he did not have to endure simple nobility in two kinsmen. The only other production

I have been able to trace is that at the Antioch Area Theatre, Antioch College, Ohio, which was given eight times in August and September 1955 under the direction of Arthur Lithgow. I am most grateful to Mr. Lithgow, now of the McCarter Theatre at Princeton, and to Miss Marcia Overstreet and Miss Ernestine C. Brecht of Antioch College, for writing to me about this production. Mr. Lithgow reports that the play proved "very stage-worthy," particularly the scenes involving the Jailer's Daughter, and that Mr. Ellis Rabb was "very grand" as Palamon. Some cutting had to be done of "repetitive passages," but Shakespeare's hand was felt in the "high imagery."

This is a relatively inglorious stage history for a play in which Shakespeare was concerned, and we must honor the Old Vic and Antioch College for going against the current. Despite the coldness of the London reviewers (MacDonell was typical), it is evident that something happened to the Jailer's Daughter scenes when they got on the stage, and this was confirmed at Antioch College, where indeed the play as a whole seems to have found itself at home. It is more than time that a further attempt was made to see it in action. It does, after all, contain the invocations to the gods in V.i, passages of dramatic verse outstanding even in 1613, a good time for dramatic verse; it contains some of Fletcher's most skillful and characteristic writing; it will one day, perhaps, come to be recognized as throwing a new kind of light on Shakespeare's concluding work in the theater. It needs a large and flexible stage: there is a most suitable one at Stratford, Ontario, another at Chichester in England, and others—both indoor and outdoor—easily found in the United States. One of these might well meet the challenge of what was perhaps Shakespeare's (though only partly Shakespeare's) last play.

It has some good verse and a fairly realistic picture of the onset of madness, but the director contemplating a revival will want to be assured of more than that. It is true that he must face difficulties. The play has the appearance of a romantic story, as Beaumont and Fletcher's *Philaster* has, but in neither instance does the romantic effect properly work. With *Philaster* that was because Beaumont and Fletcher were determined on a sophisticated undercutting of the romantic gesture; with *The Two Noble Kinsmen* there is the complication that two men of widely differing temperaments shared the writing. Shakespeare had used "romance" with high authority in *The Winter's Tale* and *The Tempest,* involving his audience in a love story in a setting that was both natural and strange, and at the same time making them feel that they were in the presence of stern and unknowable powers. But now he was working with Fletcher, whose sights were lower, essentially those that had characterized *Philaster*. For Shakespeare, we can assume it was the sense of the inscrutable that made the story attractive to him; for Fletcher, it was its essential, often painful, but never overwhelming, absurdity. Because it seems likely that Fletcher had the task of putting together his and Shakespeare's work on the play, the overriding effect is Fletcherian: we are taken to high realms of thought, and deliberately let down, as we are so often, but less extravagantly, in the other plays in which Fletcher had a main hand. It is a paradox that Shakespeare seems to have planned *The Two Noble Kinsmen* and that Fletcher gave it its dominant tone. But that tone is dominant, not exclusive: from Shakespeare we get the solemn pageant of the Queens' mission in I.i, the sage talk of Emilia and Hippolyta in I.iii, the sharp magniloquence of the prayers in V.i; and Fletcher's deflations do not take them from our memory.

But what has probably put off most readers and potential directors has been the nature of the characterization. Shakespeare's handling of character from *Pericles* onwards was lacking in the complexity and verisimilitude that had marked the comedies and frequently the tragedies of his middle and mature years. But audiences have been ready to accept Leontes in place of Othello, Miranda in place of Rosalind, Prospero in place of Hamlet, because in these plays they are led consistently toward the idea of "great creating Nature," toward a sense of epiphany, toward an austere assertion that to accept what is remains the best hope, the highest wisdom, we have. But Fletcher has been little more successful on the stage from the eighteenth to the twentieth century, either alone or in collaboration with Beaumont, than he has been in association with Shakespeare. Reviewing the Old Vic performance of *The Two Noble Kinsmen* in 1928, James Agate asked how any actress could make anything of Emilia, passed from hero to hero as from pillar to post.[7] A. G. MacDonell, we have seen, found even one manifestly noble kinsman enough to bear. Fletcher offers nothing in the way of obvious compensation for his stereotyping of human characters: these are, he suggests, the types that men fall into, or imagine they fall into, or try to live up to the idea of falling into. The Fletcherian drama is a drama about men's refusal to live as individuals. In his plays, men avoid nakedness by doing what they feel the codes and traditions of society demand from them. We may differentiate Palamon from Arcite: one is more rough, the other ready to see himself as sinning because he devoted himself to Emilia a few seconds after his friend did. But each keeps within a stereotype, a notion that belongs to the playhouse of the mind that men are always imagining for themselves: they are alike victims and worshipers of Bacon's Idols of the Theater. It is a kind of characterization that in recent years Brecht has familiarized us with, and we should now therefore be the more fitted to respond to the mode and to see what the play as a whole is saying.

It is indeed a well-arranged play, despite the duality of authorship and the dichotomy of attitude that in this instance is thus imposed. Instead of the loose story-telling we might expect, we have a fairly tight structure, and in "A Note on the Source" (p. 187) we shall see that this has been achieved partly through the changes made in adapting Chaucer. The action involves three interwoven strands: (1) the prologue-action, as we may call it, concerning the conflict between Athens and Thebes; (2) the story of the rivalry for Emilia; (3) the story of the Jailer's Daughter. The first makes the play begin in a manner of high seriousness and formal rhetoric, and it is in manifest contrast with the slighter, more personal stories of the

7 *Brief Chronicles*, London, 1943, pp. 53–56.

knights and the girls. The subplot, as we have seen, reflects ironically on the plot of the knights.

The act division throughout is firm, and is related to the play's changes of locality. Act I concerns itself with the conflict between Athens (chivalrous) and Thebes (ignoble), ending with the imprisonment of the nearly dead Palamon and Arcite (noble on the wrong side). Act II gives us their falling in love and release from prison, and introduces the subplot. Act III is wholly outside the town: it shows how Palamon and Arcite meet again, how the Jailer's Daughter loses Palamon, how Theseus and his court are entertained by a group of rustics including the Daughter, and finally how the Duke comes upon the kinsmen and decrees their final trial. Act IV, which is briefly and quietly indeterminate, makes toward the cure of the Daughter and emphasizes the perplexity of Emilia: it is, as often with a fourth act, a halting place before the catastrophe. Act V gives us the tournament and its curious consequences, with both girls in some sense pledged to Palamon. Athens and Thebes are the localities of Act I, Athens and the country nearby those of Act II; the country consistently is the place of action in Act III, the city of Athens (but alternating between palace and prison) in Acts IV and V. As the play progresses its range of locality shrinks, so that what begins as an opposition of Thebes and Athens ends as an opposition of palace and prison within a single city. The point of rest toward which we move is marked by death and bereavement and acquiescence: the Jailer who freed Arcite in Act II, and put Palamon under further restraint, is prominently in the stage picture when Palamon is prepared for execution and then, at the news of Arcite's death, for marriage.

The play's recurrent irony is supported by other details of the planning. Theseus is ceremoniously petitioned by the Queens in I.i and by Hippolyta, Emilia, and Pirithous in III.vi: he yields in both instances, though with eloquence in the earlier, Shakespearian passage and with the cleverness of compromise in Fletcher's III.vi. The talk between Palamon and Arcite in I.ii, where they show their wish to leave a corrupt Thebes, becomes ironic when in fighting for Thebes they come near death and are sentenced to life imprisonment. The discussion of friendship by Hippolyta and Emilia in I.iii not only anticipates the dominant friendship motif in the play as a whole, but casts an ironic light on the knights' subsequent devotion to Emilia. And just as the subplot as a whole reflects on Emilia and her ultimate disposal, so the entertainment devised by the Schoolmaster, which brings Theseus and the Jailer's Daughter together on the stage for the only time, is not only a contrast to and an anticipation of the wryly presented tournament of Act V: it also gives a distorted image of the entertainment that the kinsmen and the Duke and his ladies offer to the audience in the theater.

Of course, this is a Blackfriars play. The King's Men had taken over that "private" theater (previously used by the child actors) around 1610 and had begun by using it as their winter house, keeping the Globe for the summer. The title page of 1634 mentions only the Blackfriars, and we may assume that at least by the 1620's this play had found its right home there. It is a sophisticated—even, we have seen, a dislocated—play, not firm, ultimately, in its implications but surely fascinating, if disturbing and at times irritating, to watch. Its epilogue calls it "the tale we have told—/For 'tis no other." That was what Shakespeare had insistently, in the text as well as in the title, called *The Winter's Tale*. *The Two Noble Kinsmen,* like that earlier "romance," is a strange story with many reversals of fortune, but like that too it has its unromantic aftertaste and is more carefully structured than a casual glance suggests. The Blackfriars audience was at times most gullible, ready to lose itself in a merely romanticized wonderland, but it could rise to the appreciation of something complex: it welcomed Fletcher's masterpiece in comedy, *The Humorous Lieutenant* (c. 1619–20), and, though we cannot be sure that it much liked the experience, it saw Ford's *The Broken Heart* some dozen years after that. There were doubtless moments of puzzlement with *The Two Noble Kinsmen* in 1613 and the following years, but some at least of the spectators must have noticed that the supreme dramatist and his more than clever successor were not failing them.

Nor would they, I think, fail us now if we put their joint play again on the stage.[8]

CLIFFORD LEECH
University of Toronto

[8] Since this Introduction was written, Paul Bertram has published a substantial book with the title *Shakespeare and The Two Noble Kinsmen* (New Brunswick, 1965), arguing that Shakespeare was the sole author of the play. It is a piece of well-informed writing, and Bertram has scored some good points in showing how the nineteenth-century scholars seized on the idea of dual authorship because of a reluctance to imagine Shakespeare writing the franker sections of the play. He argues, moreover, that the play has unity in its plotting (as indeed it has) and that throughout there is the same full use of Chaucer. Less successfully, he disposes of the evidence of verse tests by insisting that some of the scenes treated by the editors as verse are really in prose (as they are presented in the quarto): this is, I think, to disregard the strong blank-verse character of much of the writing. The reader of the present edition will be able to decide whether the scenes involving the Countrymen and the Jailer and his Daughter (apart from the beginning of II.i and the whole of IV.iii) are legitimately printed as verse. Moreover, Bertram is one of the, alas, many who have a low regard for Fletcher: he insists on Shakespeare's sole authorship of *Henry VIII* and *The Two Noble Kinsmen,* but will let Fletcher have *Cardenio,* which seems to him of minor weight. And he does not successfully meet the evidence of the 1634 title page. It is possible to quote, as he does, the statement of Leonard Digges, in the 1640 edition of Shakespeare's *Poems,* that Shakespeare did not beg "from each witty friend a Scene/To peece his Acts with," but that is another matter than the frank and equal sharing of a play with his obvious successor in 1613. It used to be necessary to argue for Shakespeare's participation in *The Two Noble Kinsmen:* now we have to safeguard Fletcher's right to a part of it. And the argument of this Introduction is that there are, despite close cooperation, a difference of view and a difference of style which indicate two authors, one of them supreme and the other at least major in his time.

The Two Noble Kinsmen

[*Dramatis Personae*

Theseus, Duke of Athens
Pirithous, friend to Theseus
Artesius, an Athenian
Palamon, Arcite — kinsmen, nephews to Creon, King of Thebes
Valerius, a Theban
Six Knights
Jailer
Wooer to the Jailer's Daughter
Doctor
Brother, Two Friends — to the Jailer
Schoolmaster
A Herald, Messengers, Countrymen, Hymen, a Boy, an Executioner, Guard, Taborer, Bavian or Fool, Lords and Attendants
Hippolyta, an Amazon, bride to Theseus
Emilia, her sister
Three Queens
The Jailer's Daughter
Waiting-woman to Emilia
Maids, Country Wenches, and Nymphs

Scene: Athens and the country nearby; Thebes]

PROLOGUE

Flourish.°[1]

New plays and maidenheads are near akin:
Much followed° both, for both much money gi'en,
If they stand sound and well. And a good play—
Whose modest scenes blush on his marriage day,
And shake to lose his honor—is like her *5*
That after holy tie and first night's stir
Yet still is modesty, and still retains
More of the maid to sight than husband's pains.°
We pray our play may be so, for I am sure
It has a noble breeder, and a pure, *10*
A learnèd, and a poet never went
More famous yet 'twixt Po and silver Trent.
Chaucer, of all admired, the story gives:
There constant to eternity it lives.
If we let fall° the nobleness of this,° *15*
And the first sound this child hear be a hiss,
How will it shake the bones of that good man,
And make him cry from under ground, "O fan
From me the witless chaff of such a writer°
That blasts my bays, and my famed works makes
lighter *20*

[1] The degree sign (°) indicates a footnote, which is keyed to the text by line number. Text references are printed in **boldface** type; the annotation follows in roman type.

Prologue s.d. **Flourish** i.e., of trumpets 2 **followed** pursued, cultivated 8 **pains** endeavors 15 **let fall** fail to maintain 15 **this** i.e., Chaucer's poem 19 **such a writer** (the singular is notable, but by no means decisive on the question of authorship)

Than Robin Hood!" This is the fear we bring;
For, to say truth, it were an endless° thing,
And too ambitious, to aspire to him.
Weak as we are, and almost breathless swim
25 In this deep water, do but you hold out
Your helping hands, and we shall tack about,°
And something do to save us. You shall hear
Scenes, though below his art, may yet appear
Worth two hours' travail.° To his bones sweet sleep;
30 Content to you. If this play do not keep
A little dull time from us, we perceive
Our losses fall so thick we must needs leave.°

Flourish.

22 **endless** purposeless, vain 26 **tack about** change direction 29 **travail** labor (with a suggestion of "travel," as the play's action moves from place to place) 32 **leave** give up acting

ACT I

[Scene I. *Athens. Before a temple.*]

Enter Hymen° with a torch burning; a boy in a white robe before, singing and strewing flowers; after Hymen, a nymph, encompassed in her tresses,° bearing a wheaten garland;° then Theseus between two other nymphs with wheaten chaplets° on their heads; then Hippolyta the bride, led by Pirithous, and another holding a garland over her head, her tresses likewise hanging; after her, Emilia holding up her train; [*Artesius and Attendants*]. *Music.*

The Song

Roses, their sharp spines being gone,
Not royal in their smells alone,
But in their hue;
Maiden pinks, of odor faint,
Daisies smell-less, yet most quaint,° *5*
And sweet thyme true;

Primrose, first-born child of Ver,°
Merry spring-time's harbinger,
With harebells dim;
Oxlips, in their cradles growing, *10*
Marigolds, on death-beds blowing,°
Lark's-heels trim;°

I.i. s.d. **Hymen** god of marriage **encompassed in her tresses** with hair loose, in token of virginity **wheaten garland** a symbol of fertility and peace **chaplets** wreaths 5 **quaint** pretty 7 **Ver** spring 11 **on death-beds blowing** blooming on graves 12 **trim** neat

All dear Nature's children sweet
Lie 'fore bride and bridegroom's feet, *Strew flowers.*
15 Blessing their sense;
Not an angel° of the air,
Bird melodious, or bird fair,
Is° absent hence;

The crow, the sland'rous cuckoo, nor
20 The boding raven, nor chough hoar,
Nor chatt'ring pie,
May on our bridehouse° perch or sing,
Or with them any discord bring,
But from it fly.

Enter three Queens in black, with veils stained, with imperial crowns. The first Queen falls down at the foot of Theseus; the second falls down at the foot of Hippolyta; the third before Emilia.

25 *First Queen.* For pity's sake and true gentility's,°
Hear and respect° me.

Second Queen. For your mother's sake,
And as you wish your womb may thrive with fair ones,
Hear and respect me.

Third Queen. Now for the love of him whom Jove hath marked
30 The honor of your bed,° and for the sake
Of clear° virginity, be advocate
For us, and our distresses. This good deed
Shall raze you° out o' th' Book of Trespasses°
All you are set down there.

Theseus. Sad lady, rise.

Hippolyta. Stand up.

16 **angel** here a synonym for "bird" 18 **Is** (often emended to "Be," but the indicative seems acceptable) 22 **bridehouse** house where a wedding is celebrated 25 **gentility** nobleness 26 **respect** give attention to 29–30 **whom . . . bed** for whom Jove has destined the honor of wedding you 31 **clear** pure 33 **raze you** delete for you 33 **Book of Trespasses** recording angel's register of sins

Emilia. No knees to me. 35
What woman I may stead° that is distressed
Does bind me to her.

Theseus. What's your request? Deliver you for all.

First Queen. We are three queens, whose sovereigns fell before
The wrath of cruel Creon;° who endured° 40
The beaks of ravens, talons of the kites,
And pecks of crows, in the foul fields of Thebes.
He will not suffer us to burn their bones,
To urn their ashes, nor to take th' offense
Of mortal loathsomeness from the blest eye 45
Of holy Phoebus,° but infects the winds
With stench of our slain lords. O pity, duke,
Thou purger of the earth, draw thy feared sword
That does good turns to th' world; give us the bones
Of our dead kings, that we may chapel° them; 50
And of thy boundless goodness take some note
That for our crownèd heads we have no roof,
Save this which is the lion's and the bear's,
And vault° to everything.

Theseus. Pray you kneel not.
I was transported with your speech, and suffered 55
Your knees to wrong themselves. I have heard the fortunes
Of your dead lords, which gives me such lamenting
As wakes my vengeance and revenge for 'em.
King Capaneus° was your lord. The day
That he should° marry you, at such a season 60
As now it is with me, I met your groom.
By Mars's altar, you were that time fair:
Not Juno's mantle° fairer than your tresses,

36 **stead** help 40 **Creon** king of Thebes after Oedipus 40 **endured** have endured 45–46 **blest eye/Of holy Phoebus** i.e., the sun 50 **chapel** bury in a chapel 54 **vault** arched roof (here the sky) 59 **Capaneus** (here four syllables, though classically three) 60 **should** was to 63 **Juno's mantle** (Juno was goddess of marriage and her mantle is described in *Iliad,* XIV; but the peacock was sacred to Juno, and "mantle" also suggests the bird's spread tail)

Nor in more bounty spread her; your wheaten wreath
Was then nor threshed° nor blasted;° Fortune at
65 you
Dimpled her cheek with smiles. Hercules our kinsman,°
Then weaker than your eyes, laid by his club:
He tumbled down upon his Nemean hide°
And swore his sinews thawed. O grief and time,
70 Fearful consumers, you will all devour.

First Queen. O I hope some god,
Some god hath put his mercy in your manhood,
Whereto he'll infuse pow'r, and press you forth
Our undertaker.°

Theseus. O no knees, none, widow,
75 Unto the helmeted Bellona° use them,
And pray for me your soldier.
Troubled I am. *Turns away.*
[*The Queens rise.*]

Second Queen. Honored Hippolyta,
Most dreaded Amazonian, that hast slain
The scythe-tusked boar, that with thy arm as strong
80 As it is white, wast near to make the male
To thy sex captive, but that this thy lord,
Born to uphold creation in that honor
First Nature 'stilled it in,° shrunk thee into
The bound° thou wast o'erflowing, at once subduing
85 Thy force and thy affection; soldieress,
That equally canst poise° sternness with pity,

65 **threshed** beaten so as to separate grain from husks (here an image for fertilizing: cf. I.i opening s.d.) 65 **blasted** i.e., by widowhood 66 **kinsman** (according to Plutarch's "Life of Theseus," both he and Hercules were descended on their mothers' side from Pelops; moreover, Theseus as alleged son of Poseidon could claim kinship with Hercules, son of Zeus) 68 **Nemean hide** (Hercules customarily wore the hide of the lion of Nemea, which he had slain) 73–74 **press you forth/ Our undertaker** impel you to champion our cause 75 **Bellona** goddess of war 83 **'stilled it in** instilled in it 84 **bound** limit, as bank of a river 86 **equally canst poise** canst justly balance

Whom° now I know hast much more power on him
Than ever he had on thee, who ow'st° his strength
And his love too, who is a servant for
The tenor of thy speech;° dear glass of° ladies, 90
Bid him that we whom flaming war doth scorch
Under the shadow of his sword may cool us;
Require him he advance it o'er our heads;
Speak't in a woman's key, like such a woman
As any of us three; weep ere you fail; 95
Lend us a knee;
But° touch the ground for us no longer time
Than a dove's motion when the head's plucked off;
Tell him if he i' th' blood-sized° field lay swoll'n,
Showing the sun his teeth, grinning at the moon, 100
What you would do.

Hippolyta. Poor lady, say no more.
I had as lief trace° this good action with you
As that whereto I am going, and never yet
Went I so willing way.° My lord is taken
Heart-deep with your distress. Let him consider. 105
I'll speak anon.

Third Queen. (*Kneel*[*s*] *to Emilia*) O my petition was
Set down in ice, which by hot grief uncandied°
Melts into drops, so sorrow wanting form
Is pressed with deeper matter.°

Emilia. Pray stand up,
Your grief is written in your cheek.

Third Queen. O woe, 110
You cannot read it there; there through my tears,°
Like wrinkled pebbles in a glassy stream

87 **Whom** (usual in seventeenth century before a parenthetic clause) 88 **ow'st** possessest 89–90 **who . . . speech** who is obedient to everything you say 90 **glass of** mirror for (as in "mirror for magistrates," etc.) 97 **But** only 99 **blood-sized** spread with blood 102 **trace** pursue 104 **so willing way** any way so willingly 106–09 **O my . . . deeper matter** i.e., the formality of her previous speech (lines 29–34) now melts into tears, but grief in its formlessness can receive the imprint of a "deeper matter" (in this instance the desire for funeral rites and vengeance) 107 **uncandied** dissolved 111 **there through my tears** i.e., in her eyes

You may behold 'em.° Lady, lady, alack!
He that will all the treasure know o' th' earth
115 Must know the center° too; he that will fish
For my least minnow, let him lead his line°
To catch one at my heart. O pardon me,
Extremity that sharpens sundry wits
Makes me a fool. [*She rises.*]

Emilia. Pray you say nothing, pray you.
120 Who cannot feel nor see the rain, being in't,
Knows neither wet nor dry. If that you were
The ground-piece° of some painter, I would buy
you
T' instruct me 'gainst a capital grief indeed
Such heart-pierced° demonstration.° But alas,
125 Being a natural sister of our sex,°
Your sorrow beats so ardently upon me
That it shall make a counter-reflect° 'gainst
My brother's heart, and warm it to some pity
Though it were made of stone. Pray have good
comfort.

130 *Theseus.* Forward to th' temple, leave not out a jot
O' th' sacred ceremony.

First Queen. O this celebration
Will long last, and be more costly than
Your suppliants' war. Remember that your fame
Knolls in the ear o' th' world; what you do quickly
135 Is not done rashly; your first thought is more
Than others' labored meditance,° your premedi-
tating
More than their actions. But O Jove, your actions,
Soon as they move, as ospreys do the fish,°

113 **'em** i.e., her eyes, where her grief is imaged 115 **center** i.e., of the earth 116 **lead his line** weight it with lead 122 **ground-piece** flat representation (?) 124 **heart-pierced** heart-piercing 124 **demonstration** i.e., your demonstration of grief would instruct me how to bear any great grief 125 **Being . . . sex** since you are a woman like me (but "sifter" may be the right reading: see Textual Note) 127 **counter-reflect** reflection 136 **meditance** meditation, planning 138 **ospreys do the fish** (the osprey was believed to fascinate the fish before catching it)

Subdue before they touch. Think, dear duke, think
What beds our slain kings have.

Second Queen. What griefs our beds 140
That our dear lords have none.

Third Queen. None fit for th' dead.
Those that with cords, knives, drams' precipitance,°
Weary of this world's light, have to themselves
Been death's most horrid agents, human grace°
Affords them dust and shadow.°

First Queen. But our lords 145
Lie blist'ring 'fore the visitating° sun,
And were good kings when living.

Theseus. It is true,
And I will give you comfort, to give° your dead lords graves.
The which to do, must make some work with Creon.

First Queen. And that work presents itself to th' doing.° 150
Now 'twill take form,° the heats are gone tomorrow.
Then bootless toil must recompense itself
With its own sweat. Now he's secure,°
Not dreams we stand before your puissance,
Rinsing our holy begging in our eyes 155
To make petition clear.

Second Queen. Now you may take him,
Drunk with his victory.

Third Queen. And his army full
Of bread° and sloth.

Theseus. Artesius, that best knowest

142 **drams' precipitance** suicide by taking poison 144 **grace** mercy 145 **shadow** shelter 146 **visitating** inflicting harm (?) 148 **to give** by giving 150 **presents itself to th' doing** offers itself to be done at once 151 **form** shape 153 **secure** confident 158 **bread** food, feasting

How to draw out° fit to this enterprise
160 The prim'st for this proceeding, and the number
To carry° such a business, forth and levy
Our worthiest instruments, whilst we dispatch
This grand act of our life, this daring deed
Of fate° in wedlock.

First Queen. Dowagers, take hands,
165 Let us be widows to our woes,° delay
Commends us to a famishing hope.

All [*Queens*]. Farewell.

Second Queen. We come unseasonably, but when could grief
Cull forth,° as unpanged° judgment can, fitt'st time
For best solicitation?

Theseus. Why, good ladies,
170 This is a service whereto I am going
Greater than any was; it more imports me
Than all the actions that I have foregone°
Or futurely° can cope.

First Queen. The more proclaiming
Our suit shall be neglected. When her arms,
175 Able to lock Jove from a synod,° shall
By warranting° moonlight corslet thee, O when
Her twining cherries shall their sweetness fall°
Upon thy tasteful° lips, what wilt thou think
Of rotten kings or blubbered queens, what care
For what thou feel'st not, what thou feel'st being
180 able
To make Mars spurn his drum? O if thou couch
But one night with her, every hour in't will
Take hostage of thee for a hundred,° and

159 **draw out** select 161 **carry** carry out 163–64 **daring deed/Of fate** deed challenging fate 165 **be widows to our woes** live with our woes like widows (as we are) 168 **Cull forth** choose 168 **unpanged** untormented 172 **foregone** previously experienced 173 **futurely** in the future 175 **synod** council 176 **warranting** authorizing 177 **fall** let fall 178 **tasteful** tasting 183 **Take . . . hundred** i.e., you will feel committed to spend a hundred more with her

Thou shalt remember nothing more than what
That banquet bids thee to.

Hippolyta. [*Kneels*] Though much unlike 185
You should be so transported, as much sorry
I should be such a suitor;° yet I think,
Did I not by th' abstaining of my joy,
Which breeds a deeper longing, cure their surfeit
That craves a present med'cine, I should pluck 190
All ladies' scandal° on me. Therefore, sir,
As I shall here make trial of my pray'rs,
Either presuming them to have some force
Or sentencing for aye their vigor dumb,°
Prorogue° this business we are going about, and
hang 195
Your shield afore your heart, about that neck
Which is my fee,° and which I freely lend
To do these poor queens service.

All Queens. [*To Emilia*] O help now,
Our cause cries for your knee.

Emilia. [*Kneels*] If you grant not
My sister her petition in that force,° 200
With that celerity and nature which
She makes it in,° from henceforth I'll not dare
To ask you anything, nor be so hardy°
Ever to take a husband.

Theseus. Pray stand up.
[*Hippolyta and Emilia rise.*]
I am entreating of myself to do 205
That which you kneel to have me. Pirithous,
Lead on the bride; get you and pray the gods
For success, and return; omit not anything
In the pretended° celebration. Queens,

185–87 **Though . . . suitor** i.e., my reluctance to ask this is as great as my doubt that you would be so moved by our lovemaking 191 **scandal** disgrace 194 **sentencing . . . dumb** declaring that they shall never be uttered again 195 **Prorogue** postpone 197 **fee** property 200 **in that force** with that vigor 201–02 **nature which/She makes it in** condition of mind in which she makes it 203 **hardy** bold 209 **pretended** intended

Follow your soldier, as before.° [*To Artesius*]
210 Hence you,
And at the banks of Aulis° meet us with
The forces you can raise, where we shall find
The moiety of a number for a business
More bigger-looked.° [*Exit Artesius.*]
Since that our theme is haste,
215 I stamp this kiss upon thy current° lip.
Sweet, keep it as my token. [*Kisses Hippolyta.*]
Set you forward,
For I will see you gone.

[*Hippolyta, Emilia, Pirithous and Attendants begin to move*] *towards the temple.*

Farewell, my beauteous sister. Pirithous,
Keep the feast full,° bate not an hour on't.

Pirithous. Sir,
220 I'll follow you at heels. The feast's solemnity
Shall want° till your return.

Theseus. Cousin, I charge you
Budge not from Athens. We shall be returning
Ere you can end this feast, of which I pray you
Make no abatement. Once more, farewell all.
[*The procession enters the temple.*]

First Queen. Thus dost thou still make good the
225 tongue o' th' world.°

Second Queen. And earn'st a deity equal with Mars.

Third Queen. If not above him, for
Thou being but mortal makest affections bend

210 **as before** as I have already declared myself 211 **banks of Aulis** (see Textual Note: Aulis was a seaport, but "banks" could refer to the shore; however, this was an odd way to proceed from Athens to Thebes) 212–14 **where . . . bigger-looked** while I shall gather the other half of a force that would serve for a larger undertaking than this 215 **current** fleeting (transferred from Theseus, who is in haste), with a suggestion also of putting his royal stamp on her lip as on a coin 219 **full** fully 221 **want** be incomplete 225 **make good the tongue o' th' world** justify what the world says of you

To godlike honors.° They themselves,° some say,
Groan under such a mast'ry.°

Theseus. As we are men, 230
Thus should we do. Being sensually subdued,
We lose our human title.° Good cheer, ladies.
Now turn we towards your comforts.
Flourish. Exeunt.

Scene II. [*Thebes.*]

Enter Palamon and Arcite.

Arcite. Dear Palamon, dearer in love than blood°
And our prime° cousin, yet° unhardened in
The crimes of nature, let us leave the city
Thebes, and the temptings in't, before we further
Sully our gloss of youth; 5
And here to keep in abstinence we shame
As in incontinence:° for not to swim
I' th' aid o'° th' current were almost to sink,
At least to frustrate striving;° and to follow
The common stream, 'twould bring us to an eddy 10
Where we should turn° or drown; if labor through,
Our gain but life and weakness.

Palamon. Your advice
Is cried up° with example: what strange ruins
Since first we went to school may we perceive
Walking in Thebes? Scars and bare weeds 15

228–29 **makest . . . honors** turn your natural inclinations toward the winning of divine honors 229 **They themselves** i.e., the gods 230 **mast'ry** i.e., as yours 231–32 **Being . . . title** by yielding to our senses we lose our claim to be considered men I.ii.1 **blood** kinship 2 **prime** closest 2 **yet** as yet 6–7 **here . . . incontinence** here it is as shameful to abstain from vice as (elsewhere) to indulge in it 8 **I' th' aid o'** i.e., with 9 **frustrate striving** make our efforts useless 11 **turn** i.e., turn and begin to swim with the current 13 **cried up** supported

The gain o' th' Martialist,° who did propound
To his bold ends honor and golden ingots,
Which though he won he had not, and now flirted°
By peace for whom he fought: who then shall offer
20 To Mars's so scorned altar? I do bleed
When such I meet, and wish great Juno would
Resume her ancient fit of jealousy°
To get the soldier work, that peace might purge
For her repletion,° and retain° anew
25 Her charitable heart, now hard and harsher
Than strife or war could be.

Arcite. Are you not out?°
Meet you no ruin but the soldier in
The cranks and turns° of Thebes? You did begin
As if you met decays of many kinds.
30 Perceive you none that do arouse your pity
But th' unconsidered° soldier?

Palamon. Yes, I pity
Decays where'er I find them, but such most
That sweating in an honorable toil
Are paid with ice° to cool 'em.

Arcite. 'Tis not this
35 I did begin to speak of: this is virtue
Of no respect in Thebes. I spake of Thebes,
How dangerous if we will keep our honors
It is for our residing, where every evil
Hath a good color,° where every seeming good's
40 A certain evil, where not to be ev'n jump°
As they° are, here were to be° strangers, and

16 **Martialist** follower of Mars (i.e., soldier) 18 **flirted** mocked 21–22 **Juno . . . jealousy** (Juno's jealousy was a contributing factor to the Trojan War) 23–24 **peace might purge/For her repletion** (a common image: war was seen as a recurrent necessity so that society might "purge" itself of the results of too self-indulgent living: "for" here means "as a remedy for") 24 **retain** take into service 26 **Are you not out?** are you not mistaking the matter? 28 **cranks and turns** winding streets and passages 31 **unconsidered** neglected 34 **Are paid with ice** i.e., are treated coolly (ironically appropriate, because they have been sweating) 39 **color** appearance 40 **jump** exactly 41 **they** i.e., the Thebans 41 **were to be** would be

Such things to be,° mere° monsters.

Palamon. 'Tis in our power
(Unless we fear that apes can tutor's) to
Be masters of our manners. What need I
Affect° another's gait, which is not catching 45
Where there is faith, or to be fond upon
Another's way of speech, when by mine own
I may be reasonably conceived°—saved too,
Speaking it truly?° Why am I bound
By any generous bond° to follow him 50
Follows his tailor,° haply so long until
The followed make pursuit?° Or let me know
Why mine own barber is unblest, with him
My poor chin too, for° 'tis not scissored just
To such a favorite's glass.° What canon° is there 55
That does command my rapier from my hip
To dangle't in my hand, or to go tiptoe
Before the street be foul?° Either I am
The fore-horse in the team, or I am none
That draw i' th' sequent trace.° These poor slight
sores 60
Need not a plantain.° That which rips my bosom
Almost to th' heart's—

Arcite. Our uncle Creon.

Palamon. He,

42 **Such things to be** to be such things as they (the Thebans) are 42 **mere** absolute 45 **Affect** imitate 48 **conceived** understood 49 **Speaking it truly** i.e., if I speak the truth 50 **generous bond** nobleman's obligation 50–51 **follow him/Follows his tailor** imitate a man who takes instruction about conduct from his tailor 51–52 **until/The followed make pursuit** until the tailor, not having been paid, pursues his client to dun him 54 **for** because 54–55 **just/To such a favorite's glass** exactly in the fashion affected by such-and-such a favored person 55 **canon** law (particularly divine or ecclesiastical law) 57–58 **go tip-toe/Before the street be foul** (suggestive either of a mincing gait or of a way of walking so as to avoid noise, for purposes of surprise attack) 58–60 **Either . . . trace** either I shall lead or I shall refuse to be one that merely follows (the image being from a team of horses) 61 **plantain** (the leaves of the plantain herb were much used for treating wounds, stanching blood, etc.)

A most unbounded tyrant, whose successes
Makes heaven unfeared, and villainy assured
65 Beyond its power there's nothing; almost puts
Faith in a fever, and deifies alone
Voluble° chance; who° only attributes
The faculties of other instruments
To his own nerves and act;° commands men service,
70 And what they win in't, boot° and glory; one
That fears not to do harm; good, dares not.° Let
The blood of mine that's sib° to him be sucked
From me with leeches, let them break and fall
Off me with that corruption.

Arcite. Clear-spirited° cousin,
75 Let's leave his court, that we may nothing share
Of his loud infamy; for our milk
Will relish of the pasture,° and we must
Be vile or disobedient, not his kinsmen
In blood unless in quality.°

Palamon. Nothing truer.
80 I think the echoes of his shames have deafed
The ears of heav'nly justice: widows' cries
Descend again into their throats, and have not
Due audience of° the gods.

Enter Valerius.

Valerius!

Valerius. The king calls for you; yet be leaden-footed°
85 Till his great rage be off him. Phoebus, when
He broke his whipstock° and exclaimed against

67 **Voluble** inconstant 67 **who** i.e., the "tyrant" of line 63 67–69 **who . . . act** i.e., who takes what his subjects do as his own achievement 70 **boot** profit, booty 71 **good, dares not** dares not do good 72 **sib** related 74 **Clear-spirited** noble-spirited 76–77 **our milk/ Will relish of the pasture** i.e., what we produce will be affected by our environment 78–79 **not his kinsmen . . . quality** i.e., we must not hold the position of members of his family unless we are like him in character 83 **Due audience of** fitting attention from 84 **be leaden-footed** do not hasten 86 **whipstock** (here) whip

The horses of the sun, but whispered to°
The loudness of his fury.

Palamon. Small winds shake him,
But what's the matter?°

Valerius. Theseus, who where he threats appalls, hath sent 90
Deadly defiance to him and pronounces
Ruin to Thebes, who is at hand to seal
The promise of his wrath.°

Arcite. Let him approach.
But that we fear the gods in him,° he brings not
A jot of terror to us. Yet what° man 95
Thirds° his own worth (the case is each of ours)
When that his action's dregged,° with mind assured
'Tis bad he goes about.

Palamon. Leave that unreasoned.°
Our services stand now for Thebes, not Creon.
Yet to be neutral to him were dishonor, 100
Rebellious to oppose: therefore we must
With him stand to the mercy of our Fate,
Who hath bounded our last minute.°

Arcite. So we must.
Is't said this war's afoot, or it shall be
On fail of some condition?°

Valerius. 'Tis in motion: 105
The intelligence of state came in the instant
With the defier.°

87 **to** in comparison with 89 **the matter** the cause of disturbance 92–93 **seal/The promise of his wrath** confirm what his angry words have spoken 94 **fear the gods in him** fear him as an emissary of the gods 95 **what** here equivalent to "every" 96 **Thirds** reduces to a third of its former strength 97 **dregged** accompanied by dross matter 98 **unreasoned** unspoken, not argued about 103 **Who hath bounded our last minute** who has already settled the time when our lives end 105 **On fail of some condition** if stated terms of peace are not agreed to 106–07 **The intelligence . . . defier** i.e., the news that the war had started came at the same time as the declaration

Palamon. Let's to the king, who were he
A quarter carrier of that honor which
His enemy come in, the blood we venture
110 Should be as for our health, which were not spent,
Rather laid out for purchase.° But alas,
Our hands advanced before our hearts,° what will
The fall o' th' stroke do damage?

Arcite. Let th' event,°
That never erring arbitrator, tell us
115 When we know all ourselves, and let us follow
The becking of our chance. *Exeunt.*

Scene III. [*Athens.*]

Enter Pirithous, Hippolyta, Emilia.

Pirithous. No further.

Hippolyta. Sir, farewell. Repeat my wishes
To our great lord, of whose success I dare not
Make any timorous question, yet I wish him
Excess and overflow of power, and't might be
5 To dure° ill-dealing Fortune. Speed° to him:
Store never hurts good governors.°

Pirithous. Though I know
His ocean needs not my poor drops, yet they
Must yield their tribute there. [*To Emilia*] My precious maid,
Those best affections° that the heavens infuse

111 **laid out for purchase** invested for profit 112 **Our hands advanced before our hearts** i.e., our hands being engaged rather than our desires 113 **event** result I.iii.4–5 **and't might be/To dure** in case it were necessary to undergo 5 **Speed** hasten 6 **Store never hurts good governors** plenty is never a handicap to good leaders 9 **affections** inclinations

In their best-tempered pieces,° keep enthroned 10
In your dear heart.

Emilia. Thanks, sir. Remember me
To our all-royal brother, for whose speed°
The great Bellona I'll solicit; and
Since in our terrene° state petitions are not
Without gifts understood, I'll offer to her 15
What I shall be advised° she likes: our hearts
Are in his army, in his tent.

Hippolyta. In's bosom.
We have been soldiers, and we cannot weep
When our friends don their helms, or put to sea,
Or tell of babes broached on the lance, or women 20
That have sod° their infants in—and after eat
them—
The brine they wept at killing 'em.° Then if
You stay to see of us such spinsters,° we
Should hold you here forever.

Pirithous. Peace be to you
As I pursue this war, which shall be then 25
Beyond further requiring.° *Exit Pirithous.*

Emilia. How his longing
Follows his friend! Since his depart,° his sports,
Though craving seriousness and skill, passed slightly
His careless execution,° where nor gain
Made him regard, or loss consider, but 30
Playing one business in his hand, another
Directing in his head—his mind nurse equal
To these so diff'ring twins.° Have you observed
him,

10 **best-tempered pieces** most harmoniously wrought creatures 12 **speed** success 14 **terrene** earthly 16 **shall be advised** am told 21 **sod** boiled 22 **brine they wept at killing 'em** tears they shed as they killed them 23 **spinsters** i.e., weak women 25–26 **which . . . requiring** i.e., peace will be ensured 27 **depart** departure 28–29 **passed slightly/His careless execution** i.e., were given only slight and careless attention 32–33 **his mind . . . twins** i.e., his mind was equally concerned with what he was doing and with what he was imagining (fighting with Theseus)

Since our great lord departed?

Hippolyta. With much labor;°

35 And I did love him for't. They two have cabined°
In many as dangerous as poor a corner,
Peril and want contending.° They have skiffed
Torrents whose roaring tyranny and power
I' th' least of these° was dreadful; and they have
40 Fought out together where Death's self was lodged,
Yet Fate hath brought them off.° Their knot of love,
Tied, weaved, entangled, with so true, so long,
And with a finger of so deep a cunning,
May be outworn, never undone.° I think
45 Theseus cannot be umpire to himself,
Cleaving his conscience° into twain and doing
Each side like° justice, which he loves best.°

Emilia. Doubtless
There is a best, and Reason has no manners
To say it is not you.° I was acquainted
50 Once with a time when I enjoyed a playfellow.
You were at wars, when she the grave enriched
Who made too proud the bed, took leave o' th' moon
(Which then looked pale at parting) when our count°
Was each eleven.

Hippolyta. 'Twas Flavina.

Emilia. Yes.

34 **labor** attention 35 **cabined** lodged together 37 **contending** i.e., being comparable in degree 39 **I' th' least of these** (referring either to "Peril and want," line 37, or to "tyranny and power," line 38) 41 **brought them off** brought them to safety 44 **May be outworn, never undone** i.e., may be worn out by death, not unknotted before 45–47 **Theseus . . . best** i.e., even Theseus cannot judge whether he loves best himself or Pirithous 46 **conscience** consciousness 47 **like** equal 49 **To say it is not you** (Emilia, taking Hippolyta's remark in a different way from that intended, suggests that Theseus must love Hippolyta best of all; lines 95–96 make it less likely that "you" is indefinite, meaning that Theseus must in reason love himself better than his friend) 53 **our count** the number of our years

You talk of Pirithous' and Theseus' love. 55
Theirs has more ground,° is more maturely seasoned,
More buckled° with strong judgment, and their needs
The one of th' other may be said to water
Their intertangled roots of love. But I
And she I sigh and spoke of were things innocent, 60
Loved for we did,° and like the elements
That know not what, nor why, yet do effect
Rare issues by their operance,° our souls
Did so to one another: what she liked
Was then of me approved, what not condemned— 65
No more arraignment;° the flow'r that I would pluck
And put between my breasts, O then but beginning
To swell about the blossom, she would long
Till she had such another, and commit it
To the like innocent cradle, where phoenix-like 70
They died in perfume;° on my head no toy°
But was her pattern;° her affections°—pretty
Though happily her careless were°—I followed
For my most serious decking;° had mine ear
Stol'n some new air, or at adventure hummed on 75
From musical coinage,° why, it was a note
Whereon her spirits would sojourn, rather dwell on,
And sing it in her slumbers. This rehearsal,°
Which—every innocent° wots well—comes in
Like old importment's bastard,° has this end 80

56 **ground** foundation 57 **buckled** supported 61 **for we did** merely because we did 62–63 **effect/Rare issues by their operance** produce strange happenings through their operation 65–66 **what not condemned—/No more arraignment** what she did not like was condemned by me, without further consideration of the case 70–71 **phoenix-like/They died in perfume** (referring to the legendary phoenix, from whose fragrant funeral pyre the next phoenix was born) 71 **toy** trifling ornament 72 **pattern** i.e., for imitation 72 **affections** inclinations, preferences 73 **Though happily her careless were** though her preferences might be carelessly made 74 **decking** adornment 75–76 **hummed on/From musical coinage** i.e., improvised 78 **rehearsal** recital 79 **innocent** child 80 **Like old importment's bastard** like a feeble imitation of the experience itself

That the true love 'tween maid and maid may be
More than in sex dividual.°

Hippolyta. Y' are out of breath,
And this high-speeded pace is but to say
That you shall never, like the maid Flavina,
Love any that's called man.

85 *Emilia.* I am sure I shall not.

Hippolyta. Now alack, weak sister,
I must no more believe thee in this point,
Though in't I know thou dost believe thyself,
Than I will trust a sickly appetite
90 That loathes even as it longs. But sure, my sister,
If I were ripe for your persuasion, you
Have said enough to shake me from the arm
Of the all-noble Theseus, for whose fortunes
I will now in and kneel, with great assurance
95 That we, more than his Pirithous, possess
The high throne in his heart.

Emilia. I am not against
Your faith, yet I continue mine. *Exeunt.*

81–82 **That . . . dividual** i.e., that their love may be greater than the love of those different in sex

Scene IV. [*Thebes.*]

Cornets. A battle struck° within. Then a retreat. Flourish. Then enter Theseus (victor) [with a Herald, Lords and Attendants and with Palamon and Arcite carried on hearses].° The three Queens meet him, and fall on their faces before him.

First Queen. To thee no star be dark!°

Second Queen. Both heaven and earth
Friend° thee forever!

Third Queen. All the good that may
Be wished upon thy head, I cry "amen" to't!

Theseus. Th' impartial gods, who from the mounted° heavens
View us their mortal herd, behold who err *5*
And in their time chastise. Go and find out
The bones of your dead lords, and honor them
With treble ceremony; rather than a gap
Should be in their dear° rites, we would supply't.
But those we will depute which shall invest *10*
You in your dignities, and even° each thing
Our haste does leave imperfect. So adieu,
And heaven's good eyes look on you.
Exeunt Queens.
What are those?

Herald. Men of great quality, as may be judged
By their appointment.° Some of Thebes have told's *15*
They are sisters' children, nephews to the king.

I.iv. s.d. **struck** sounded **hearses** carriages 1 **To thee no star be dark** let all stars be favorable to you 2 **Friend** befriend 4 **mounted** high (with a suggestion of the gods on horseback looking down on men as beasts under their control) 9 **dear** valued 11 **even** make right 15 **appointment** accouterment

Theseus. By th' helm of Mars, I saw them in the war,
Like to a pair of lions smeared with prey,
Make lanes in troops aghast. I fixed my note°
20 Constantly on them, for they were a mark
Worth a god's view. What prisoner was't that told me°
When I enquired their names?

Herald. We 'lieve° they're called
Arcite and Palamon.

Theseus. 'Tis right: those, those;
They are not dead?

25 *Herald.* Nor in a state of life: had they been taken
When their last hurts were given, 'twas possible
They might have been recovered. Yet they breathe
And have the name of men.°

Theseus. Then like men use 'em.
The very lees of such—millions of rates°—
30 Exceed the wine of others. All our surgeons
Convent° in their behoof, our richest balms,
Rather than niggard, waste. Their lives concern us
Much more than Thebes is worth. Rather than have 'em
Freed of this plight and in their morning state,°
35 Sound and at liberty, I would 'em dead,°
But forty-thousandfold we had rather have 'em
Prisoners to us than Death.° Bear 'em speedily
From our kind air, to them unkind,° and minister
What man to man may do—for our sake more,
40 Since I have known frights, fury, friends' behests,
Love's provocations, zeal, a mistress' task,
Desire of liberty, a fever, madness,
Hath set a mark which Nature could not reach to

19 **fixed my note** directed my attention 21 **What . . . me** i.e., what was it that a prisoner told me 22 **'lieve** believe 28 **have the name of men** can still be called men 29 **millions of rates** millions of times 31 **Convent** summon 34 **in their morning state** as they were this morning 35 **would 'em dead** would rather they were dead 37 **Death** i.e., prisoners to Death 38 **kind air, to them unkind** i.e., the open air is healthy to us but not to them

Without some imposition—sickness in will
O'er-wrestling strength in reason.° For our love 45
And great Apollo's° mercy, all our best
Their best skill tender.° Lead into the city,
Where, having bound things scattered, we will post
To Athens 'fore our army. *Flourish. Exeunt.*

Scene V. [*Thebes.*]

Music. Enter the Queens with the hearses of their knights, in a funeral solemnity, &c.

[*Song*]

Urns and odors bring away,°
Vapors, sighs, darken the day;
Our dole more deadly looks than dying:
Balms and gums° and heavy cheers,°
Sacred vials filled with tears, 5
And clamors through the wild air flying.

Come, all sad and solemn shows
That are quick-eyed Pleasure's foes:
We convent° nought else but woes,
We convent, &c. 10

Third Queen. [*To Second Queen*] This funeral path brings° to your household's grave.
Joy seize on you again. Peace sleep with him.

Second Queen. [*To First Queen*] And this to yours.°

40–45 **Since . . . reason** i.e., since I have known cases where unusual physical or emotional disturbance has produced results that Nature could not produce without some special stimulus ("imposition"), this disturbance being able to overcome what could be reasonably expected 46 **Apollo** as god of healing 47 **tender** minister I.v.1 **bring away** accompany us 4 **gums** (used for perfume at the funeral rites) 4 **heavy cheers** sad faces 9 **convent** summon, bring together 11 **brings** leads 13 **this to yours** (the Queens now take their different paths home)

First Queen. [*To Third Queen*] Yours this way. Heavens lend°
A thousand differing ways to one sure end.

Third Queen. This world's a city full of straying°
15 streets,
And death's the market place where each one meets. *Exeunt severally.*

13 lend provide **15 straying** winding

ACT II

Scene I. [*Athens. A garden with a room in a prison above.*]

Enter Jailer and Wooer.

Jailer. I may depart with° little while I live: something I may cast to you, not much. Alas, the prison I keep, though it be for great ones, yet they seldom come. Before one salmon you shall take a number of minnows. I am given out to be better lined than *5* it can appear to me report is a true speaker.° I would I were really that I am delivered° to be. Marry,° what I have, be it what it will, I will assure° upon my daughter at the day of my death.

Wooer. Sir, I demand no more than your own offer, *10* and I will estate° your daughter in what I have promised.

Jailer. Well, we will talk more of this when the solemnity° is passed. But have you a full promise of her?

Enter Daughter.

When that shall be seen, I tender my consent. *15*

Wooer. I have, sir. Here she comes.

II.i.1 **depart with** give 5–6 **I am . . . speaker** I am generally believed to be better off than there seems to me cause for rumor to assert 7 **delivered** said 8 **Marry** indeed 8–9 **assure** i.e., bestow 11 **estate** endow 13–14 **solemnity** i.e., wedding

Jailer. Your friend and I have chanced to name you here, upon the old business; but no more of that now. So soon as the court-hurry° is over, we will
20 have an end of it. I' th' meantime look tenderly to the two prisoners. I can tell you they are princes.

Daughter. These strewings° are for their chamber. 'Tis pity they are in prison, and 'twere pity they should be out. I do think they have patience to
25 make any adversity ashamed: the prison itself is proud of 'em, and they have all the world in their chamber.°

Jailer. They are famed to be a pair of absolute° men.

Daughter. By my troth, I think Fame but stammers
30 'em:° they stand a grize° above the reach of report.

Jailer. I heard them reported in the battle to be the only doers.°

Daughter. Nay, most likely, for they are noble suff'rers. I marvel how they would have looked had
35 they been victors, that with such a constant nobility enforce a freedom out of bondage, making misery their mirth, and affliction a toy to jest at.

Jailer. Do they so?

Daughter. It seems to me they have no more sense of
40 their captivity than I of ruling Athens. They eat well, look merrily, discourse of many things, but nothing of their own restraint° and disasters. Yet sometime a divided° sigh, martyred as 'twere i' th' deliverance, will break from one of them—when
45 the other presently° gives it so sweet a rebuke that I could wish myself a sigh to be so chid, or at least a sigher to be comforted.

19 **court-hurry** celebrations at court (?) 22 **strewings** rushes 26–27 **they . . . chamber** their nobility makes their chamber into a whole world (?), everyone visits them (?) 28 **absolute** complete 29–30 **Fame but stammers 'em** i.e., their reputation falls short of their worth 30 **grize** step 32 **only doers** unique performers 42 **restraint** imprisonment 43 **divided** broken off 45 **presently** at once

Wooer. I never saw 'em.

Jailer. The duke himself came privately in the night, and so did they:° what the reason of it is I know not. 50

Enter Palamon and Arcite above.

Look, yonder they are. That's Arcite looks out.

Daughter. No, sir, no! That's Palamon! Arcite is the lower° of the twain. You may perceive a part of him. 55

Jailer. Go to, leave your pointing. They would not make us their object.° Out of their sight!

Daughter. It is a holiday to look on them. Lord, the diff'rence of men!

Exeunt [*Jailer, Wooer, Daughter*].

Palamon. How do you, noble cousin?

Arcite. How do you, sir? 60

Palamon. Why, strong enough to laugh at misery,
And bear the chance of war. Yet we are prisoners
I fear forever, cousin.

Arcite. I believe it,
And to that destiny have patiently
Laid up my hour to come.°

Palamon. O cousin Arcite, 65
Where is Thebes now? Where is our noble country?
Where are our friends, and kindreds?° Never more
Must we behold those comforts, never see
The hardy youths strive for the games of honor,
Hung with the painted favors of their ladies, 70

49–50 **The duke . . . they** i.e., Theseus brought the princes secretly to the prison 54 **lower** shorter 56–57 **They would not make us their object** they would not point at us 65 **Laid up my hour to come** i.e., resolved myself 66–67 **Where is Thebes . . . kindreds** (these references to Thebes are very different from those in the princes' conversation of I.ii)

Like tall ships under sail; then start amongst 'em
And as an east wind leave 'em all behind us,
Like lazy clouds, whilst Palamon and Arcite,
Even in the wagging of a wanton leg,°
75 Outstripped the people's praises, won the garlands
Ere they have time to wish 'em ours. O never
Shall we two exercise, like twins of Honor,
Our arms again, and feel our fiery horses
Like proud seas under us! Our good swords now—
80 Better the red-eyed god of war ne'er wore!—
Ravished our sides, like age must run to rust
And deck the temples of those gods that hate us.
These hands shall never draw 'em out like lightning
To blast whole armies more.

Arcite. No, Palamon,
85 Those hopes are prisoners with us: here we are
And here the graces of our youths must wither
Like a too timely° spring; here age must find us,
And which is heaviest, Palamon, unmarried;
The sweet embraces of a loving wife,
90 Loaden with kisses, armed with thousand Cupids,
Shall never clasp our necks, no issue° know us,
No figures of ourselves shall we e'er see,
To glad our age, and like young eagles teach 'em
Boldly to gaze against bright arms,° and say:
95 "Remember what your fathers were, and conquer."
The fair-eyed maids shall weep our banishments,
And in their songs curse ever-blinded Fortune
Till she for shame see what a wrong she has done
To youth and nature. This is all our world:
100 We shall know nothing here but one another,
Hear nothing but the clock that tells° our woes.
The vine shall grow, but we shall never see it;
Summer shall come, and with her all delights;
But dead-cold winter must inhabit here still.

74 **Even . . . leg** as quickly as a leg might be wantonly or idly moved 87 **too timely** too early 91 **issue** children 94 **arms** weapons and armor (with an allusion to the eagle's ability to look directly at the sun) 101 **tells** counts

Palamon. 'Tis too true, Arcite. To our Theban hounds, *105*
That shook the agèd forest with their echoes
No more now must we halloo, no more shake
Our pointed javelins, whilst the angry swine°
Flies like a Parthian quiver° from our rages,
Struck with our well-steeled darts. All valiant uses,° *110*
The food and nourishment of noble minds,
In us two here shall perish. We shall die—
Which is the curse of honor—lastly,°
Children of grief and ignorance.

Arcite. Yet, cousin,
Even from the bottom of these miseries, *115*
From all that Fortune can inflict upon us,
I see two comforts rising, two mere° blessings,
If the gods please: to hold here a brave patience,
And the enjoying of our griefs together.
Whilst Palamon is with me, let me perish *120*
If I think this our prison.

Palamon. Certainly,
'Tis a main° goodness, cousin, that our fortunes
Were twined together. 'Tis most true, two souls
Put in two noble bodies, let 'em suffer
The gall of hazard,° so° they grow together, *125*
Will never sink; they must not, say° they could.
A willing man dies sleeping, and all's done.°

Arcite. Shall we make worthy uses of this place
That all men hate so much?

Palamon. How, gentle cousin?

Arcite. Let's think this prison holy sanctuary, *130*
To keep us from corruption of worse men.
We are young and yet desire the ways of honor

108 **angry swine** wild boar 109 **Parthian quiver** (the Parthian bowman was famed for shooting his arrows while retreating: here the fleeing boar, with the arrows stuck in it, is seen as the Parthian's quiver) 110 **uses** customs, practices 113 **lastly** (three syllables) 117 **mere** pure 122 **main** principal 125 **The gall of hazard** the bitterness of misadventure 125 **so** provided that 126 **say** even if 127 **A willing . . . done** a man resigned to his fate dies as gently as falling asleep (but the tone of this line is not resigned)

That liberty and common conversation,
The poison of pure spirits, might like women
135 Woo us to wander from. What worthy blessing
Can be but our imaginations
May make it ours? And here being thus together,
We are an endless mine° to one another;
We are one another's wife, ever begetting
New births of love; we are father, friends, acquain-
140 tance;
We are in one another families;
I am your heir, and you are mine. This place
Is our inheritance; no hard oppressor
Dare take this from us; here with a little patience
145 We shall live long, and loving; no surfeits seek us;
The hand of war hurts none here, nor the seas
Swallow their youth. Were we at liberty,
A wife might part us lawfully, or business,
Quarrels consume us, envy of ill men
150 Crave our acquaintance.° I might sicken, cousin,
Where you should never know it, and so perish
Without your noble hand to close mine eyes,
Or prayers to the gods. A thousand chances,
Were we from hence, would sever us.

Palamon. You have made me—
155 I thank you, cousin Arcite—almost wanton°
With my captivity. What a misery
It is to live abroad, and everywhere!
'Tis like a beast, methinks. I find the court here,
I am sure a more content,° and all those pleasures
160 That woo the wills of men to vanity
I see through now, and am sufficient°
To tell the world 'tis but a gaudy shadow
That old Time, as he passes by, takes with him.
What had we been old° in the court of Creon,

138 **mine** source of wealth 150 **Crave our acquaintance** i.e., contaminate by impact on us (editors have variously emended, e.g. to "Grave" = bury, "Cleave" = separate) 155 **wanton** i.e., delighted 159 **a more content** i.e., a court more contented than the real one 161 **sufficient** able 164 **What had we been old** what if we had been old (editors have emended to "What had we been, old . . .")

Where sin is justice, lust and ignorance 165
The virtues of the great ones! Cousin Arcite,
Had not the loving gods found this place for us,
We had died as they do, ill old men, unwept,
And had their epitaphs, the people's curses.
Shall I say more?

Arcite. I would hear you still.

Palamon. Ye shall. 170
Is there record of any two that loved
Better than we do, Arcite?

Arcite. Sure there cannot.

Palamon. I do not think it possible our friendship
Should ever leave us.

Arcite. Till our deaths it cannot,

Enter Emilia and her Woman [below].

And after death our spirits shall be led 175
To those that love eternally.° Speak on, sir.
[*Palamon sees Emilia.*]

Emilia. This garden has a world of pleasures in't.
What flow'r is this?

Woman. 'Tis called Narcissus, madam.

Emilia. That was a fair boy certain, but a fool
To love himself:° were there not maids enough? 180

Arcite. Pray, forward.°

Palamon. Yes.

Emilia. Or were they all hard-hearted?

Woman. They could not be to one so fair.

Emilia. Thou wouldst not.

175–76 **our . . . eternally** our souls shall be with famous lovers in Elysium 178–80 **Narcissus . . . himself** (Narcissus fell in love with his own reflection in water, and drowned in trying to embrace it) 181 **forward** i.e., continue

Woman. I think I should not, madam.

Emilia. That's a good wench;
But take heed to your kindness, though.

Woman. Why, madam?

Emilia. Men are mad things.

185 *Arcite*. Will ye go forward, cousin?

Emilia. Canst not thou work such flowers in silk, wench?

Woman. Yes.

Emilia. I'll have a gown full of 'em and of these.
This is a pretty color, will't not do
Rarely upon a skirt, wench?

Woman. Dainty, madam.

Arcite. Cousin, cousin, how do you, sir? Why, Pala-
190 mon!

Palamon. Never till now I was in prison, Arcite.

Arcite. Why, what's the matter, man?

Palamon. Behold, and wonder.
By heaven, she is a goddess.

Arcite. [*Seeing Emilia*] Ha!

Palamon. Do reverence.
She is a goddess, Arcite.

Emilia. Of all flow'rs
Methinks a rose is best.

195 *Woman*. Why, gentle madam?

Emilia. It is the very emblem of a maid.
For when the west wind courts her gently°
How modestly she blows,° and paints° the sun

197 **gently** (three syllables) 198 **blows** opens into flower 198 **paints** gives an image of

With her chaste blushes! When the north comes
near her,
Rude and impatient, then like chastity 200
She locks her beauties in her bud again,
And leaves him to base briers.°

Woman. Yet, good madam,
Sometimes her modesty will blow so far
She falls for't:° a maid,
If she have any honor, would be loath 205
To take example by her.

Emilia. Thou art wanton.

Arcite. She is wondrous fair.

Palamon. She is all the beauty extant.°

Emilia. The sun grows high, let's walk in. Keep these
flowers:
We'll see how mere art can come near their colors.
I am wondrous merry-hearted, I could laugh now. 210

Woman. I could lie down,° I am sure.

Emilia. And take one with you?°

Woman. That's as we bargain,° madam.

Emilia. Well, agree° then.
Exeunt Emilia and Woman.

Palamon. What think you of this beauty?

Arcite. 'Tis a rare one.

Palamon. Is't but a rare one?

Arcite. Yes, a matchless beauty.

Palamon. Might not a man well lose himself and love
her? 215

202 **leaves him to base briers** leaves only base briers for him 204 **for't** as a result of it 207 **extant** in existence 210–11 **laugh . . . lie down** (the waiting-woman turns Emilia's merriment into an allusion to the proverb "laugh and lie down") 211 **And take one with you** i.e., lie down with a (male) companion 212 **bargain, agree** come to terms

Arcite. I cannot tell what you have done. I have.
Beshrew mine eyes for't, now I feel my shackles.

Palamon. You love her, then?

Arcite. Who would not?

Palamon. And desire her?

Arcite. Before my liberty.

Palamon. I saw her first.

Arcite. That's nothing.

Palamon. But it shall be.

220 *Arcite.* I saw her too.

Palamon. Yes, but you must not love her.

Arcite. I will not as you do, to worship her,
As she is heavenly and a blessèd goddess:
I love her as a woman, to enjoy her.
225 So both may love.

Palamon. You shall not love at all.

Arcite. Not love at all?
Who shall deny me?

Palamon. I that first saw her, I that took possession
First with mine eye of all those beauties
230 In her revealed to mankind. If thou lov'st her,
Or entertain'st a hope to blast my wishes,
Thou art a traitor, Arcite, and a fellow°
False as thy title to her. Friendship, blood°
And all the ties between us I disclaim
If thou once think upon her.

235 *Arcite.* Yes, I love her,
And if the lives of all my name° lay on it,
I must do so, I love her with my soul.
If that will lose ye,° farewell, Palamon:
I say again, I love, and in loving her maintain

232 **fellow** (often used contemptuously at this time) 233 **blood** kinship 236 **name** family 238 **lose ye** make me lose you

I am as worthy and as free a lover 240
And have as just a title to her beauty
As any Palamon or any living
That is a man's son.

Palamon. Have I called thee friend?

Arcite. Yes, and have found me so; why are you moved thus?
Let me deal coldly° with you: am not I 245
Part of your blood, part of your soul? You have told me
That I was Palamon and you were Arcite.

Palamon. Yes.

Arcite. Am not I liable to those affections,°
Those joys, griefs, angers, fears, my friend shall suffer?

Palamon. Ye may be.

Arcite. Why then would you deal so cunningly, 250
So strangely, so unlike a noble kinsman,
To love alone? Speak truly, do you think me
Unworthy of her sight?

Palamon. No, but unjust,
If thou pursue that sight.

Arcite. Because another
First sees the enemy, shall I stand still 255
And let mine honor down, and never charge?

Palamon. Yes, if he be but one.

Arcite. But say that one
Had rather combat me?

Palamon. Let that one say so,
And use thy freedom; else if thou pursuest her,
Be as that cursèd man that hates his country, 260
A branded villain.

245 **coldly** rationally 248 **affections** emotions

Arcite. You are mad.

Palamon. I must be,
Till thou art worthy, Arcite: it concerns me.°
And in this madness if I hazard thee°
And take thy life, I deal but truly.

Arcite. Fie, sir.
265 You play the child extremely. I will love her,
I must, I ought to do so, and I dare,
And all this justly.

Palamon. O that now, that now
Thy false self and thy friend had but this fortune
To be one hour at liberty, and grasp
Our good swords in our hands, I would quickly
270 teach thee
What 'twere to filch affection from another.
Thou art baser in it than a cutpurse.
Put but thy head out of this window more,
And as I have a soul, I'll nail thy life to't.

Arcite. Thou dar'st not, fool, thou canst not, thou art
275 feeble.
Put my head out? I'll throw my body out,
And leap° the garden, when I see her next

Enter Jailer [*above*].

And pitch° between her arms to anger thee.

Palamon. No more; the keeper's coming; I shall live
To knock thy brains out with my shackles.

280 *Arcite.* Do.

Jailer. By your leave, gentlemen.

Palamon. Now, honest keeper?

Jailer. Lord Arcite, you must presently° to th' duke;
The cause I know not yet.

262 **it concerns me** it is of importance to me 263 **hazard thee** put your life in danger (?), risk losing your friendship (?) 277 **leap** leap down into 278 **pitch** plant myself 282 **presently** immediately

Arcite. I am ready, keeper.

Jailer. Prince Palamon, I must awhile bereave you
Of your fair cousin's company.
Exeunt Arcite and Jailer.

Palamon. And me too, 285
Even when you please, of life. Why is he sent for?
It may be he shall marry her, he's goodly,°
And like enough the duke hath taken notice
Both of his blood and body. But his falsehood—
Why should a friend be treacherous? If that 290
Get him a wife so noble and so fair,
Let honest men ne'er love again. Once more
I would but see this fair one. Blessed garden,
And fruit, and flowers more blessed that still° blossom
As her bright eyes shine on ye! Would I were 295
For° all the fortune of my life hereafter
Yon little tree, yon blooming apricock!
How I would spread, and fling my wanton arms
In at her window! I would bring her fruit
Fit for the gods to feed on; youth and pleasure 300
Still as she tasted should be doubled on her,
And if she be not heavenly I would make her
So near the gods in nature, they should fear her.

Enter Jailer [*above*].

And then I am sure she would love me. How now, keeper,
Where's Arcite?

Jailer. Banished. Prince Pirithous 305
Obtained his liberty; but never more
Upon his oath and life must he set foot
Upon this kingdom.

Palamon. [*Aside*] He's a blessed man,
He shall see Thebes again, and call to arms
The bold young men, that when he bids 'em charge 310

287 **goodly** handsome 294 **still** ever 296 **For** in exchange for

Fall on like fire. Arcite shall have a fortune,°
If he dare make himself a worthy lover,
Yet in the field to strike a battle° for her,
And if he lose her then, he's a cold coward.
315 How bravely may he bear himself to win her
If he be noble Arcite! Thousand ways.°
Were I at liberty, I would do things
Of such a virtuous greatness that this lady,
This blushing virgin, should take manhood to her
And seek to ravish me.

320 *Jailer.* My lord, for you
I have this charge too.

Palamon. To discharge my life?

Jailer. No, but from this place to remove your lordship:
The windows are too open.°

Palamon. Devils take 'em
That are so envious° to me! Prithee kill me.

Jailer. And hang for't afterward.

325 *Palamon.* By this good light,
Had I a sword I would kill thee.

Jailer. Why, my lord?

Palamon. Thou bring'st such pelting° scurvy news continually
Thou art not worthy life. I will not go.

Jailer. Indeed you must, my lord.

Palamon. May I see the garden?

Jailer. No.

330 *Palamon.* Then I am resolved, I will not go.

311 **a fortune** a chance 313 **strike a battle** sound a call to battle 316 **Thousand ways** i.e., there are a thousand ways in which he may show himself brave 323 **open** easy to escape from 324 **envious** malicious 327 **pelting** paltry, contemptible

Jailer. I must constrain you then; and for you are dangerous,
I'll clap more irons on you.

Palamon. Do, good keeper.
I'll shake 'em so, ye shall not sleep,
I'll make ye a new morris.° Must I go?

Jailer. There is no remedy.

Palamon. Farewell, kind window. 335
May rude wind never hurt thee. O my lady,
If ever thou hast felt what sorrow was,
Dream how I suffer. Come; now bury me.
Exeunt Palamon and Jailer.

Scene II. [*The open country*.]

Enter Arcite.

Arcite. Banished the kingdom! 'Tis a benefit,
A mercy I must thank 'em for; but banished
The free enjoying of that face I die for,
O 'twas a studied punishment, a death
Beyond imagination! Such a vengeance 5
That, were I old and wicked, all my sins
Could never pluck upon me. Palamon,
Thou has the start now, thou shalt stay and see
Her bright eyes break each morning 'gainst thy window,
And let in life into thee; thou shalt feed 10
Upon the sweetness of a noble beauty
That Nature ne'er exceeded, nor ne'er shall.
Good gods! What happiness has Palamon!
Twenty to one, he'll come to speak to her,
And if she be as gentle as she's fair, 15

334 **make ye a new morris** dance a new morris dance for you (in which bells would jingle on the dancer's coat)

I know she's his: he has a tongue will tame
Tempests, and make the wild rocks wanton. Come what can come,
The worst is death. I will not leave the kingdom.
I know mine own° is but a heap of ruins,
20 And no redress there. If I go, he has her.
I am resolved another shape° shall make me,°
Or end my fortunes. Either way I am happy:
I'll see her and be near her, or no more.

Enter four country people, and one with a garland before them.

First Countryman. My masters, I'll be there, that's certain.

25 *Second Countryman.* And I'll be there.

Third Countryman. And I.

Fourth Countryman. Why, then, have with ye,° boys. 'Tis but a chiding.°
Let the plough play today; I'll tickle't out
Of the jades'° tails tomorrow.

First Countryman. I am sure
30 To have my wife as jealous as a turkey,
But that's all one.° I'll go through,° let her mumble.

Second Countryman. Clap her aboard° tomorrow night, and stow° her,
And all's made up again.

Third Countryman. Aye, do but put
A fescue in her fist,° and you shall see her

II.ii.19 **mine own** i.e., Thebes 21 **another shape** a disguise 21 **make me** bring good fortune to me 27 **have with ye** i.e., I'll be there too 27 **'Tis but a chiding** the worst that can happen is a chiding 29 **jades'** nags' 31 **that's all one** that's a matter of indifference 31 **go through** i.e., go through with it 32 **Clap her aboard** board her (as a conquered ship) 32 **stow** fill the hold with cargo (continuing the metaphor) 33–34 **put/A fescue in her fist** (a "fescue" was a small stick, etc., which a teacher used as a pointer: here it indicates a penis, the idea being "give *her* something to point with")

Take a new lesson out° and be a good wench. 35
Do we all hold,° against° the Maying?

Fourth Countryman. Hold?
What should ail us?°

Third Countryman. Arcas will be there.

Second Countryman. And Sennois
And Rycas, and three better lads ne'er danced
Under green tree; and ye know what wenches, ha?
But will the dainty dominie,° the schoolmaster, 40
Keep touch,° do you think? For he does all,° ye
know.

Third Countryman. He'll eat a hornbook° ere he fail.
Go to,
The matter's too far driven between
Him and the tanner's daughter to let slip now,°
And she must see the duke, and she must dance too. 45

Fourth Countryman. Shall we be lusty!°

Second Countryman. [*Dances*] All the boys in Athens
Blow wind i' th' breech on's,° and here I'll be
And there I'll be, for our town, and here again
And there again! Ha, boys, hey for the weavers!°

First Countryman. This must be done i' th' woods.

Fourth Countryman. O pardon me.° 50

Second Countryman. By any means.° Our thing of
learning° says so,

35 **Take a new lesson out** learn a new lesson (continuing the metaphor) 36 **hold** hold to our purposes 36 **against** in regard to 37 **ail us** make us incapable 40 **dainty dominie** fine schoolmaster 41 **Keep touch** hold to his word 41 **does all** i.e., is indispensable 42 **hornbook** sheet of paper protected by a sheet of transparent horn, used in teaching the alphabet, etc. 43–44 **The matter's . . . slip now** i.e., their love affair cannot fail to lead to marriage 46 **lusty** vigorous 46–47 **All . . . breech on's** i.e., all the boys in Athens are supporting us (literally, are helping us to dance by blowing us from the ground) 49 **hey for the weavers** (the Second Countryman, like Bottom, is a weaver and will dance in honor of his craft) 50 **pardon me** (indicating dissent) 51 **By any means** in any case 51 **Our thing of learning** i.e., the schoolmaster

Where he himself will edify the duke
Most parlously° in our behalfs. He's excellent i' th' woods;
Bring him to th' plains,° his learning makes no cry.°

Third Countryman. We'll see the sports, then every
55 man to's tackle.°
And, sweet companions, let's rehearse by any means
Before the ladies see us, and do sweetly,°
And God knows what may come on't.

Fourth Countryman. Content;
The sports once ended, we'll perform. Away, boys, and hold!°

Arcite. [*Comes forward*] By your leaves, honest
60 friends. Pray you, whither go you?

Fourth Countryman. Whither? Why, what a question's that!

Arcite. Yes, 'tis a question to me that know not.

Third Countryman. To the games, my friend.

Second Countryman. Where were you bred you know it not?

Arcite. Not far, sir.
Are there such games today?

65 *First Countryman.* Yes, marry are there,
And such as you never saw. The duke himself
Will be in person there.

Arcite. What pastimes are they?

53 **parlously** amazingly 53–54 **He's excellent . . . plains** (a *double-entendre* is fairly obvious, implying that the schoolmaster is better in the earlier than in the later stages of sexual activity) 54 **makes no cry** wins no applause (and, continuing the metaphor, he will not make a girl cry out) 55 **every man to's tackle** let every man keep his engagement 57 **sweetly** delectably 59 **hold** hold to your purposes

Second Countryman. Wrestling and running. [*Aside*]
'Tis a pretty fellow.

Third Countryman. Thou wilt not go along?

Arcite. Not yet, sir.

Fourth Countryman. Well, sir,
Take your own time. Come, boys.

First Countryman. My mind misgives me. 70
This fellow has a vengeance° trick o' th' hip:
Mark how his body's made for't.°

Second Countryman. I'll be hanged, though,
If he dare venture. Hang him! Plum porridge,°
He wrestle? He roast eggs!° Come, let's be gone,
lads. *Exeunt* [*the*] *four* [*Countrymen*].

Arcite. This is an offered opportunity 75
I durst not wish for. Well, I could have wrestled,°
The best men called it excellent, and run
Swifter than wind upon a field of corn,
Curling the wealthy ears, never flew.° I'll venture,
And in some poor disguise be there. Who knows 80
Whether my brows may not be girt with garlands,
And happiness° prefer me to a place
Where I may ever dwell in sight of her?
Exit Arcite.

71 **vengeance** confounded 72 **for't** i.e., for wrestling 73 **Plum porridge** dish made of plums thickened with barley, etc. (here used as a term of contempt for one not likely to excel in wrestling) 74 **He roast eggs** i.e., he would be more capable of cooking an egg 76 **could have wrestled** used to be able to wrestle 78–79 **Swifter . . . flew** swifter than wind . . . ever flew (the illogical negative "never" is idiomatic in the seventeenth century, but editors have frequently emended) 82 **happiness** good fortune

Scene III. [*The prison.*]

Enter Jailer's Daughter alone.

Daughter. Why should I love this gentleman? 'Tis odds
He never will affect° me; I am base,°
My father the mean keeper of his prison,
And he a prince; to marry him is hopeless,
5 To be his whore is witless. Out upon't,
What pushes° are we wenches driven to
When fifteen once has found us!° First I saw him:
I, seeing, thought he was a goodly man:
He has as much to please a woman in him,
10 If he please to bestow it so, as ever
These eyes yet looked on. Next, I pitied him,
And so would any young wench o' my conscience
That ever dreamed, or vowed her maidenhead
To a young handsome man. Then I loved him,
15 Extremely loved him, infinitely loved him.
And yet he had a cousin, fair as he too.
But in my heart was Palamon, and there,
Lord, what a coil he keeps!° To hear him
Sing in an evening, what a heaven it is!
20 And yet his songs are sad ones. Fairer spoken
Was never gentleman. When I come in
To bring him water in a morning, first
He bows his noble body, then salutes me thus:
"Fair, gentle maid, good-morrow, may thy goodness
25 Get thee a happy husband." Once he kissed me.
I loved my lips the better ten days after—
Would he would do so ev'ry day! He grieves much,

II.iii.2 **affect** love 2 **base** of low birth 6 **pushes** shifts 7 **When fifteen once has found us** when we have reached the age of fifteen 18 **coil he keeps** disturbance he makes

And me as much to see his misery.
What should I do to make him know I love him,
For I would fain enjoy him? Say I ventured 30
To set him free? What says the law then? Thus much
For law, or kindred!° I will do it,
And this night, or tomorrow, he shall love me.
Exit.

Scene IV. [*At the games.*]

Short flourish of cornets,° and shouts within. Enter Theseus, Hippolyta, Pirithous, Emilia, Arcite [disguised] with a garland, &c.

Theseus. You have done worthily. I have not seen,
Since Hercules, a man of tougher sinews.
Whate'er you are, you run the best and wrestle
That these times can allow.°

Arcite. I am proud to please you.

Theseus. What country bred you?

Arcite. This; but far off, prince. 5

Theseus. Are you a gentleman?

Arcite. My father said so,
And to those gentle uses gave me life.°

Theseus. Are you his heir?

Arcite. His youngest, sir.

Theseus. Your father

31–32 **Thus much/For law, or kindred** (we can imagine her clicking her fingers, thus filling out line 32) II.iv.s.d. **cornets** hunting horns 4 **allow** acknowledge, praise 7 **to those gentle uses gave me life** brought me up to practice such noble customs

Sure is a happy sire, then. What proves you?°

10 *Arcite.* A little of all noble qualities:°
I could have kept° a hawk, and well have halloo'd
To a deep cry° of dogs; I dare not praise
My feat in horsemanship, yet they that knew me
Would say it was my best piece;° last, and greatest,
I would be thought a soldier.

15 *Theseus.* You are perfect.

Pirithous. Upon my soul, a proper man.

Emilia. He is so.

Pirithous. How do you like him, lady?

Hippolyta. I admire° him:
I have not seen so young a man so noble,
If he say true, of his sort.

Emilia. I believe
20 His mother was a wondrous handsome woman:
His face methinks goes that way.°

Hippolyta. But his body
And fiery mind illustrate° a brave father.

Pirithous. Mark how his virtue,° like a hidden sun,
Breaks through his baser garments.

Hippolyta. He's well got,° sure.

Theseus. What made you seek this place, sir?

25 *Arcite.* Noble Theseus,
To purchase name,° and do my ablest service
To such a well-found° wonder as thy worth,
For only in thy court, of all the world,
Dwells fair-eyed Honor.

9 **What proves you** what can you show for yourself 10 **qualities** abilities 11 **could have kept** was able to keep 12 **deep cry** loud pack 14 **piece** feature, accomplishment 17 **admire** wonder at 21 **goes that way** suggests that 22 **illustrate** confer honor on (stressed on second syllable) 23 **virtue** nobility 24 **well got** nobly descended 26 **purchase name** win reputation 27 **well-found** well-reputed

Pirithous. All his words are worthy.

Theseus. Sir, we are much indebted to your travel,° 30
Nor shall you lose your wish. Pirithous,
Dispose of° this fair gentleman.

Pirithous. Thanks, Theseus.
[*To Arcite*] Whate'er you are y' are mine, and I shall give you
To a most noble service, to this lady,
This bright young virgin; pray observe her goodness; 35
You have honored her fair birthday with your virtues,
And as your due y' are hers. Kiss her fair hand, sir.

Arcite. Sir, y' are a noble giver. Dearest beauty,
Thus let me seal my vowed faith. [*Kisses her hand.*] When your servant,
Your most unworthy creature, but offends you, 40
Command him die: he shall.

Emilia. That were too cruel.
If you deserve well, sir, I shall soon see't.
Y' are mine, and somewhat better than your rank I'll use you.

Pirithous. I'll see you furnished,° and because you say
You are a horseman, I must needs entreat you 45
This afternoon to ride, but 'tis a rough one.°

Arcite. I like him better, prince: I shall not then
Freeze in my saddle.

Theseus. Sweet, you must be ready,
And you, Emilia, and you, friend, and all,
Tomorrow by the sun° to do observance 50
To flow'ry May in Dian's wood. Wait well, sir,
Upon your mistress. Emily, I hope
He shall not go afoot.

30 **travel** journey (or, perhaps, labor) 32 **Dispose of** take charge of 44 **furnished** provided (with what you need) 46 **a rough one** i.e., an untrained or unruly horse 50 **by the sun** by sunrise

Emilia. That were a shame, sir,
While I have horses. [*To Arcite*] Take your choice, and what
55 You want at any time, let me but know it.
If you serve faithfully, I dare assure you
You'll find a loving mistress.

Arcite. If I do not,
Let me find that my father ever hated,
Disgrace and blows.

Theseus. Go, lead the way: you have won it.°
60 It shall be so; you shall receive all dues
Fit for the honor you have won; 'twere wrong else.
Sister, beshrew my heart, you have a servant
That, if I were a woman, would be master.
But you are wise.

Emilia. I hope too wise for that,° sir.
Flourish. Exeunt omnes.

Scene V. [*The prison.*]

Enter Jailer's Daughter alone.

Daughter. Let all the dukes, and all the devils, roar:
He is at liberty. I have ventured for him,
And out I have brought him to a little wood
A mile hence. I have sent him where a cedar,
5 Higher than all the rest, spreads like a plane
Fast by a brook, and there he shall keep close°
Till I provide him files and food, for yet
His iron bracelets are not off. O Love,
What a stout-hearted child thou art! My father

59 **you have won it** i.e., your success in the games makes you deserve to lead the way 64 **I hope too wise for that** (Emilia rejects Theseus' suggestion of marriage) II.v.6 **keep close** stay in hiding

Durst better have endured cold iron° than done it. 10
I love him, beyond love and beyond reason,
Or wit,° or safety: I have made him know it.
I care not, I am desperate. If the law
Find me,° and then condemn me for't, some
wenches,
Some honest-hearted maids, will sing my dirge, 15
And tell to memory my death was noble,
Dying almost a martyr. That way he takes
I purpose is my way too. Sure he cannot
Be so unmanly as to leave me here.
If he do, maids will not so easily 20
Trust men again. And yet he has not thanked me
For what I have done—no, not so much as kissed
me,
And that methinks is not so well. Nor scarcely
Could I persuade him to become a freeman,
He made such scruples of the wrong he did 25
To me, and to my father. Yet I hope,
When he considers more, this love of mine
Will take more root within him. Let him do
What he will with me, so he use me kindly,
For use me so he shall, or I'll proclaim him, 30
And to his face, no man.° I'll presently°
Provide him necessaries, and pack my clothes up,
And where there is a path of ground° I'll venture,
So° he be with me. By him, like a shadow,
I'll ever dwell. Within this hour the hubbub 35
Will be all o'er the prison: I am then
Kissing the man they look for. Farewell, father;
Get many more such prisoners, and such daughters,
And shortly you may keep yourself.° Now to him.
[*Exit.*]

10 endured cold iron suffered death with sword or ax **12 wit** good sense **14 Find me** bring me to judgment **31 no man** impotent **31 presently** at once **33 path of ground** way through woods, etc. (some editors emend to "patch of ground") **34 So** provided that **39 shortly you may keep yourself** i.e., you will lose all of them and will have only yourself to look after

ACT III

Scene I. [*The open country.*]

Cornets in sundry places. Noise and hallooing° as people a-Maying. Enter Arcite alone.

Arcite. The duke has lost Hippolyta; each took
A several° laund.° This is a solemn rite
They owe bloomed May, and the Athenians pay it
To th' heart of ceremony.° O Queen Emilia,
5 Fresher than May, sweeter
Than her gold buttons° on the boughs or all
Th' enameled knacks° o' th' mead or garden—yea,
We challenge too the bank of any nymph
That makes the stream seem flowers!° Thou, O jewel
O' th' wood, o' th' world, hast likewise° blest a
10 place
With thy sole presence, in thy rumination,°
That I, poor man, might eftsoons° come between
And chop on some cold thought.° Thrice blessed chance

III.i. s.d. **hallooing** cries of people calling to each other from a distance, or urging dogs in the chase 2 **several** different 2 **laund** open space among woods (obsolete form of "lawn") 4 **To th' heart of ceremony** most ceremoniously 6 **buttons** buds 7 **enameled knacks** trifles of various colors 8–9 **the bank . . . flowers** i.e., by the stream reflecting the flowers on its bank 10 **likewise** like the "nymph" of line 8 11 **in thy rumination** as you meditate there 12 **eftsoons** quickly 12–13 **come . . . thought** ("chop" was a hunting term meaning to seize prey before it was away from cover: here the idea is apparently that Arcite hopes merely to come into Emilia's chaste ["cold"] thoughts)

To drop on° such a mistress, expectation
Most guiltless on't!° Tell me, O lady Fortune, 15
Next after Emily my sovereign, how far
I may be proud. She takes strong note of° me,
Hath made me near her;° and this beauteous morn,
The prim'st° of all the year, presents me with
A brace of horses: two such steeds might well 20
Be by a pair of kings backed, in a field
That their crowns' titles tried.° Alas, alas,
Poor cousin Palamon, poor prisoner, thou
So little dream'st upon my fortune that
Thou think'st thyself the happier thing, to be 25
So near Emilia! Me thou deem'st at Thebes,
And therein wretched, although free. But if
Thou knew'st my mistress breathed on me, and that
I eared° her language, lived in her eye°—O coz,
What passion would enclose thee!°

Enter Palamon as out of a bush, with his shackles. [He] bends his fist at Arcite.

Palamon. Traitor kinsman, 30
Thou shouldst perceive my passion, if these signs
Of prisonment were off me, and this hand
But owner of a sword. By all oaths in one,
I and the justice of my love would make thee
A confessed traitor, O thou most perfidious 35
That ever gently° looked, the void'st of honor
That e'er bore gentle token!° Falsest cousin
That ever blood made kin, call'st thou her thine?
I'll prove it in my shackles, with these hands

14 **drop on** come upon 14–15 **expectation/Most guiltless on't** i.e., without at all expecting it 17 **takes strong note of** observes closely 18 **made me near her** made me attend on her 19 **prim'st** supreme 22 **That their crowns' titles tried** where their claims to the crowns were being decided 29 **eared** listened to, with also a suggestion of "ear" = to plow 29 **in her eye** where she can see me, but with the suggestion of being so close as to see his reflection in her eye 30 **enclose thee** i.e., imprison you (doubly ironic in that Arcite thinks Palamon physically in prison while he is actually free but is "enclosed" by the passion indicated) 36 **gently** nobly 37 **bore gentle token** showed outward sign of nobility

40 Void of appointment,° that thou liest, and art
A very thief in love, a chaffy° lord,
Nor worth the name of villain—had I a sword,
And these house-clogs° away.

Arcite. Dear cousin Palamon—

Palamon. Cozener Arcite, give me language such
As thou hast showed me feat.°

45 *Arcite.* Not finding in
The circuit of my breast any gross stuff
To form me like your blazon,° holds me to
This gentleness of answer: 'tis your passion
That thus mistakes, the which to you being enemy
50 Cannot to me be kind;° honor and honesty
I cherish, and depend on, howsoe'er
You skip° them in me, and with them, fair coz,
I'll maintain my proceedings. Pray be pleased
To show in generous° terms your griefs,° since that
55 Your question's° with your equal, who professes
To clear his own way,° with the mind and sword
Of a true gentleman.

Palamon. That thou durst, Arcite!

Arcite. My coz, my coz, you have been well advertised°
How much I dare. Y' have seen me use my sword
60 Against th' advice° of fear. Sure° of another
You would not hear me doubted, but your silence
Should break out, though i' th' sanctuary.°

Palamon. Sir,

40 **Void of appointment** without weapons to fight with 41 **chaffy** worthless 43 **house-clogs** i.e., his shackles 44–45 **give . . . feat** i.e., let your language correspond with your actions 47 **your blazon** your description of me 49–50 **the which . . . kind** as your passion is your enemy, it cannot be kind to me, your friend and other self 52 **skip** overlook 54 **generous** noble 54 **griefs** grievances 55 **question's** quarrel's 55–56 **professes/To clear his own way** claims to justify his conduct 58 **advertised** informed (stressed on second syllable) 60 **advice** warning 60 **Sure** surely 62 **i' th' sanctuary** in a church, but also with the suggestion of breaking out of "sanctuary" (a place of safety) for the sake of righting his friend

I have seen you move in such a place° which well
Might justify your manhood: you were called
A good knight and a bold. But the whole week's not
fair 65
If any day it rain. Their valiant temper°
Men lose when they incline° to treachery,
And then they fight like compelled° bears, would
fly
Were they not tied.

Arcite. Kinsman, you might as well
Speak this and act it in your glass, as to 70
His ear which now disdains you.

Palamon. Come up to me,
Quit me of these cold gyves,° give me a sword,
Though it be rusty, and the charity
Of one meal lend me. Come before me then,
A good sword in thy hand, and do but say 75
That Emily is thine, I will forgive
The trespass thou hast done me, yea my life
If then thou carry't;° and brave souls in shades
That have died manly, which will seek of me
Some news from earth, they shall get none but this, 80
That thou art brave and noble.

Arcite. Be content.
Again betake you to your hawthorn house.°
With counsel of the night,° I will be here
With wholesome viands. These impediments°
Will I file off. You shall have garments, and 85
Perfumes to kill the smell o' th' prison. After,
When you shall stretch yourself and say but "Arcite,
I am in plight,"° there shall be at your choice
Both sword and armor.

63 **in such a place** i.e., in battle or tournament 66 **temper** character 67 **incline** yield 68 **compelled** i.e., in bear-baiting (stressed on first syllable here) 72 **gyves** fetters 78 **If then thou carry't** i.e., if you then kill me 82 **hawthorn house** shelter in the hawthorn bush 83 **With counsel of the night** with only night as my confidant 84 **These impediments** Palamon's shackles 88 **in plight** in good condition, ready

Palamon. O you heavens, dares any
90 So noble bear° a guilty business? None
But only Arcite. Therefore none but Arcite
In this kind is so bold.

Arcite. Sweet Palamon!

Palamon. I do embrace you and your offer. For
Your offer do't I only, sir. Your person
95 Without hypocrisy I may not wish
Wind horns off.
More than my sword's edge on't.

Arcite. You hear the horns.
Enter your musit° lest this match between's
Be crossed ere met.° Give me your hand. Farewell.
I'll bring you every needful thing. I pray you
Take comfort and be strong.

100 *Palamon.* Pray hold your promise,
And do the deed with a bent brow°—most certain
You love me not; be rough with me, and pour
This oil° out of your language. By this air,
I could for each word give a cuff,° my stomach°
Not reconciled by reason.

105 *Arcite.* Plainly spoken,
Yet pardon me hard language.° When I spur
Wind horns.
My horse, I chide him not. Content and anger
In me have but one face.° Hark, sir, they call
The scattered to the banquet:° you must guess
I have an office° there.

110 *Palamon.* Sir, your attendance
Cannot please heaven, and I know your office
Unjustly is achieved.°

90 **bear** carry out 97 **musit** gap in a hedge through which a hare, etc., might pass when hunted 98 **crossed ere met** i.e., prevented before begun 101 **with a bent brow** sternly 103 **oil** courtesy, gentleness 104 **cuff** blow 104 **stomach** anger 106 **pardon me hard language** allow me not to use hostile language 108 **one face** the same outward manifestation 109 **banquet** light repast, as for a hunting party 110 **office** duty to perform 112 **Unjustly is achieved** has been unfairly won

Arcite. If a good title°—
I am persuaded this question, sick between's,
By bleeding must be cured.° I am a suitor
That to your sword you will bequeath this plea,° 115
And talk of it no more.

Palamon. But this one word:
You are going now to gaze upon my mistress,
For, note you, mine she is.

Arcite. Nay, then.

Palamon. Nay, pray you,
You talk of feeding me to breed me strength.
You are going now to look upon a sun 120
That strengthens what it looks on: there you have
A vantage o'er me, but enjoy't till
I may enforce my remedy. Farewell.
Exeunt [*severally*].

Scene II. [*The open country.*]

Enter Jailer's Daughter alone.

Daughter. He has mistook the brake° I meant, is gone
After his fancy.° 'Tis now well nigh morning.
No matter, would it were perpetual night,
And darkness lord o' th' world. Hark! 'Tis a wolf!
In me hath grief slain fear, and but for one thing 5
I care for nothing, and that's Palamon.
I reck not if the wolves would jaw me, so
He had this file. What if I halloo'd for him?
I cannot halloo. If I whooped, what then?

112 **If a good title** (either Arcite interrupts himself or, as some editors have done, we should emend "If" to "I've") 113–14 **this question . . . cured** (Arcite sees the quarrel as a sick person standing between them: they must cure the sickness by letting blood from it) 115 **plea** lawsuit III.ii.1 **brake** thicket 2 **After his fancy** where his fancy has led him

10 If he not answered, I should call a wolf
And do him but that service.° I have heard
Strange howls this live-long night: why may't not be
They have made prey of him? He has no weapons,
He cannot run, the jingling of his gyves
15 Might call fell° things to listen, who have in them
A sense to know a man unarmed, and can
Smell where resistance° is. I'll set it down°
He's torn to pieces: they howled many together
And then they fed on him. So much for that;
20 Be bold to ring the bell.° How stand I then?
All's chared° when he is gone. No, no, I lie.
My father's to be hanged for his escape,
Myself to beg, if I prized life so much
As to deny my act, but that I would not,
25 Should I try death by dozens.° I am moped:°
Food took I none these two days,
Sipped some water. I have not closed mine eyes
Save when my lids scoured off their brine.° Alas,
Dissolve my life, let not my sense unsettle,
30 Lest I should drown, or stab, or hang myself.
O state of nature,° fail together° in me,
Since thy best props are warped! So which way
now?
The best way is the next° way to a grave:
Each errant step beside° is torment. Lo,
The moon is down, the crickets chirp, the screech-
35 owl
Calls in° the dawn. All offices° are done
Save what I fail in. But the point is this:
An end, and that is all.° *Exit.*

11 **do him but that service** i.e., (ironically) bring a wolf to him 15 **fell** savage 17 **resistance** the power to resist 17 **set it down** take it as settled 20 **ring the bell** i.e., toll the bell for his death 21 **All's chared** all tasks are ended 25 **Should I try death by dozens** should I have to die many times or in many ways 25 **moped** bewildered, numbed 28 **when my lids scoured off their brine** when I closed them to get rid of my tears 31 **state of nature** condition of being alive 31 **together** altogether 33 **next** nearest 34 **Each errant step beside** i.e., each step that does not lead directly to my grave 36 **Calls in** summons (the owl, doing duty for the cock, indicates the upside-downness of her world) 36 **offices** tasks 38 **An end, and that is all** i.e., only death is to come

Scene III. [*The open country.*]

Enter Arcite, with meat, wine, and files.

Arcite. I should be near the place. Ho, cousin Palamon!

Enter Palamon.

Palamon. Arcite?

Arcite. The same. I have brought you food and files.
Come forth and fear not; here's no Theseus.

Palamon. Nor none so honest, Arcite.

Arcite. That's no matter,
We'll argue that hereafter. Come, take courage, 5
You shall not die thus beastly;° here, sir, drink,
I know you are faint; then I'll talk further with you.

Palamon. Arcite, thou mightst now poison me.

Arcite. I might;
But I must° fear you first. Sit down, and good now,°
No more of these vain parleys: let us not, 10
Having our ancient reputation with us,
Make talk for fools and cowards.° To your health, &c. [*He drinks.*]

Palamon. Do.°

III.iii.6 **thus beastly** in your present beastlike condition 9 **must** should have to 9 **good now** please 12 **Make talk for fools and cowards** give matter for fools and cowards to talk about 13 **Do** i.e., do drink

Arcite. Pray sit down then, and let me entreat you,
By all the honesty and honor in you,
15 No mention of this woman, 'twill disturb us;
We shall have time enough.

Palamon. Well, sir, I'll pledge you.
[*He drinks.*]

Arcite. Drink a good hearty draught, it breeds good blood, man.
Do not you feel it thaw you?

Palamon. Stay, I'll tell you
After a draught or two more.

Arcite. Spare it not,
The duke has more, coz. Eat now.

Palamon. Yes. [*He eats.*]

20 *Arcite.* I am glad
You have so good a stomach.°

Palamon. I am gladder
I have so good meat to't.

Arcite. Is't not mad° lodging
Here in the wild woods, cousin?

Palamon. Yes, for them
That have wild° consciences.

Arcite. How tastes your victuals?
Your hunger needs no sauce, I see.

25 *Palamon.* Not much.
But if it did, yours° is too tart. Sweet cousin,
What is this?

Arcite. Venison.

Palamon. 'Tis a lusty° meat.

21 **stomach** appetite 22 **mad** fantastic 24 **wild** disordered 26 **yours** i.e., the sauce you bring in your words and presence 27 **lusty** hearty, invigorating

Give me more wine. [*Arcite gives him the wine.*]
Here, Arcite, to the wenches
We have known in our days. The Lord Steward's daughter,
Do you remember her?
[*He offers the wine to Arcite.*]

Arcite. After you, coz. 30

Palamon. She loved a black-haired man.

Arcite. She did so. Well, sir?

Palamon. And I have heard some call him Arcite, and—

Arcite. Out with't, 'faith.

Palamon. She met him in an arbor:
What did she there, coz? Play o' th' virginals?°

Arcite. Something she did, sir.

Palamon. Made her groan a month for't; 35
Or two, or three, or ten.°

Arcite. The Marshal's sister
Had her share too, as I remember, cousin,
Else there be tales° abroad. You'll pledge her?

Palamon. Yes.
[*He drinks.*]

Arcite. A pretty brown wench 'tis. There was a time
When young men went a-hunting—and a wood, 40
And a broad beech, and thereby hangs a tale.
Heigh ho!

Palamon. For Emily, upon my life! Fool,
Away with this strained mirth! I say again
That sigh was breathed for Emily. Base cousin,

34 **Play o' th' virginals** ("virginals" was the name of a small instrument like a spinet: here punningly used with reference to sexual intercourse) 35–36 **groan . . . ten** (Palamon leads archly to the idea of gestation) 38 **tales** false reports

Dar'st thou break° first?

Arcite. You are wide.°

45 *Palamon.* By heaven and earth,
There's nothing in thee honest.

Arcite. Then I'll leave you:
You are a beast° now.

Palamon. As thou mak'st me, traitor.

Arcite. There's all things needful: files and shirts and perfumes.
I'll come again some two hours hence, and bring
That that shall quiet all.

50 *Palamon.* A sword and armor?

Arcite. Fear me not; you are now too foul;° farewell.
Get off your trinkets,° you shall want nought.

Palamon. Sirrah°—

Arcite. I'll hear no more. *Exit.*

Palamon. If he keep touch,° he dies for't. *Exit.*

Scene IV. [*The open country.*]

Enter Jailer's Daughter.

Daughter. I am very cold, and all the stars are out too,
The little stars and all, that look like aglets.°
The sun has seen my folly. Palamon!

45 **break** break our agreement not to refer to Emilia (but also with a suggestion of emotion breaking out) 45 **wide** wide of the mark 47 **beast** i.e., not fit for conversation 51 **foul** unwashed, etc. 52 **trinkets** i.e., shackles 52 **Sirrah** (contemptuous form of address) 53 **keep touch** keep his promise III.iv.2 **aglets** jewels used as hair ornaments and for tags to laces

Alas, no, he's in heaven. Where am I now?
Yonder's the sea, and there's a ship: how't tumbles, 5
And there's a rock lies watching under water;
Now, now, it beats upon it;° now, now, now!
There's a leak sprung, a sound° one; how they cry!
Spoon° her before the wind, you'll lose all else!
Up with a course° or two, and tack about,° boys! 10
Good night, good night, y' are gone. I am very hungry.
Would I could find a fine frog; he would tell me
News from all parts o' th' world; then would I make
A carack° of a cockleshell, and sail
By east and north-east to the King of Pigmies, 15
For he tells fortunes rarely. Now my father
Twenty to one is trussed up in a trice°
Tomorrow morning. I'll say never a word.

(*Sing*[*s*]) For I'll cut my green coat, a foot above my knee,
And I'll clip my yellow locks, an inch below mine eye. 20
Hey, nonny, nonny, nonny!
He's° buy me a white cut,° forth for to ride,
And I'll go seek him, through the world that is so wide.
Hey, nonny, nonny, nonny!

O for a prick now like a nightingale, 25
To put my breast against!° I shall sleep like a top else. *Exit.*

7 it beats upon it i.e., the ship strikes the rock 8 **sound** great 9 **Spoon** scud 10 **course** sail attached to the lower yards of a ship 10 **tack about** change direction 14 **carack** ship of large burden 17 **trussed up in a trice** hanged immediately 22 **He's** (vulgar form of "He'll") 22 **cut** laboring horse, so called because either with docked tail or gelded 25–26 **prick . . . against** (alluding to the common belief that the nightingale presses against a thorn in order to stay awake and sing)

Scene V. [*The open country.*]

Enter a Schoolmaster, four Countrymen and Bavian,° five wenches, with a Taborer.°

Schoolmaster. Fie, fie,
What tediosity and disensanity°
Is here among ye? Have my rudiments
Been labored so long with ye, milked unto ye,
5 And, by a figure,° even the very plumbroth°
And marrow of my understanding laid upon ye?
And do you still cry "where" and "how" and "wherefore"?
You most coarse frieze° capacities, ye jean° judgments,
Have I said "thus let be," and "there let be,"
10 And "then let be," and no man understand me?
Proh deum, medius fidius,° ye are all dunces!
For why, here stand I. Here the duke comes; there are you
Close° in the thicket; the duke appears; I meet him
And unto him I utter learnèd things,
15 And many figures; he hears, and nods, and hums,
And then cries "Rare!", and I go forward; at length
I fling my cap up—mark there—then do you,
As once did Meleager and the boar,°
Break comely° out before him—like true lovers,°

III.v. s.d. **Bavian** the fool in the morris dance (the word signifying either "driveler" or "baboon") **Taborer** one who plays a small drum 2 **disensanity** insanity ("dis-" here being intensive) 5 **figure** i.e., of speech 5 **plumbroth** (as "plum porridge," II.ii.73) 8 **frieze** rough woollen cloth 8 **jean** a kind of fustian (also spelt "jane") 11 **Proh deum, medius fidius** O God, most certainly 13 **Close** secretly 18 **Meleager and the boar** (alluding to Meleager's killing the Calydonian boar, and his bringing the boar's head to Atalanta) 19 **comely** fittingly 19 **lovers** i.e., of Theseus

Cast yourselves in a body° decently, 20
And sweetly, by a figure, trace and turn,° boys.

First Countryman. And sweetly we will do it, Master Gerald.

Second Countryman. Draw up the company. Where's the taborer?

Third Countryman. Why, Timothy!

Taborer. Here, my mad boys, have at ye!°

Schoolmaster. But, I say, where's their women?

Fourth Countryman. Here's Friz and Maudlin. 25

Second Countryman. And little Luce with the white legs, and bouncing° Barbary.

First Countryman. And freckled Nell, that never failed her master.°

Schoolmaster. Where be your ribands, maids? Swim° with your bodies,
And carry it° sweetly and deliverly,°
And now and then a favor,° and a frisk.° 30

Nell. Let us alone,° sir.

Schoolmaster. Where's the rest o' th' music?°

Third Countryman. Dispersed° as you commanded.

Schoolmaster. Couple° then,
And see what's wanting. Where's the Bavian?
My friend, carry your tail without offense
Or scandal to the ladies; and be sure 35
You tumble with audacity, and manhood,
And when you bark do it with judgment.

20 **Cast yourselves in a body** arrange yourselves in a group for the dance 21 **trace and turn** dance and revolve 24 **have at ye** i.e., I am ready for you 26 **bouncing** large of body 27 **that never failed her master** i.e., did whatever he wanted of her 28 **Swim** move flowingly 29 **carry it** i.e., perform the dance 29 **deliverly** nimbly 30 **favor** (presumably a kiss) 30 **frisk** caper 31 **Let us alone** leave it to us 31 **music** musicians 32 **Dispersed** i.e., scattered in arranged places 32 **Couple** take your partners

Bavian. Yes, sir.

Schoolmaster. Quo usque tandem?° Here is a woman wanting.°

Fourth Countryman. We may go whistle.° All the fat's i' th' fire.

40 *Schoolmaster.* We have,
As learnèd authors utter, washed a tile,°
We have been *fatuus,*° and labored vainly.

Second Countryman. This is that scornful piece,° that scurvy hilding,°
That gave her promise faithfully she would be here,
45 Cicely the sempster's° daughter.
The next gloves that I give her shall be dogskin.
Nay, and° she fail me once! You can tell, Arcas,°
She swore by wine and bread she would not break.°

Schoolmaster. An eel and woman,
50 A learnèd poet says,° unless by th' tail
And with thy teeth thou hold, will either° fail.
In manners this was false position.°

First Countryman. A fire ill° take her! Does she flinch now?

Third Countryman. What
Shall we determine,° sir?

Schoolmaster. Nothing.
55 Our business is become a nullity,
Yea, and a woeful, and a piteous nullity.

38 **Quo usque tandem** how long now 38 **wanting** missing 39 **We may go whistle** we have occupied ourselves to no purpose 41 **washed a tile** labored in vain (Latin "*laterem lavare*") 42 **fatuus** foolish 43 **piece** creature 43 **hilding** good-for-nothing 45 **sempster's** probably here = sempstress's 47 **and** if 47 **Arcas** (the name of one of the Countrymen: cf. II.ii.37) 48 **break** break her word 50 **A learnèd poet says** (no one has identified the "poet," if he existed; but Fletcher used the proverb in other plays) 51 **either** both 52 **position** statement of a proposition, affirmation (the Schoolmaster means that Cicely's breaking her word was the equivalent in manners to the stating of a false proposition in logic) 53 **fire ill** (perhaps equivalent to "pox," or "ill" may be adverbial) 54 **determine** decide to do

Fourth Countryman. Now when the credit of our town lay on it,
Now to be frampel,° now to piss o' th' nettle!°
Go thy ways, I'll remember thee, I'll fit thee!°

Enter Jailer's Daughter.

Daughter.

[*Sings*] The George Alow° came from the south, 60
From the coast of Barbary-a,
And there he met with brave gallants of war,
By one, by two, by three-a.
Well hailed, well hailed, you jolly gallants,
And whither now are you bound-a? 65
O let me have your company
Till we come to the sound-a.

There was three fools fell out about an owlet.

The one said it was an owl;
The other he said nay; 70
The third he said it was a hawk,
And her bells° were cut away.

Third Countryman. There's a dainty° mad woman, master,
Comes i' th' nick,° as mad as a march hare.
If we can get her dance, we are made again:° 75
I warrant her, she'll do the rarest° gambols.

First Countryman. A mad woman? We are made, boys.

Schoolmaster. And are you mad, good woman?

58 **frampel** peevish, froward 58 **piss o' th' nettle** give herself occasion to show bad temper 59 **fit thee** punish you as you deserve 60 **George Alow** (this was the name of a ship in a ballad published in 1611) 72 **bells** (used on a hawk for ease in tracing it) 73 **dainty** fine 74 **i' th' nick** i.e., just when we need her 75 **we are made again** our fortune is once more secure 76 **rarest** finest

Daughter. I would be sorry else.
Give me your hand.

Schoolmaster. Why?

Daughter. I can tell your fortune.
80 You are a fool. Tell ten. I have posed him.° Buzz.°
Friend, you must eat no white bread; if you do,
Your teeth will bleed extremely. Shall we dance, ho?
I know you, y' are a tinker: sirrah tinker,
Stop no more holes but what you should.°

Schoolmaster. *Dii boni!*°
A tinker, damsel?

85 *Daughter.* Or a conjuror.
Raise me a devil now, and let him play
Qui passa,° o' th' bells and bones.°

Schoolmaster. Go take her,
And fluently° persuade her to a peace.
Et opus exegi, quod nec Iovis ira, nec ignis.°
Strike up,° and lead her in.°

90 *Second Countryman.* Come, lass, let's trip it.

Daughter. I'll lead.

Third Countryman. Do, do.

Schoolmaster. Persuasively, and cunningly!°
Wind horns.

80 **Tell ten. I have posed him** (counting on one's fingers was a common method of testing idiocy: the Jailer's Daughter decides the Schoolmaster cannot pass the test) 80 **Buzz** (exclamation commanding silence) 84 **Stop . . . should** (alluding to the proverb "A tinker stops one hole and makes others"; but with an obvious double meaning here) 84 **Dii boni** good gods 87 **Qui passa** (the song "Chi passa per questa strada") 87 **bells and bones** (similar to Bottom's "the tongs and the bones," *A Midsummer Night's Dream,* IV.i.32: "bones" were bone clappers held between the fingers) 88 **fluently** quickly 89 **Et . . . ignis** I have achieved something which neither Jove's anger nor fire . . . (from Ovid's *Metamorphoses,* xv. 871, where it reads "*Jamque opus . . . nec ignes*") 90 **Strike up** begin the music 90 **in** offstage, into the thicket where the dancers will wait 91 **cunningly** skillfully

Away, boys! I hear the horns.
Give me some meditation,° and mark your cue.
Exeunt all but Schoolmaster.
Pallas° inspire me!

Enter Theseus, Pirithous, Hippolyta, Emilia, Arcite, and train. [*A chair and stools are brought out.*]°

Theseus. This way the stag took.

Schoolmaster. Stay, and edify!°

Theseus. What have we here? 95

Pirithous. Some country sport, upon my life, sir.

Theseus. Well, sir, go forward, we will edify.
Ladies, sit down; we'll stay it.° [*They sit.*]

Schoolmaster. Thou doughty duke, all hail! All hail, sweet ladies!

Theseus. This is a cold beginning.° 100

Schoolmaster. If you but favor, our country pastime made is.
We are a few of those collected here
That ruder tongues distinguish° villager.
And to say verity, and not to fable,
We are a merry rout, or else a rabble 105
Or company, or by a figure *Chorus,*°
That 'fore thy dignity will dance a morris.
And I that am the rectifier° of all,
By title Pedagogus, that let fall
The birch upon the breeches of the small ones, 110
And humble with a ferula° the tall ones,

93 **meditation** time for meditation (?), attention (?) 94 **Pallas** as goddess of learning 94 s.d. **A chair and stools are brought out** (see Textual Note for lines 65–67) 95 **edify** (the Schoolmaster's English for "profit mentally," "be edified") 98 **stay it** wait here for it 100 **cold beginning** (deliberately taking "hail" for a reference to the weather) 103 **distinguish** classify 106 **by a figure Chorus** (the Schoolmaster's "figure" allows him to compare the morris dancers with the chorus of a classical play) 108 **rectifier** (pedant's word for "director") 111 **ferula** cane

Do here present this machine,° or this frame;°
And dainty duke, whose doughty dismal fame
From Dis to Daedalus,° from post to pillar°
115 Is blown abroad, help me, thy poor well-willer,
And with thy twinkling eyes look right and straight
Upon this mighty "Morr," of mickle weight;
"Is" now comes in—which being glued together
Makes "Morris,"° and the cause that we came hither,
120 The body of our sport of no small study.
I first appear, though rude, and raw, and muddy,
To speak before thy noble grace this tenor,°
At whose great feet I offer up my penner;°
The next° the Lord of May, and Lady bright,
125 The Chambermaid and Servingman by night
That seek out silent hanging;° then mine Host
And his fat Spouse, that welcomes to their° cost
The gallèd° Traveler, and with a beck'ning
Informs the Tapster to inflame the reck'ning;
130 Then the beest-eating° Clown, and next the Fool,
The Bavian with long tail, and eke long tool,°
Cum multis aliis° that make a dance.
Say "Aye," and all shall presently advance.

Theseus. Aye, aye, by any means, dear dominie.

Pirithous. Produce.°

112 **machine** structure, device (stressed on first syllable) 112 **frame** contrivance 114 **Dis to Daedalus** (Dis was the Greek god of the underworld, Daedalus the maker of the Labyrinth in Crete: the Schoolmaster's use of learning is indiscriminate) 114 **from post to pillar** from one resource to another (the Schoolmaster is desperate for a rhyme) 117–19 **Morr . . . Morris** (perhaps the Schoolmaster holds up two boards in turn, with the syllables "Morr" and "is" on them, and then puts them together; but the first board could show a picture of a Moor) 122 **tenor** properly, the wording of a document; drift 123 **penner** pen case (offered as a token of his services to Theseus) 124 **next** i.e., next to appear 126 **seek out silent hanging** i.e., seek out a curtain or tapestry behind which they can make love 127 **their** (perhaps plural because "Traveler" is so understood) 128 **gallèd** distressed 130 **beest-eating** (probably indicates the Clown's partiality for "beest," the milk of a cow soon after calving, used in making puddings) 131 **tool** sexual organ 132 **Cum multis aliis** with many others 134 **Produce** bring forth

Schoolmaster. *Intrate, filii!*° Come forth and foot it. 135

Knock.° *Enter the Dance. Music.* [*They*] *dance.*

Ladies, if we have been merry
And have pleased ye with a derry,
And a derry, and a down,
Say the Schoolmaster's no Clown.
Duke, if we have pleased thee too 140
And have done as good boys should do,
Give us but a tree or twain
For a maypole, and again,
Ere another year run out,
We'll make thee laugh and all this rout.° 145

Theseus. Take twenty, dominie. [*To Hippolyta*] How does my sweetheart?

Hippolyta. Never so pleased, sir.

Emilia. 'Twas an excellent dance,
And for a preface I never heard a better.

Theseus. Schoolmaster, I thank you. One see 'em all rewarded.

Pirithous. [*Gives money.*] And here's something to paint your pole withal. 150

Theseus. Now to our sports again.

Schoolmaster. May the stag thou hunt'st stand° long,
And thy dogs be swift and strong,
May they kill him without lets,°
And the ladies eat his dowsets!° *Wind horns.* 155
[*To the dancers*] Come, we are all made. *Dii deaeque omnes!*°
Ye have danced rarely, wenches. *Exeunt.*

135 **Intrate, filii** enter, my sons 135 s.d. **Knock** (the Schoolmaster gives a signal for the entry: but see Textual Note, p. 179) 145 **rout** company 152 **stand** endure 154 **lets** hindrances 155 **dowsets** testicles 156 **Dii deaeque omnes** all gods and goddesses

Scene VI. [*The open country.*]

Enter Palamon from the bush.

Palamon. About this hour my cousin gave his faith
To visit me again, and with him bring
Two swords and two good armors: if he fail,
He's neither man nor soldier. When he left me,
5 I did not think a week could have restored
My lost strength to me, I was grown so low
And crestfall'n with my wants. I thank thee, Arcite,
Thou art yet a fair foe, and I feel myself,
With this refreshing, able once again
10 To outdure° danger. To delay it longer
Would make the world think when it comes to hearing
That I lay fatting like a swine to fight,°
And not a soldier. Therefore this blest morning
Shall be the last; and that sword he refuses,°
15 If it but hold,° I kill him with: 'tis justice.
So love and Fortune for me!

Enter Arcite with armors and swords.

O good-morrow!

Arcite. Good-morrow, noble kinsman.

Palamon. I have put you
To too much pains, sir.

Arcite. That too much, fair cousin,
Is but a debt to honor, and my duty.

III.vi.10 **outdure** survive 12 **fatting like a swine to fight** being fattened to fight as a swine is fattened to be eaten 14 **that sword he refuses** (Palamon will give Arcite his choice) 15 **If it but hold** if it does not break

Palamon. Would you were so in all, sir! I could wish ye 20
As kind a kinsman as you force me find
A beneficial foe, that my embraces
Might thank ye, not my blows.

Arcite. I shall think either,
Well done, a noble recompense.

Palamon. Then I shall quit° you.

Arcite. Defy me in these fair terms, and you show° 25
More than a mistress to me. No more anger,
As you love anything that's honorable!
We were not bred° to talk, man. When we are armed
And both upon our guards, then let our fury,
Like meeting of two tides, fly strongly from us, 30
And then to whom the birthright° of this beauty
Truly pertains—without upbraidings, scorns,
Despisings of our persons, and such poutings
Fitter for girls and schoolboys—will be seen,
And quickly, yours or mine. Will't please you arm, sir? 35
Or if you feel yourself not fitting yet
And furnished with your old strength, I'll stay,° cousin,
And ev'ry day discourse you into health,
As I am spared.° Your person I am friends with,
And I could wish I had not said I loved her, 40
Though I had died.° But loving such a lady
And justifying° my love, I must not fly from't.

Palamon. Arcite, thou art so brave an enemy
That no man but thy cousin's fit to kill thee.

24 **quit** requite 25 **show** appear 28 **bred** brought up 31 **birthright** the right to possess her, given to one of us at birth 37 **stay** wait 39 **As I am spared** as long as I am alive 41 **Though I had died** i.e., as a result of my silence 42 **justifying** affirming, defending

I am well and lusty.° Choose your arms.

45 *Arcite.* Choose you, sir.

Palamon. Wilt thou exceed in all, or dost thou do it
To make me spare thee?

Arcite. If you think so, cousin,
You are deceived, for as I am a soldier
I will not spare you.

Palamon. That's well said.

Arcite. You'll find it.°

50 *Palamon.* Then as I am an honest man and love,
With all the justice of affection°
I'll pay thee soundly.° This I'll take.
[*Chooses an armor.*]

Arcite. That's mine then.
[*Takes the other.*]
I'll arm you first.

Palamon. Do. [*Arcite arms him.*] Pray thee tell me, cousin,
Where gott'st thou this good armor?

Arcite. 'Tis the duke's,
55 And to say true, I stole it. Do I pinch you?

Palamon. No.

Arcite. Is't not too heavy?

Palamon. I have worn a lighter,
But I shall make it serve.

Arcite. I'll buckle't close.

Palamon. By any means.°

Arcite. You care not for a grand guard?°

45 **lusty** vigorous 49 **find it** i.e., find it so 51 **justice of affection** justice administered by one who loves the offender 52 **soundly** fully, strongly 58 **By any means** i.e., please do 58 **grand guard** part of armor worn by knight on horseback

Palamon. No, no, we'll use no horses. I perceive
You would fain be at that fight.°

Arcite. I am indifferent.° 60

Palamon. 'Faith, so am I. Good cousin, thrust the buckle
Through far enough.

Arcite. I warrant you.

Palamon. My casque° now.

Arcite. Will you fight bare-armed?

Palamon. We shall be the nimbler.

Arcite. But use your gauntlets, though. Those are o' th' least:°
Prithee take mine, good cousin.

Palamon. Thank you, Arcite. 65
How do I look, am I fall'n much away?°

Arcite. 'Faith, very little: love has used you kindly.

Palamon. I warrant thee, I'll strike home.

Arcite. Do, and spare not;
I'll give you cause, sweet cousin.

Palamon. Now to you, sir.
[*He arms Arcite.*]
Methinks this armor's very like that, Arcite, 70
Thou wor'st that day the three kings fell, but lighter.

Arcite. That was a very good one, and that day
I well remember you outdid me, cousin.
I never saw such valor: when you charged
Upon the left wing of the enemy, 75
I spurred hard to come up, and under me

60 **at that fight** i.e., fight on horseback 60 **indifferent** i.e., as to how we fight 62 **casque** helmet 64 **Those are o' th' least** i.e., those you have are the smallest possible 66 **am I fall'n much away** have I got much thinner

I had a right good horse.

Palamon. You had indeed:
A bright bay, I remémber.

Arcite. Yes, but all
Was vainly labored in me: you outwent me,
80 Nor could my wishes reach you.° Yet a little
I did by imitation.

Palamon. More by virtue;°
You are modest, cousin.

Arcite. When I saw you charge first,
Methought I heard a dreadful clap of thunder
Break from the troop.

Palamon. But still before that flew
85 The lightning of your valor. Stay a little,
Is not this piece too strait?°

Arcite. No, no, 'tis well.

Palamon. I would have nothing hurt thee but my sword,
A bruise would be dishonor.

Arcite. Now I am perfect.°

Palamon. Stand off° then.

Arcite. Take my sword, I hold° it better.

90 *Palamon.* I thank ye. No, keep it, your life lies° on it.
Here's one: if it but hold, I ask no more
For all my hopes. My cause and honor guard me!

Arcite. And me my love!

They bow several ways;° then advance and stand.

Is there ought else to say?

80 **Nor could my wishes reach you** i.e., my wish to be by your side could not put me there 81 **virtue** natural talent 86 **strait** tight 88 **perfect** ready 89 **Stand off** stand away 89 **hold** think 90 **lies** depends 93 s.d. **bow several ways** bow formally in different directions, as in the lists

Palamon. This only, and no more. Thou art mine aunt's son,
And that blood we desire to shed is mutual, 95
In me thine, and in thee mine. My sword
Is in my hand, and if thou kill'st me
The gods and I forgive thee. If there be
A place prepared for those that sleep in honor,
I wish his weary soul that falls may win it. 100
Fight bravely, cousin. Give me thy noble hand.

Arcite. Here, Palamon. [*They take hands*.] This hand shall never more
Come near thee with such friendship.

Palamon. I commend° thee.

Arcite. If I fall, curse me, and say I was a coward,
For none but such dare die in these just trials. 105
Once more farewell, my cousin.

Palamon. Farewell, Arcite.
[*They*] *fight*.
Horns within; they stand.

Arcite. Lo, cousin, lo, our folly has undone us.

Palamon. Why?

Arcite. This is the duke, a-hunting as I told you:
If we be found, we are wretched. O retire 110
For honor's sake, and safety, presently°
Into your bush again. Sir, we shall find
Too many hours to die in, gentle cousin.
If you be seen, you perish instantly
For breaking prison, and I, if you reveal me, 115
For my contempt;° then all the world will scorn us,
And say we had a noble difference,°
But base disposers° of it.

Palamon. No, no, cousin,
I will no more be hidden, nor put off

103 **commend** praise, honor 111 **presently** at once 116 **contempt** i.e., of Theseus' banishment of him 117 **difference** quarrel 118 **disposers** controllers

120 This great adventure to a second trial.
I know your cunning, and I know your cause.°
He that faints° now, shame take him: put thyself
Upon thy present guard.°

Arcite. You are not mad?

Palamon. Or I will make th' advantage of this hour
125 Mine own, and what to come shall threaten me
I fear less than my fortune.° Know, weak cousin,
I love Emilia, and in that I'll bury
Thee, and all crosses° else.

Arcite. Then come what can come,
Thou shalt know, Palamon, I dare as well
130 Die as discourse or sleep. Only this fears me:°
The law will have the honor of our ends.
Have at thy life!

Palamon. Look to thine own well, Arcite.
[*They*] *fight again. Horns.*

Enter Theseus, Hippolyta, Emilia, Pirithous and train.

Theseus. What ignorant and mad malicious° traitors
Are you, that 'gainst the tenor° of my laws
135 Are making battle, thus like knights appointed,
Without my leave, and officers of arms?°
By Castor,° both shall die.

Palamon. Hold° thy word, Theseus.
We are certainly both traitors, both despisers
Of thee, and of thy goodness. I am Palamon
140 That cannot love thee, he that broke thy prison:
Think well what that deserves; and this is Arcite:
A bolder traitor never trod thy ground,

121 **your cause** i.e., why you wish to postpone the fight 122 **faints** draws back 123 **Upon thy present guard** on guard at once 126 **my fortune** i.e., my fortune in this fight 128 **crosses** obstacles 130 **fears me** makes me fear 133 **malicious** evilly disposed 134 **tenor** purport 136 **officers of arms** officials formally appointed to supervise a fight 137 **Castor** (son of Zeus by Leda, twin brother to Pollux) 137 **Hold** keep

A falser ne'er seemed friend. This is the man
Was begged° and banished, this is he contemns thee
And what thou dar'st do; and in this disguise 145
Against thy own edict follows thy sister,
That fortunate bright star,° the fair Emilia,
Whose servant—if there be a right in seeing,
And first bequeathing of the soul to—justly
I am, and which is more, dares think her his. 150
This treachery, like a most trusty lover,
I called him now to answer. If thou be'st
As thou art spoken, great and virtuous,
The true decider of all injuries,
Say "Fight again," and thou shalt see me, Theseus. 155
Do such a justice thou thyself wilt envy.
Then take my life, I'll woo thee to't.

Pirithous. O heaven,
What more than man is this!

Theseus. I have sworn.

Arcite. We seek not
Thy breath of mercy, Theseus: 'tis to me
A thing as soon to die as thee to say it, 160
And no more moved. Where° this man calls me traitor,
Let me say thus much: if in love be treason
In service of so excellent a beauty,
As I love most, and in that faith will perish,
As I have brought my life here to confirm it, 165
As I have served her truest, worthiest,
As I dare kill this cousin that denies it,
So let me be most traitor, and ye please me.
For° scorning thy edict, duke, ask that lady
Why she is fair, and why her eyes command me 170
Stay here to love her; and if she say "traitor,"
I am a villain fit to lie unburied.

Palamon. Thou shalt have pity of us both, O Theseus,
If unto neither thou show mercy. Stop,

144 **begged** petitioned for 147 **fortunate bright star** star bringing good fortune 161 **Where** whereas 169 **For** as for

175 As thou art just, thy noble ear against us;
As thou art valiant, for thy cousin's soul
Whose twelve strong labors crown his memory,°
Let's die together, at one instant, duke:
Only a little let him fall before me,
180 That I may tell my soul he shall not have her.

Theseus. I grant your wish, for to say true your cousin
Has ten times more offended, for I gave him
More mercy than you found, sir, your offenses
Being no more than his. None here speak for 'em,
185 For ere the sun set both shall sleep forever.

Hippolyta. Alas the pity! Now or never, sister,
Speak not to be denied: that face of yours
Will bear the curses else of after ages
For these lost cousins.

Emilia. In my face, dear sister,
190 I find no anger to 'em, nor no ruin:
The misadventure of their own eyes kill° 'em.
Yet that I will be woman, and have pity,
My knees shall grow to th' ground but° I'll get
mercy.
Help me, dear sister; in a deed so virtuous
195 The powers of all women will be with us.
[*They kneel.*]
Most royal brother!

Hippolyta. Sir, by our tie of marriage!

Emilia. By your own spotless honor!

Hippolyta. By that faith,
That fair hand, and that honest heart you gave me!

Emilia. By that you would have pity° in another,
By your own virtues infinite!

176–77 **thy cousin's . . . memory** i.e., the soul of Hercules, who legendarily performed twelve great labors 191 **kill** (plural verb through association with "eyes," despite the singular subject) 193 **but** unless (or until) 199 **By that you would have pity** by whatever you would have pity on

Hippolyta. By valor, 200
By all the chaste nights I have ever pleased you!

Theseus. These are strange conjurings.°

Pirithous. Nay, then I'll in too:
[*He kneels.*]
By all our friendship, sir, by all our dangers,
By all you love most—wars, and this sweet lady!

Emilia. By that you would have trembled to deny 205
A blushing maid!°

Hippolyta. By your own eyes; by strength,
In which you swore I went beyond all women,
Almost all men, and yet I yielded, Theseus.

Pirithous. To crown all this: by your most noble soul,
Which cannot want° due mercy! I beg first. 210

Hippolyta. Next hear my prayers.

Emilia. Last let me entreat, sir.

Pirithous. For mercy!

Hippolyta. Mercy!

Emilia. Mercy on these princes!

Theseus. Ye make my faith° reel. [*They rise.*] Say I felt
Compassion to 'em both, how would you place it?°

Emilia. Upon their lives—but with their banishments. 215

Theseus. You are a right° woman, sister. You have pity,
But want the understanding where to use it.
If you desire their lives, invent a way
Safer than banishment. Can these two live
And have the agony of love about 'em, 220

202 **conjurings** conjurations 205–06 **By that . . . maid** presumably, the love the maid asked for 210 **want** fail to get (?), lack the power to feel (?) 213 **faith** i.e., in his own judgment 214 **how would you place it** i.e., in what way would you have it bestowed 216 **right** true, typical

And not kill one another? Every day
They'd fight about you, hourly bring your honor
In public question with their swords. Be wise then,
And here forget 'em. It concerns your credit,
225 And my oath equally. I have said they die:
Better they fall by th' law than one another.
Bow° not my honor.

Emilia. O my noble brother,
That oath was rashly made, and in your anger;
Your reason will not hold° it. If such vows
230 Stand for express will,° all the world must perish.
Beside, I have another oath, 'gainst yours,
Of more authority, I am sure more love,
Not made in passion neither, but good heed.

Theseus. What is it, sister?

Pirithous. Urge it home, brave lady.

235 *Emilia.* That you would ne'er deny me anything
Fit for my modest suit, and your free granting.
I tie you to your word now: if ye fall in't,°
Think how you maim your honor—
For now I am set a-begging, sir, I am deaf
240 To all but your compassion—how their lives
Might breed the ruin of my name, opinion.°
Shall anything that loves me perish for me?
That were a cruel wisdom. Do men prune
The straight young boughs that blush with thousand blossoms
245 Because they may be rotten?° O duke Theseus,
The goodly mothers that have groaned for these,
And all the longing maids that ever loved,
If your vow stand, shall curse me and my beauty,
And in their funeral songs for these two cousins

227 **Bow** humiliate, bring disgrace on 229 **hold** hold to 230 **express will** unshakable resolve 237 **fall in't** renege on it 240–41 **how . . . opinion** i.e., how the taking away of their lives might lead to the ruin of my name and reputation (some editors emend to "name's opinion"; some take "opinion" as an exclamation of contempt) 245 **Because they may be rotten** because they may later become rotten

Despise my cruelty, and cry woe worth° me, 250
Till I am nothing but the scorn of women.
For heaven's sake save their lives, and banish 'em.

Theseus. On what conditions?

Emilia. Swear 'em never more
To make me their contention, or to know me,°
To tread upon thy dukedom, and to be, 255
Wherever they shall travel, ever strangers
To one another.

Palamon. I'll be cut a-pieces
Before I take this oath: forget I love her?
O all ye gods despise me then! Thy banishment
I not mislike, so° we may fairly carry 260
Our swords and cause along. Else never trifle,
But take our lives, duke: I must love and will,
And for that love must and dare kill this cousin
On any piece° the earth has.

Theseus. Will you, Arcite,
Take these conditions?

Palamon. He's a villain then. 265

Pirithous. These are men.°

Arcite. No, never, duke. 'Tis worse to me than begging
To take my life so basely. Though I think
I never shall enjoy her, yet I'll preserve
The honor of affection, and die for her, 270
Make° death a devil.

Theseus. What may be done? For now I feel compassion.

Pirithous. Let it not fall° again, sir.

Theseus. Say, Emilia,
If one of them were dead, as one must, are you

250 **woe worth** woe befall 254 **know me** hold me in their minds 260 **so** provided that 264 **piece** i.e., of ground 266 **men** i.e., complete men 271 **Make** though you make 273 **fall** weaken

275 Content to take th' other to your husband?
They cannot both enjoy you. They are princes
As goodly as your own eyes, and as noble
As ever Fame yet spoke of. Look upon 'em,
And if you can love, end this difference.
280 I give consent; are you content too, princes?

Both [*Cousins*]. With all our souls.

Theseus. He that she refuses
Must die then.

Both [*Cousins*]. Any death thou canst invent, duke.

Palamon. If I fall from that mouth,° I fall with favor,
And lovers yet unborn shall bless my ashes.

285 *Arcite.* If she refuse me, yet my grave will wed me,
And soldiers sing my epitaph.

Theseus. Make choice, then.

Emilia. I cannot, sir, they are both too excellent:
For me, a hair shall never fall of these men.°

Hippolyta. What will become of 'em?

Theseus. Thus I ordain it,
290 And by mine honor, once again, it stands,
Or both shall die. You shall both to your country,
And each within this month, accompanied
With three fair knights, appear again in this place,
In which I'll plant a pyramid;° and whether,°
295 Before us that are here, can force his cousin
By fair and knightly strength to touch the pillar,
He shall enjoy her; the other lose his head,
And all his friends.° Nor shall he grudge to fall,
Nor think he dies with interest in this lady.
Will this content ye?

283 **from that mouth** i.e., the sentence being spoken by her 288 **For . . . men** it will not be from me that a hair of either shall perish 294 **pyramid** obelisk 294 **whether** which of the two 298 **And all his friends** i.e., they shall lose their heads too

Palamon. Yes. Here, cousin Arcite, 300
I am friends again, till that hour.

Arcite. I embrace ye.

Theseus. Are you content, sister?

Emilia. Yes, I must, sir,
Else both miscarry.

Theseus. Come, shake hands again, then,
And take heed, as you are gentlemen, this quarrel
Sleep till the hour prefixed,° and hold your course.° 305

Palamon. We dare not fail thee, Theseus.

Theseus. Come, I'll give ye
Now usage like to princes, and to friends.
When ye return, who wins I'll settle here,°
Who loses°—yet I'll weep upon his bier. *Exeunt.*

305 **prefixed** arranged 305 **hold your course** keep to your resolve 308 **settle here** give him a home in Athens 309 **Who loses—** (Theseus, by changing the construction, shows his realization that the second half of the antithesis must be anticlimactic)

ACT IV

Scene I. [*The prison.*]

Enter Jailer and his friend.

Jailer. Hear you no more, was nothing said of me
Concerning the escape of Palamon?
Good sir, remember.

First Friend. Nothing that I heard,
For I came home before the business°
5 Was fully ended. Yet I might perceive,
Ere I departed, a great likelihood
Of both their pardons. For Hippolyta
And fair-eyed Emily upon their knees
Begged with such handsome pity that the duke
Methought stood staggering, whether he should
10 follow
His rash oath or the sweet compassion
Of those two ladies; and to second them
That truly noble prince Pirithous,
Half his own heart,° set in too,° that° I hope
15 All shall be well. Neither heard I one question
Of your name, or his 'scape.

Enter Second Friend.

Jailer. Pray heaven it hold so.

IV.i.4 **business** (three syllables) 14 **Half his own heart** i.e., the possessor of half of Theseus' heart 14 **set in too** joined in as well 14 **that** so that

Second Friend. Be of good comfort, man; I bring you news,
Good news.

Jailer. They are welcome.

Second Friend. Palamon has cleared you,
And got your pardon, and discovered° how
And by whose means he escaped, which was your daughter's, 20
Whose pardon is procured too, and the prisoner,
Not to be held ungrateful to her goodness,
Has given a sum of money to her marriage,
A large one I'll assure you.

Jailer. Ye are a good man
And ever bring good news.

First Friend. How was it ended? 25

Second Friend. Why, as it should be: they that never begged
But they prevailed had their suits fairly granted.
The prisoners have their lives.

First Friend. I knew 'twould be so.

Second Friend. But there be new conditions, which you'll hear of
At better time.

Jailer. I hope they are good.

Second Friend. They are honorable; 30
How good they'll prove I know not.

Enter Wooer.

First Friend. 'Twill be known.

Wooer. Alas, sir, where's your daughter?

Jailer. Why do you ask?

Wooer. O sir, when did you see her?

19 **discovered** revealed

Second Friend. How he looks!

Jailer. This morning.

Wooer. Was she well? Was she in health?
Sir, when did she sleep?

35 *First Friend.* These are strange questions.

Jailer. I do not think she was very well, for now
You make me mind her,° but° this very day
I asked her questions, and she answered me
So far from what she was, so childishly,
40 So sillily, as if she were a fool,
An innocent,° and I was very angry.
But what of her, sir?

Wooer. Nothing but my pity;°
But you must know it, and as good by me
As by another that less loves her.

Jailer. Well, sir?

First Friend. Not right?°

Second Friend. Not well?

45 *Wooer.* No, sir, not well.
'Tis too true, she is mad.

First Friend. It cannot be.

Wooer. Believe you'll find it so.

Jailer. I half suspected
What you have told me: the gods comfort her!
Either this was her love to Palamon,
50 Or fear of my miscarrying° on his 'scape,
Or both.

Wooer. 'Tis likely.

Jailer. But why all this haste,° sir?

37 **mind her** call her to mind 37 **but** only 41 **innocent** idiot 42 **Nothing but my pity** it is only pity that makes me speak 45 **Not right** i.e., in the head 50 **miscarrying** dying 51 **haste** (the Wooer's haste in coming to tell the Jailer)

Wooer. I'll tell you quickly. As I late was angling
In the great lake that lies behind the palace,
From the far shore, thick set with reeds and sedges,
As patiently I was attending sport, 55
I heard a voice, a shrill one, and attentive
I gave my ear, when I might well perceive
'Twas one that sung, and by the smallness of it
A boy or woman. I then left my angle
To his own skill, came near, but yet perceived not 60
Who made the sound, the rushes and the reeds
Had so encompassed it.° I laid me down
And listened to the words she sung, for then,
Through a small glade cut by the fishermen,
I saw it was your daughter.

Jailer. Pray go on, sir. 65

Wooer. She sung much, but no sense. Only I heard her
Repeat this often: "Palamon is gone,
Is gone to th' wood to gather mulberries;
I'll find him out tomorrow."

First Friend. Pretty soul!

Wooer. "His shackles will betray him, he'll be taken, 70
And what shall I do then? I'll bring a bevy,
A hundred black-eyed maids, that love as I do,
With chaplets° on their heads of daffadillies,
With cherry lips, and cheeks of damask roses,
And all we'll dance an antic° 'fore the duke, 75
And beg his° pardon." Then she talked of you, sir,
That you must lose your head tomorrow morning,
And she must gather flowers to bury you,
And see the house made handsome. Then she sung
Nothing but "Willow, willow, willow,"° and between 80
Ever was "Palamon, fair Palamon,"

62 **it** i.e., the place 73 **chaplets** wreaths 75 **antic** grotesque dance, as in an antimasque 76 **his** i.e., Palamon's 80 **Willow, willow, willow** (Desdemona's song in *Othello,* IV.iii)

And "Palamon was a tall young man."° The place
Was knee-deep where she sat; her careless tresses
A wreath of bullrush rounded; about her stuck
85 Thousand fresh water flowers of several colors—
That methought she appeared like the fair nymph
That feeds the lake with waters, or as Iris°
Newly dropped down from heaven. Rings she made
Of rushes that grew by, and to 'em spoke
90 The prettiest posies:° "Thus our true love's tied,"
"This you may loose,° not me," and many a one.
And then she wept, and sung again, and sighed,
And with the same breath smiled, and kissed her hand.

Second Friend. Alas, what pity it is!

Wooer. I made in to her.°
She saw me, and straight sought the flood; I saved
95 her,
And set her safe to land—when presently°
She slipped away, and to the city made,
With such a cry, and swiftness, that believe me
She left me far behind her. Three or four
100 I saw from far off cross° her: one of 'em
I knew to be your brother; where she stayed,°
And fell, scarce to be got away. I left them with her,

Enter Brother, Daughter, and others.

And hither came to tell you. Here they are.

Daughter.

[*Sings*] May you never more enjoy the light, &c.

82 **Palamon was a tall young man** (a variant of the song "When Samson was a tall young man," possibly referred to in *Love's Labor's Lost,* I.ii.171) 87 **Iris** goddess of the rainbow 90 **posies** mottoes engraved on rings 91 **loose** (may have the meaning "lose," the two words being commonly spelled "loose") 94 **made in to her** i.e., forced my way through the rushes to her 96 **presently** at once 100 **cross** intercept 101 **stayed** stopped

Is not this a fine song?

Brother. O, a very fine one. 105

Daughter. I can sing twenty more.

Brother. I think you can.

Daughter. Yes, truly can I. I can sing "The Broom"°
And "Bonny Robin."° Are not you a tailor?

Brother. Yes.

Daughter. Where's my wedding gown?

Brother. I'll bring it tomorrow.

Daughter. Do, very rearly,° I must be abroad else° 110
To call the maids, and pay the minstrels,
For I must lose my maidenhead by cocklight:°
'Twill never thrive else.°

(*Sings*) O fair, O sweet,° &c.

Brother. You must e'en take it patiently.

Jailer. 'Tis true. 115

Daughter. Good e'en, good men, pray did you ever hear
Of one young Palamon?

Jailer. Yes, wench, we know him.

Daughter. Is't not a fine young gentleman?

Jailer. 'Tis, love.

Brother. By no mean cross her, she is then distempered

107 **The Broom** (a popular song quoted in W. Wager's play *The Longer thou livest the more Fool thou art* [*c.* 1559] and elsewhere: "broom" here is the shrub of that name) 108 **Bonny Robin** (a song preserved in Queen Elizabeth's Virginal Book and in William Ballet's Lute Book: Ophelia sings a line of it in *Hamlet,* IV.v, where, as here, it may imply a sexual meaning for "Robin") 110 **rearly** early 110 **I must be abroad else** otherwise I shall be away from home 112 **by cocklight** before dawn 113 **'Twill never thrive else** otherwise things will never prosper with me 114 **O fair, O sweet** (a song included among "Certaine Sonets" in Sidney's 1598 Folio)

Far worse than now she shows.

120 *First Friend.* Yes, he's a fine man.

Daughter. O, is he so? You have a sister?

First Friend. Yes.

Daughter. But she shall never have him, tell her so,
For a trick that I know.° Y' had best look to her,
For if she see him once, she's gone, she's done,
125 And undone in an hour. All the young maids
Of our town are in love with him, but I laugh at 'em
And let 'em all alone.° Is't not a wise course?

First Friend. Yes.

Daughter. There is at least two hundred now with child by him,
There must be four; yet I keep close° for all this,
130 Close as a cockle;° and all these must be boys—
He has the trick° on't—and at ten years old
They must be all gelt for musicians,
And sing the wars of Theseus.

Second Friend. This is strange.

Daughter. As ever you heard, but say nothing.

First Friend. No.

Daughter. They come from all parts of the dukedom
135 to him.
I'll warrant ye, he had not so few last night
As twenty to dispatch: he'll tickle 't up°
In two hours, if his hand be in.°

Jailer. She's lost
Past all cure.

123 **For a trick that I know** because of a stratagem that I know 127 **let 'em all alone** pay no attention to them 129 **keep close** maintain secrecy 130 **Close as a cockle** (the proverb occurs also in Shirley's *The School of Compliment* [1625]: "cockle" here indicates "cockle-shell," formerly used for the shells of mollusks generally) 131 **trick** method 137 **tickle 't up** i.e., finish the task (with a strong suggestion of sexual pleasure) 138 **if his hand be in** if he is in good form

Brother. Heaven forbid, man.

Daughter. Come hither, you are a wise man.

First Friend. Does she know him? 140

Second Friend. No, would she did.

Daughter. You are master of a ship?°

Jailer. Yes.

Daughter. Where's your compass?

Jailer. Here.

Daughter. Set it to th' north.
And now direct your course to th' wood, where Palamon
Lies longing for me. For the tackling let me alone.
Come° weigh, my hearts, cheerly all! O, O, O, 'tis up!° 145
The wind's fair: top the bowling!° Out with the mainsail!
Where's your whistle, master?

Brother. Let's get her in.

Jailer. Up to the top, boy!

Brother. Where's the pilot?

First Friend. Here.

Daughter. What ken'st° thou?

141 **master of a ship** (the Daughter has taken the Schoolmaster for a tinker, III.v.83, and the Brother for a tailor, IV.i.108: Palamon is always a soldier, and she completes the proverbial four occupations by taking her father for a sailor) 145 **Come** (lines 145–49 are hardly verse, and the 1634 quarto prints mainly as prose; but a faint sense of line breaks seems to lie behind the Daughter's staccato phrases) 145 **'tis up** (i.e., the tackling: the "O, O, O" indicating the Daughter's imaginary exertions) 146 **top the bowling** slant the bowline (rope run from the middle of the perpendicular of the weather side of a sail to the larboard or starboard bow, for the purpose of keeping the sail steady in a wind) 149 **ken'st** seest

Second Friend. A fair wood.

Daughter. Bear for° it, master! Tack about!

150 (*Sings*) When Cynthia with her borrowed light, &c.

Exeunt.

Scene II. [*The palace of Theseus.*]

Enter Emilia alone, with two pictures.

Emilia. Yet I may bind those wounds up,° that must open
And bleed to death for my sake else: I'll choose,
And end their strife. Two such young handsome men
Shall never fall for me; their weeping mothers,
5 Following the dead cold ashes of their sons,
Shall never curse my cruelty. Good heaven,
What a sweet face has Arcite! If wise Nature
With all her best endowments, all those beauties
She sows into the births of noble bodies,
10 Were here a mortal woman, and had in her
The coy denials of young maids, yet doubtless
She would run mad for this man. What an eye,
Of what a fiery sparkle, and quick° sweetness,
Has this young prince! Here° Love himself sits smiling:
15 Just such another° wanton Ganymede
Set Jove a-fire with and enforced the god
Snatch up the goodly boy° and set him by him,
A shining constellation. What a brow
Of what a spacious majesty he carries—

149 **Bear for** sail toward IV.ii.1 **bind those wounds up** (proleptic for "prevent those wounds from being given") 13 **quick** vital 14 **Here** i.e., in his eye 15 **another** i.e., another smile (or eye?) 17 **the goodly boy** i.e., Ganymede

Arched like the great-eyed Juno's, but far sweeter, 20
Smoother than Pelops' shoulder!° Fame and Honor
Methinks from hence,° as from a promontory
Pointed° in heaven, should clap their wings and
sing
To all the under-world° the loves and fights
Of gods and such men near 'em.° Palamon 25
Is but his foil, to him a mere dull shadow:
He's swarth,° and meager, of an eye as heavy
As if he had lost his mother; a still temper,°
No stirring in him, no alacrity,
Of all this spritely sharpness not a smile.° 30
Yet these that we count errors may become him:
Narcissus° was a sad boy, but a heavenly.
O who can find the bent of woman's fancy?
I am a fool, my reason is lost in me,
I have no choice,° and I have lied so lewdly° 35
That women ought to beat me. On my knees
I ask thy pardon, Palamon: thou art alone,°
And only beautiful, and these the eyes,
These the bright lamps of beauty, that command
And threaten Love, and what young maid dare
cross° 'em? 40
What a bold gravity, and yet inviting,
Has this brown manly face! O Love, this only
From this hour is complexion.° Lie there, Arcite,
Thou art a changeling° to him, a mere gipsy,
And this the noble body. I am sotted,° 45
Utterly lost, my virgin's faith has fled me!
For if my brother but even now had asked me

21 **Pelops' shoulder** (Pelops was son of Tantalus and father of Atreus: Marlowe, *Hero and Leander*, i.65, mentions his shoulder as a standard of whiteness) 22 **from hence** i.e., from Arcite's brow 23 **Pointed** coming to its point 24 **the under-world** the earth 25 **such men near 'em** demigods, etc. 27 **swarth** dark-complexioned 28 **still temper** placid disposition 30 **smile** trace (with an echo of Arcite's smiling mentioned in lines 14–15) 32 **Narcissus** (cf. II.i. 178–80) 35 **choice** ability to choose 35 **lewdly** grossly 37 **alone** unique, supreme 40 **cross** gainsay 42–43 **this only/From this hour is complexion** i.e., only this complexion is acceptable 44 **changeling** child left by the fairies in place of another 45 **sotted** reduced to stupidity

Whether° I loved, I had run mad for Arcite;
Now if my sister, more for Palamon.
50 Stand both together:° now come ask me, brother.
Alas, I know not. Ask me now, sweet sister.
I may go look.° What a mere child is Fancy,
That having two fair gawds° of equal sweetness
Cannot distinguish, but must cry for both!

Enter [*a*] *Gentleman.*

How now, sir?

55 *Gentleman.* From the noble duke your brother,
Madam, I bring you news: the knights are come.

Emilia. To end the quarrel?

Gentleman. Yes.

Emilia. Would I might end first!
What sins have I committed, chaste Diana,°
That my unspotted youth must now be soiled
60 With blood of princes, and my chastity
Be made the altar where the lives of lovers,
Two greater and two better never yet
Made mothers joy, must be the sacrifice
To my unhappy beauty?

Enter Theseus, Hippolyta, Pirithous and Attendants.

Theseus. Bring 'em in
65 Quickly: by any means,° I long to see 'em.
Your two contending lovers are returned,
And with them their fair knights. Now, my fair sister,
You must love one of them.

48 **Whether** which of the two 50 **Stand both together** (she puts the two pictures side by side) 52 **I may go look** i.e., I may go seek (for I do not yet know) 53 **gawds** toys, trifles 58 **Diana** (appropriately invoked by Emilia, as in V.i, as Diana was the patron of Amazons) 65 **by any means** indeed

Emilia. I had rather both,
So° neither for my sake should fall untimely.

Enter [a] Messenger.

Theseus. Who saw 'em?

Pirithous. I a while.°

Gentleman. And I. 70

Theseus. From whence come you, sir?

Messenger. From the knights.

Theseus. Pray speak,
You that have seen them, what they are.

Mesenger. I will, sir,
And truly what I think. Six braver spirits
Than these they have brought, if we judge by the outside,
I never saw nor read of. He that stands 75
In the first place with Arcite, by his seeming
Should be a stout° man, by his face a prince.
His very looks so say him: his complexion
Nearer a brown than black; stern, and yet noble,
Which shows him hardy, fearless, proud of dangers; 80
The circles of his eyes show fire within him,
And as a heated° lion so he looks;
His hair hangs long behind him, black and shining
Like ravens' wings; his shoulders broad and strong,
Armed long and round,° and on his thigh a sword 85
Hung by a curious baldric,° when he frowns
To seal his will with:° better o' my conscience
Was never soldier's friend.°

Theseus. Thou hast well described him.

69 **So** provided that 70 **a while** briefly 77 **stout** bold, strong 82 **heated** enraged (with perhaps a suggestion of "in heat") 85 **Armed long and round** with long, round arms 86 **baldric** belt 86–87 **when he frowns/To seal his will with** to effect his desire with when he is angry 87–88 **better . . . friend** i.e., no soldier has had a better, more trustworthy sword

Pirithous. Yet a great deal short,
90 Methinks, of him that's first with Palamon.

Theseus. Pray speak him, friend.

Pirithous. I guess he is a prince too,
And if it may be, greater;° for his show°
Has all the ornament of honor in't.
He's somewhat bigger than the knight he° spoke of,
95 But of a face far sweeter. His complexion
Is, as a ripe grape, ruddy. He has felt
Without doubt what he fights for,° and so apter
To make this cause his own. In's face appears
All the fair hopes of what he undertakes,°
100 And when he's angry, then a settled° valor,
Not tainted with extremes, runs through his body
And guides his arm to brave things. Fear he cannot,
He shows no such soft temper. His head's yellow,
Hard-haired, and curled, thick twined like ivy tods,°
105 Not to undo° with thunder. In his face
The livery of the warlike maid° appears,
Pure red and white, for yet no beard has blest him;
And in his rolling eyes sits Victory,
As if she ever meant to court his valor.°
110 His nose stands high, a character° of honor;
His red lips, after fights,° are fit for ladies.

Emilia. Must these men die too?

Pirithous. When he speaks, his tongue
Sounds like a trumpet. All his lineaments
Are as a man would wish 'em, strong and clean.
115 He wears a well-steeled ax, the staff of gold.
His age some five and twenty.

92 **greater** i.e., more than a prince 92 **show** appearance 94 **he** i.e., the Messenger 97 **what he fights for** i.e., love 98–99 **In's face . . . undertakes** i.e., he shows great hope of success 100 **settled** steady 104 **ivy tods** ivy bushes 105 **Not to undo** not to be undone, not disheveled 106 **the warlike maid** (the goddess of war, Bellona) 109 **court his valor** (if "court" is right—see Textual Note—the image is strained: the look in his eyes seems in love with his own valor) 110 **character** token 111 **after fights** when fighting is over

Messenger. There's another,
A little man, but of a tough soul, seeming
As great as any: fairer promises
In such a body yet I never looked on.

Pirithous. O, he that's freckle-faced?

Messenger. The same, my lord. 120
Are they° not sweet ones?

Pirithous. Yes, they are well.

Messenger. Methinks,
Being so few and well disposed,° they show
Great and fine art in nature. He's white-haired,°
Not wanton white, but such a manly color
Next to an auburn;° tough, and nimble set, 125
Which shows an active soul. His arms are brawny,
Lined with strong sinews: to the shoulder-piece
Gently they swell, like women new-conceived,°
Which speaks him prone to labor,° never fainting
Under the weight of arms; stout-hearted, still,° 130
But when he stirs, a tiger. He's gray-eyed,
Which yields compassion where he conquers;° sharp
To spy advantages, and where he finds 'em
He's swift to make 'em his. He does no wrongs,
Nor takes none.° He's round-faced, and when he smiles 135
He shows° a lover, when he frowns a soldier.
About his head he wears the winner's oak,°
And in it stuck the favor of his lady.
His age some six and thirty. In his hand
He bears a charging staff,° embossed with silver. 140

121 **they** i.e., the freckles 122 **disposed** arranged 123 **white-haired** blond 125 **auburn** yellowish white 128 **new-conceived** recently made pregnant 129 **labor** toil (but continuing the image of "new-conceived") 130 **still** quiet 131–32 **gray-eyed . . . conquers** (apparently gray eyes were considered a sign of mercy) 134–35 **He does no wrongs/Nor takes none** he neither inflicts nor submits to an unfair attack 136 **shows** appears 137 **winner's oak** wreath of oak leaves bestowed for valor 140 **charging staff** spear used in charging an enemy

Theseus. Are they all thus?

Pirithous. They are all the sons of Honor.

Theseus. Now as I have a soul I long to see 'em!
Lady, you shall see men fight now.°

Hippolyta. I wish it,
But not the cause, my lord. They would show
145 Bravely about the titles of two kingdoms;°
'Tis pity Love should be so tyrannous.
O my soft-hearted sister, what think you?
Weep not till they weep blood. Wench, it must be.

Theseus. You have steeled 'em with your beauty. Honored friend,
150 To you I give the field:° pray order it
Fitting the persons that must use it.

Pirithous. Yes, sir.

Theseus. Come, I'll go visit 'em: I cannot stay,°
Their fame has fired me so. Till they appear,
Good friend, be royal.°

Pirithous. There shall want no bravery.°

155 *Emilia.* Poor wench, go weep, for whosoever wins
Loses a noble cousin, for thy sins. *Exeunt.*

143 **you shall see men fight now** (Hippolyta, as an Amazon, would have a prejudice in favor of women as fighters: Theseus assures her she will now see fighting on a higher level than she has known) 144–45 **would . . . kingdoms** i.e., would be good to watch if they were fighting to win each other's kingdoms 150 **give the field** assign the task of arranging the tournament 152 **stay** wait 154 **be royal** make the arrangements with magnificence 154 **bravery** splendor

Scene III. [*The prison.*]

Enter Jailer, Wooer, Doctor.

Doctor. Her distraction is more at some time of the moon than at other some, is it not?

Jailer. She is continually in a harmless distemper, sleeps little, altogether without appetite, save often drinking, dreaming of another world, and a better; 5 and what broken° piece of matter soe'er she's about, the name Palamon lards it,° that she farces° ev'ry business withal, fits it to every question.

Enter Daughter.

Look where she comes, you shall perceive her behavior. 10

Daughter. I have forgot it quite. The burden° on't was "Down-a down-a," and penned by no worse man than Geraldo, Emilia's schoolmaster.° He's as fantastical° too, as ever he may go upon's legs,° for in the next world will Dido see Palamon, and then 15 will she be out of love with Aeneas.°

Doctor. What stuff's here? Poor soul!

Jailer. E'en thus all day long.

Daughter. Now for this charm that I told you of, you must bring a piece of silver on the tip of your 20

IV.iii.6 **broken** disconnected 7 **lards it** fills it (is rubbed into it like lard) 7 **farces** stuffs 11 **burden** refrain 13 **Emilia's schoolmaster** (the Daughter is of course mistaken) 13–14 **fantastical** fanciful 14 **as ever he may go upon's legs** i.e., as he could possibly be 14–16 **for . . . Aeneas** (she imagines that the Schoolmaster has taught her a song about Dido after death loving Palamon, now dead too, instead of Aeneas)

tongue, or no ferry.° Then if it be your chance to come where the blessed spirits—as there's a sight now°—we maids that have our livers perished,° cracked to pieces with love, we shall come there, 25 and do nothing all day long but pick flowers with Proserpine.° Then will I make Palamon a nosegay, then let him mark me°—then!

Doctor. How prettily she's amiss! Note her a little further.

30 *Daughter*. 'Faith, I'll tell you, sometime we go to barley-break,° we of the blessed. Alas, 'tis a sore life they have i' th' other place, such burning, frying, boiling, hissing, howling, chatt'ring, cursing—O they have shrewd measure;° take heed! If one be 35 mad, or hang or drown themselves, thither they go, Jupiter bless us, and there shall we be put in a cauldron of lead and usurers' grease,° amongst a whole million of cutpurses, and there boil like a gammon of bacon that will never be enough.° *Exit.*

40 *Doctor*. How her brain coins!°

[*Enter Daughter*.]

Daughter. Lords and courtiers, that have got maids with child, they are in this place, they shall stand in fire up to the navel, and in ice up to th' heart, and there th' offending part burns, and the deceiv- 45 ing part freezes: in troth a very grievous punish-

21 **no ferry** (Charon, the ferryman of the underworld, will not take you across the Styx) 22–23 **as there's a sight now** i.e., as I can see them now ("as" may be merely exclamatory, and possibly "sight" here means "great number") 23 **perished** shriveled up (the liver was believed to be the seat of the affections) 25–26 **pick flowers with Proserpine** (Proserpine was picking flowers when Pluto carried her off to be queen of the underworld) 27 **mark me** pay attention to me 31 **barley-break** (a game played by six persons in couples, in which one couple occupies a marked space called "hell") 34 **shrewd measure** harsh punishment 37 **usurers' grease** fat sweated by usurers 39 **enough** done, cooked 40 **coins** spins fancies

ment, as one would think, for such a trifle. Believe me, one would marry a leprous witch to be rid on't, I'll assure you.

Doctor. How she continues this fancy! 'Tis not an engraffed° madness, but a most thick and profound melancholy.° 50

Daughter. To hear there a proud lady, and a proud city wife, howl together! I were a beast and° I'd call it good sport. One cries "O this smoke!", another "This fire!" One cries "O that ever I did it behind the arras!" and then howls; th' other curses a suing fellow° and her garden house.° 55

(*Sings*) I will be true, my stars, my fate, &c.

Exit Daughter.

Jailer. What think you of her, sir?

Doctor. I think she has a perturbed mind, which I cannot minister to. 60

Jailer. Alas, what then?

Doctor. Understand you she ever affected any man ere she beheld Palamon?

Jailer. I was once, sir, in great hope she had fixed her liking on this gentleman my friend. 65

Wooer. I did think so too, and would account I had a great penn'orth° on't, to give half my 'state° that both she and I at this present stood unfeignedly on the same terms. 70

Doctor. That intemperate surfeit of her eye° hath distempered the other senses: they may return and settle again to execute their preordained faculties, but they are now in a most extravagant vagary.

50 **engraffed** implanted, firmly planted 50–51 **thick and profound melancholy** (morbid condition known as "melancholy," to be distinguished from the normal "melancholy" humor) 53 **and** if 57 **suing fellow** persistent wooer 57 **garden house** (notoriously used for assignations) 68 **penn'orth** bargain 68 **'state** property 71 **intemperate surfeit of her eye** i.e., by seeing Palamon

75 This you must do: confine her to a place where the light may rather seem to steal in than be permitted; take upon you, young sir her friend, the name of Palamon; say you come to eat with her, and to commune of love. This will catch her attention, for
80 this her mind beats upon:° other objects that are inserted 'tween her mind and eye become the pranks and friskins° of her madness. Sing to her such green° songs of love as she says Palamon hath sung in prison. Come to her, stuck in° as sweet
85 flowers as the season is mistress of, and thereto make an addition of some other compounded° odors, which are grateful° to the sense. All this shall become° Palamon, for Palamon can sing, and Palamon is sweet and ev'ry good thing. Desire to eat
90 with her, carve her,° drink to her, and, still among,° intermingle your petition of grace and acceptance into her favor. Learn what maids have been her companions and play-feres,° and let them repair to her with "Palamon" in their mouths, and appear
95 with tokens, as if they suggested° for him. It is a falsehood she is in, which is with falsehoods to be combated. This may bring her to eat, to sleep, and reduce° what's now out of square° in her into their former law and regiment.° I have seen it ap-
100 proved,° how many times I know not, but to make the number more I have great hope in this. I will between the passages° of this project come in with my appliance.° Let us put it in execution and hasten the success,° which doubt not will bring
105 forth comfort. *Exeunt.*

80 **beats upon** is preoccupied with 82 **friskins** vagaries 83 **green** youthful 84 **stuck in** adorned with 86 **compounded** mixed 87 **grateful** pleasing 87–88 **become** be suitable for 90 **carve her** carve for her 90 **still among** ever betweenwhiles 93 **play-feres** playfellows 95 **suggested** interceded 98 **reduce** bring back 98 **out of square** irregular 99 **regiment** government, order 99–100 **approved** confirmed 102 **passages** separate stages 103 **appliance** device, stratagem (presumably his device of making the disguised Wooer sleep with her) 104 **success** result

ACT V

Scene I. [*Before the altars of Mars, Venus and Diana.*]

Flourish. Enter Theseus, Pirithous, Hippolyta, Attendants.

Theseus. Now let 'em enter, and before the gods
Tender their holy prayers. Let the temples
Burn bright with sacred fires, and the altars
In hallowed clouds commend their swelling incense°
To those above us. Let no due be wanting: 5
They have a noble work in hand, will honor°
The very powers that love 'em.

Flourish of cornets. Enter Palamon and Arcite and their Knights.

Pirithous. Sir, they enter.

Theseus. You valiant and strong-hearted enemies,
You royal german-foes,° that this day come
To blow that nearness° out that flames between ye, 10
Lay by your anger for an hour, and dove-like
Before the holy altars of your helpers,
The all-feared gods, bow down your stubborn bodies.
Your ire is more than mortal: so your help be;

V.i.4 **swelling incense** incense that swells into clouds 6 **will honor** i.e., which will honor 9 **german-foes** foes who are of the same family 10 **nearness** kinship and friendship (editors have suggested "furnace" and "fierceness" as emendations)

15 And as the gods regard ye,° fight with justice.
I'll leave you to your prayers, and betwixt ye
I part° my wishes.

Pirithous. Honor crown the worthiest!

Exit Theseus and his train.

Palamon. The glass° is running now that cannot finish
Till one of us expire. Think you but thus,
20 That were there ought in me which strove to show°
Mine enemy in this business, were't one eye
Against another, arm oppressed by arm,°
I would destroy th' offender, coz, I would
Though parcel° of myself. Then from this gather
How I should tender° you.

25 *Arcite.* I am in labor°
To push your name, your ancient love, our kindred
Out of my memory, and i' th' self same place
To seat something I would confound.° So hoist we°
The sails that must these vessels° port° even where
The heavenly limiter° pleases.

30 *Palamon.* You speak well.
Before I turn,° let me embrace thee, cousin.

[*They embrace.*]

This I shall never do again.

Arcite. One farewell.

Palamon. Why, let it be so: farewell, coz.

Exeunt Palamon and his Knights.

Arcite. Farewell, sir.

15 **as the gods regard ye** i.e., as they are just to you 17 **part** divide 18 **glass** hourglass 20 **show** i.e., show itself 22 **arm oppressed by arm** if one of my arms were tyrannized over by the other 24 **parcel** part 25 **tender** treat (with an ironical suggestion of the adjectival sense) 25 **in labor** endeavoring (as a woman in childbed endeavors to give birth) 28 **confound** destroy 28 **hoist we** let us hoist 29 **these vessels** our fortunes and persons 29 **port** bring to port 30 **limiter** (the god who sets limits to things) 31 **turn** turn away

Knights, kinsmen, lovers, yea my sacrifices,
True worshippers of Mars—whose spirit in you 35
Expels the seeds of fear, and th' apprehension,
Which still is farther off it°—go with me
Before the god of our profession. There
Require of him the hearts of lions, and
The breath of tigers, yea the fierceness too, 40
Yea the speed also—to go on,° I mean,
Else wish we to be snails. You know my prize
Must be dragged out of blood, force and great feat
Must put my garland on, where she sticks
The queen of flowers:° our intercession then 45
Must be to him that makes the camp a cistern
Brimmed with the blood of men. Give me your aid
And bend your spirits towards him.

They [*prostrate themselves and then*] *kneel* [*before Mars's altar*].

Thou mighty one, that with thy power hast turned
Green Neptune° into purple, [whose approach] 50
Comets prewarn,° whose havoc in vast field
Unearthèd skulls proclaim, whose breath blows down
The teeming Ceres' foison,° who dost pluck
With hand armipotent from forth blue clouds°
The masoned turrets, that both mak'st and break'st 55
The stony girths° of cities! Me thy pupil,
Youngest follower of thy drum, instruct this day
With military skill, that to thy laud
I may advance my streamer,° and by thee
Be styled the lord o' th' day! Give me, great Mars, 60
Some token of thy pleasure.

37 **farther off it** (the idea of fear is farther from fear itself than its "seeds," or first beginnings, are) 41 **go on** advance 44–45 **where she sticks/The queen of flowers** where Emilia places her favor (the queen of flowers because it is hers) 50 **Green Neptune** i.e., the sea (as the Textual Note explains, the bracketed words at the end of this line are not in the quarto, but some such words seem necessary) 51 **prewarn** give warning of 53 **The teeming Ceres' foison** the harvest (whose goddess Ceres was) 54 **from forth blue clouds** from their height in the sky 56 **stony girths** walls 59 **streamer** banner, pennon

Here they fall on their faces as formerly,° and there is heard clanging of armor, with a short thunder as the burst of a battle, whereupon they all rise and bow to the altar.

O great corrector of enormous° times,
Shaker of o'er-rank° states, thou grand decider
Of dusty and old titles, that heal'st with blood
65 The earth when it is sick, and cur'st the world
O' th' plurisy° of people! I do take
Thy signs auspiciously and, in thy name,
To my design° march boldly. Let us go. *Exeunt.*

Enter Palamon and his Knights, with the former observance.°

Palamon. Our stars must glister with new fire, or be
70 Today extinct. Our argument is love,
Which if the goddess of it grant, she gives
Victory too: then blend your spirits with mine,
You whose free nobleness do make my cause
Your personal hazard; to the goddess Venus
75 Commend we our proceeding, and implore
Her power unto our party.

Here they kneel as formerly° [*to Venus's altar*].

Hail sovereign queen of secrets, who hast power
To call the fiercest tyrant from his rage
And weep unto a girl;° that hast the might
80 Even with an eye-glance to choke Mars's drum
And turn th' alarm to whispers; that canst make
A cripple flourish with° his crutch, and cure him
Before Apollo;° that may'st force the king

61 s.d. **as formerly** (suggesting they had done so at line 48) 62 **enormous** monstrous, degenerate 63 **o'er-rank** overripe 66 **plurisy** plethora 68 **design** goal 68 s.d. **former observance** (the prostration and kneeling used by Arcite and his Knights, but paid now to Venus's altar, at line 76) 76 s.d. **as formerly** (again referring to Arcite and his Knights) 79 **weep unto a girl** i.e., make him weep like a girl 82 **flourish with** brandish 83 **Before Apollo** sooner than Apollo (the god of healing)

To be his subject's vassal, and induce
Stale Gravity to dance: the pollèd° bachelor 85
Whose youth like wanton boys through bonfires
Have° skipped thy flame, at seventy thou canst
catch
And make him, to the scorn of his hoarse throat,°
Abuse° young lays of love; what godlike power
Hast thou not power upon? To Phoebus° thou 90
Add'st flames, hotter than his; the heavenly fires
Did scorch his mortal son,° thine him;° the hunt-
ress,°
All moist and cold, some say began to throw
Her bow away, and sigh. Take to thy grace
Me thy vowed soldier, who do bear thy yoke 95
As 'twere a wreath of roses, yet is heavier
Than lead itself, stings more than nettles.
I have never been foul-mouthed against thy law,
Ne'er revealed secret, for I knew none; would not,
Had I kenned all that were;° I never practiced° 100
Upon man's wife, nor would the libels read
Of liberal wits;° I never at great feasts
Sought to betray a beauty,° but have blushed
At simp'ring sirs that did. I have been harsh
To large confessors,° and have hotly asked them 105
If they had mothers: I had one, a woman,
And women 'twere they wronged. I knew a man
Of eighty winters, this I told them, who
A lass of fourteen brided. 'Twas thy power
To put life into dust: the aged cramp 110

85 **pollèd** bald 87 **Have** (plural through the influence of "boys") 88 **to the scorn of his hoarse throat** so that his hoarseness is mocked 89 **Abuse** employ in a ludicrous fashion 90 **Phoebus** (as sun god) 92 **his mortal son** Phäethon, who was destroyed when Phoebus allowed him to drive the sun chariot 92 **thine him** (Phoebus was made to feel the heat of love) 92 **huntress** (Diana, who loved Endymion) 100 **all that were** all secrets in existence 100 **practiced** entered into designs 101–02 **the libels read/Of liberal wits** read the abusive writings of licentious wits 103 **betray a beauty** i.e., reveal her frailty 105 **large confessors** those who boasted much of their love conquests

Had screwed his square foot round,°
The gout had knit his fingers into knots,
Torturing convulsions from his globy eyes
Had almost drawn their spheres,° that what was life
115 In him seemed torture. This anatomy°
Had by his young fair fere° a boy, and I
Believed it was his, for she swore it was,
And who would not believe her? Brief,° I am
To those that prate and have done no companion;
120 To those that boast and have not a defier;
To those that would and cannot a rejoicer.
Yea him I do not love, that tells close offices°
The foulest way, nor names concealments° in
The boldest language. Such a one I am,
125 And vow that lover never yet made sigh
Truer than I. O then most soft sweet goddess,
Give me the victory of this question, which
Is true love's merit,° and bless me with a sign
Of thy great pleasure.

Here music is heard, doves° are seen to flutter; they fall again upon their faces, then on their knees.

130 O thou that from eleven to ninety reign'st
In mortal bosoms, whose chase° is this world
And we in herds thy game,° I give thee thanks
For this fair token, which being laid unto
Mine innocent true heart, arms in assurance
135 My body to this business. Let us rise
And bow before the goddess. *They bow.*
Time comes on. *Exeunt.*

111 screwed his square foot round (the play on "square" and "round" makes the image more grotesque) 113–14 **globy . . . spheres** ("globy" suggests "swollen," and here "spheres" must be the eyes themselves, drawn from their sockets; but there is a suggestion of the spheres of the Ptolemaic universe being distorted through pain) 115 **anatomy** skeleton 116 **fere** mate 118 **Brief** in brief 122 **close offices** secret actions 123 **concealments** things that should be concealed 128 **merit** reward 129 s.d. **doves** (birds sacred to Venus) 131 **chase** place of hunting 132 **in herds thy game** (cf. the similar image at I.iv.5)

Still° music of records.° Enter Emilia in white, her hair about her shoulders, a wheaten wreath;° one in white holding up her train, her hair stuck° with flowers; one before her carrying a silver hind,° in which is conveyed incense and sweet odors, which being set upon the altar [*of Diana*], *her maids standing aloof, she sets fire to it; then they curtsy and kneel.*

Emilia. O sacred, shadowy, cold and constant queen,
Abandoner of revels, mute contemplative,
Sweet, solitary, white as chaste, and pure
As wind-fanned snow, who to thy female knights 140
Allow'st no more blood than will make a blush,
Which is their order's robe! I here thy priest
Am humbled 'fore thine altar. O vouchsafe
With that thy rare green eye, which never yet
Beheld thing maculate, look on thy virgin; 145
And sacred silver mistress, lend thine ear—
Which ne'er heard scurrile term, into whose port°
Ne'er entered wanton sound—to my petition
Seasoned with holy fear. This is my last
Of vestal office: I am bride-habited, 150
But maiden-hearted; a husband I have 'pointed,°
But do not know him; out of two I should
Choose one, and pray for his success, but I
Am guiltless of election.° Of mine eyes
Were I to lose one, they are equal precious, 155
I could doom neither: that which perished should
Go to't unsentenced. Therefore, most modest queen,
He of the two pretenders° that best loves me
And has the truest title° in't, let him
Take off my wheaten garland, or else grant 160

136 s.d. **still** soft **records** recorders **her hair about her shoulders, a wheaten wreath** (cf. I.i s.d.) **stuck** adorned **hind** female red deer, emblem of virginity, sacred to Diana 147 **port** portal 151 **'pointed** had appointed for me 154 **Am guiltless of election** have made no choice (with the suggestion that she would betray Diana if she made a choice) 158 **pretenders** claimants 159 **truest title** best claim

The file and quality° I hold I may
Continue° in thy band.

Here the hind vanishes under the altar, and in the place ascends a rose tree, having one rose upon it.

See what our general of ebbs and flows°
Out from the bowels of her holy altar
165 With sacred act advances: but one rose.
If well inspired,° this battle shall confound°
Both these brave knights, and I a virgin flow'r
Must grow alone, unplucked.

Here is heard a sudden twang of instruments, and the rose falls from the tree.

The flow'r is fall'n, the tree descends. O mistress,
170 Thou here dischargest me, I shall be gathered.
I think so, but I know not thine own will:
Unclasp thy mystery.
I hope she's pleased, her signs were gracious.
They curtsy and exeunt.

Scene II. [*The prison.*]

Enter Doctor, Jailer, and Wooer (in habit of Palamon).

Doctor. Has this advice I told you done any good upon her?

Wooer. O very much. The maids that kept her company
Have half-persuaded her that I am Palamon.
Within this half-hour she came smiling to me,

161 **file and quality** station and character 162 **Continue** continue to have 163 **general of ebbs and flows** (Diana as goddess of the moon) 166 **well inspired** prompted by the goddess 166 **confound** destroy

And asked me what I would eat, and when I would
kiss her. 5
I told her presently,° and kissed her twice.

Doctor. 'Twas well done. Twenty times had been far
better,
For there the cure lies mainly.

Wooer. Then she told me
She would watch° with me tonight, for well she
knew
What hour my fit would take me.

Doctor. Let her do so, 10
And when your fit comes, fit her home,° and
presently.

Wooer. She would have me sing.

Doctor. You did so?

Wooer. No.

Doctor. 'Twas very ill done, then:
You should observe° her ev'ry way.

Wooer. Alas,
I have no voice, sir, to confirm° her that way. 15

Doctor. That's all one,° if ye make a noise.
If she entreat again, do anything:
Lie with her if she ask you.

Jailer. Ho° there, doctor!

Doctor. Yes, in the way of cure.

Jailer. But first, by your leave,
I' th' way of honesty.°

Doctor. That's but a niceness:° 20
Ne'er cast your child away for honesty;

V.ii.6 **presently** at once 9 **watch** stay awake **11 fit her home** give her the right treatment (lie with her) 14 **observe** humor 15 **confirm** convince 16 **That's all one** that is a matter of indifference 18 **Ho** hold, stop 20 **honesty** chastity (i.e., in marriage) 20 **niceness** overscrupulousness

Cure her first this way, then if she will be honest,
She has the path before her.°

Jailer. Thank ye, doctor.

Doctor. Pray bring her in and let's see how she is.

25 *Jailer.* I will, and tell her her Palamon stays for her.
But, doctor, methinks you are i' th' wrong still.

Exit Jailer.

Doctor. Go, go.
You fathers are fine fools! Her honesty?
And° we should give her physic till we find that—

Wooer. Why, do you think she is not honest, sir?

Doctor. How old is she?

Wooer. She's eighteen.

30 *Doctor.* She may be,
But that's all one, 'tis nothing to our purpose.
Whate'er her father says, if you perceive
Her mood inclining that way that I spoke of,
Videlicet,° the way of flesh—you have me?°

Wooer. Yet very well, sir.

35 *Doctor.* Please her appetite
And do it home:° it cures her° *ipso facto*°
The melancholy humor that infects her.

Wooer. I am of your mind, doctor.

Enter Jailer, Daughter, Maid.

Doctor. You'll find it so. She comes: pray humor her.

40 *Jailer.* Come, your love Palamon stays° for you, child,
And has done this long hour, to visit you.

Daughter. I thank him for his gentle patience.

23 **has the path before her** i.e., can marry afterwards 28 **And** if 34 **Videlicet** namely 34 **have me** understand me 36 **do it home** do it thoroughly 36 **her** (an "ethic" dative) 36 **ipso facto** in itself, through its own power 40 **stays** waits

He's a kind gentleman, and I am much bound to
him.
Did you ne'er see the horse he gave me?

Jailer. Yes.

Daughter. How do you like him?

Jailer. He's a very fair° one. 45

Daughter. You never saw him dance?

Jailer. No.

Daughter. I have often.
He dances very finely, very comely,
And for a jig°—come cut and long tail to him°—
He turns ye like a top.

Jailer. That's fine indeed.

Daughter. He'll dance the morris twenty mile an hour, 50
And that will founder the best hobby-horse,
If I have any skill,° in all the parish;
And gallops to the tune of "Light o' Love."°
What think you of this horse?

Jailer. Having these virtues,
I think he might be brought to play at tennis. 55

Daughter. Alas, that's nothing.

Jailer. Can he write and read too?

Daughter. A very fair hand, and casts° himself th'
accounts
Of all his hay and provender: that ostler
Must rise betime that cozens him. You know
The chestnut mare the duke has?

Jailer. Very well. 60

45 **fair** fine 48 **jig** (a boisterous dance, often accompanied by song and used after a play) 48 **come cut and long tail to him** i.e., whatever the competition ("cut and long tail," derived from the practice of docking horses' and dogs' tails, means "all kinds," "everybody") 52 **have any skill** know anything about it 53 **Light o' Love** (a well-known song, referred to in *The Two Gentlemen of Verona,* I.ii.83) 57 **casts** makes up

Daughter. She is horribly in love with him, poor beast,
But he is like his master, coy and scornful.

Jailer. What dowry has she?

Daughter. Some two hundred bottles,°
And twenty strike° of oats; but he'll ne'er have her.
65 He lisps in's neighing able to entice
A miller's mare:° he'll be the death of her.°

Doctor. What stuff she utters!

Jailer. Make curtsy, here your love comes.

Wooer. [*Comes forward.*] Pretty soul,
How do ye? That's a fine maid! There's a curtsy!

70 *Daughter.* Yours to command i' th' way of honesty.
How far is't now to th' end o' th' world, my masters?

Doctor. Why, a day's journey, wench.

Daughter. [*To Wooer*] Will you go with me?

Wooer. What shall we do there, wench?

Daughter. Why, play at stool-ball.°
What is there else to do?

Wooer. I am content,
If we shall keep our wedding there.

75 *Daughter.* 'Tis true,
For there, I will assure you, we shall find
Some blind° priest for the purpose, that will venture
To marry us, for here they are nice° and foolish.

63 **bottles** bundles 64 **strike** (measure usually equivalent to the bushel) 66 **miller's mare** (a mare used for turning a mill wheel would be the least likely to behave wantonly) 66 **he'll be the death of her** (this passage on a wonderful horse, lines 44–66, looks back to the famous horse of John Banks, whose tricks and apparent intelligence are frequently referred to in Elizabethan literature: it performed at least between 1588 and 1600, and was remembered) 73 **stool-ball** (ball game played most often by women, and requiring a stool or stools) 77 **blind** (so that he should not recognize them) 78 **nice** overscrupulous

Besides, my father must be hanged tomorrow,
And that would be a blot i' th' business. 80
Are not you Palamon?

Wooer. Do not you know me?

Daughter. Yes, but you care not for me. I have nothing
But this poor petticoat and two coarse smocks.°

Wooer. That's all one, I will have you.

Daughter. Will you surely?

Wooer. Yes, by this fair hand will I.
[*Takes her hand.*]

Daughter. We'll to bed, then. 85

Wooer. E'en when you will. [*Kisses her.*]

Daughter. O sir, you would fain be nibbling.

Wooer. Why do you rub my kiss off?

Daughter. 'Tis a sweet one,
And will perfume me finely against the wedding.
Is not this your cousin Arcite?

Doctor. Yes, sweetheart,
And I am glad my cousin Palamon 90
Has made so fair a choice.

Daughter. Do you think he'll have me?

Doctor. Yes, without doubt.

Daughter. Do you think so too?

Jailer. Yes.

Daughter. We shall have many children. [*To the Doctor*] Lord, how y' are grown!°
My Palamon I hope will grow, too, finely
Now he's at liberty. Alas, poor chicken,° 95

83 **smocks** undergarments, shifts 93 **how y' are grown** (she noted that Arcite was shorter than Palamon at II.i.53–54 95 **chicken** child

He was kept down with hard meat° and ill lodging,
But I'll kiss him up again.°

Enter a Messenger.

Messenger. What do you here? You'll lose the noblest sight
That e'er was seen.

Jailer. Are they i' th' field?

Messenger. They are.
You bear a charge° there, too.

100 *Jailer.* I'll away straight.
I must e'en leave you here.

Doctor. Nay, we'll go with you:
I will not lose the fight.°

Jailer. How did you like her?°

Doctor. I'll warrant you within these three or four days
I'll make her right again. [*To Wooer*] You must not from her,
But still preserve her in this way.

105 *Wooer.* I will.

Doctor. Let's get her in.

Wooer. Come, sweet, we'll go to dinner,
And then we'll play at cards.

Daughter. And shall we kiss too?

Wooer. A hundred times.

Daughter. And twenty?

96 **hard meat** coarse food 97 **kiss him up again** make him grow with kissing (with a phallic suggestion) 100 **bear a charge** have a duty 102 **fight** (the emendation "sight" has been suggested and may be right: cf. line 98 and V.iii.1) 102 **How did you like her** what did you think of her condition

Wooer. Aye, and twenty.

Daughter. And then we'll sleep together?

Doctor. Take her offer.

Wooer. Yes, marry will we.

Daughter. But you shall not hurt me. 110

Wooer. I will not, sweet.

Daughter. If you do, love, I'll cry. *Exeunt.*

Scene III. [*Near the place of the tournament.*]

Flourish. Enter Theseus, Hippolyta, Emilia, Pirithous, and some Attendants.

Emilia. I'll no step further.

Pirithous. Will you lose this sight?

Emilia. I had rather see a wren hawk at a fly
Than this decision: ev'ry blow that falls
Threats a brave life, each stroke laments the place
Whereon it falls, and sounds more like a bell° 5
Than blade. I will stay here. It is enough
My hearing shall be punishèd with what
Shall happen, 'gainst the which there is
No deafing°—but to hear, not taint mine eye
With dread sights it may shun.

Pirithous. Sir, my good lord, 10
Your sister will no further.

Theseus. O she must.
She shall see deeds of honor in their kind,°
Which sometime show well, penciled.° Nature now

V.iii.5 **bell** i.e., a bell that tolls for the dead 9 **deafing** i.e., closing the ear 12 **in their kind** in their true shape 13 **penciled** when portrayed in art

Shall make and act the story, the belief
Both sealed with eye and ear.° [*To Emilia*] You
15 must be present.
You are the victor's meed,° the price,° and garland
To crown the question's title.°

Emilia. Pardon me.
If I were there, I'd wink.°

Theseus. You must be there:
This trial is as 'twere i' th' night, and you
The only star to shine.

20 *Emilia.* I am extinct.°
There is but envy° in that light which shows
The one the other: Darkness, which ever was
The dam° of Horror, who does stand accursed
Of many mortal millions, may even now,
25 By casting her black mantle over both,
That° neither could find other, get herself
Some part of a good name,° and many a murder
Set off° whereto she's guilty.

Hippolyta. You must go.

Emilia. In faith, I will not.

Theseus. Why, the knights must kindle
30 Their valor at your eye. Know of this war
You are the treasure, and must needs be by
To give the service pay.°

Emilia. Sir, pardon me,
The title of a kingdom may be tried
Out of itself.°

14–15 **the belief/Both sealed with eye and ear** (i.e., so that we both see and hear the action, while a painting merely gives us the dumb sight) 16 **meed** reward 16 **price** prize 17 **crown the question's title** bestow the title which is in question 18 **wink** close my eyes 20 **extinct** no longer shining (continuing the image of the star) 21 **envy** malice 23 **dam** mother 26 **That** so that 27 **Some part of a good name** a partly good reputation 28 **Set off** atone for 32 **give the service pay** reward the service 33–34 **The title . . . itself** a claim to a kingdom may be settled in a battle fought outside the kingdom

Theseus. Well, well, then, at your pleasure.
Those that remain with you could wish their office 35
To any of their enemies.

Hippolyta. Farewell, sister.
I am like to know your husband 'fore yourself
By some small start of time. He whom the gods
Do of the two know best,° I pray them he
Be made your lot. 40
Exeunt Theseus, Hippolyta, Pirithous, &c.

Emilia. Arcite is gently visaged; yet his eye
Is like an engine° bent, or a sharp weapon
In a soft sheath: mercy and manly courage
Are bedfellows in his visage. Palamon
Has a most menacing aspect,° his brow 45
Is graved,° and seems to bury what it frowns on;
Yet sometime 'tis not so, but alters to
The quality of his thoughts:° long time his eye
Will dwell upon his object; melancholy
Becomes him nobly. So does Arcite's mirth, 50
But Palamon's sadness is a kind of mirth,
So mingled° as if mirth did make him sad,
And sadness merry. Those darker humors that
Stick misbecomingly on others, on him
Live in fair dwelling. 55
Cornets. Trumpets sound as to a charge.
Hark how yon spurs to spirit do incite
The princes to their proof!° Arcite may win me,
And yet may Palamon wound Arcite to
The spoiling of his figure.° O what pity
Enough for such a chance?° If I were by, 60
I might do hurt, for they would glance their eyes
Toward my seat, and in that motion might

38–39 **He . . . best** the one known by the gods to be best 42 **engine** instrument (here suggesting "bow") 45 **aspect** (stressed on second syllable) 46 **graved** engraved, furrowed (with the play on "grave," suggesting that he kills) 47–48 **alters to/The quality of his thoughts** changes according to the character of his thoughts 52 **mingled** complex 57 **proof** test 59 **figure** body 59–60 **O what . . . chance** i.e., how much pity would be sufficient for such a happening

Omit a ward,° or forfeit an offense°
Which craved that very time. It is much better
65 I am not there. O better never born
Than minister to such harm!

Cornets. A great cry and noise within, crying "A Palamon!" Enter [*a*] *Servant.*

What is the chance?

Servant. The cry's "A Palamon!"

Emilia. Then he has won: 'twas ever likely.
He looked all grace° and success, and he is
70 Doubtless the prim'st of men. I prithee run
And tell me how it goes.
Shout, and cornets. Crying "A Palamon!"

Servant. Still "Palamon!"

Emilia. Run and inquire. [*Exit Servant.*] Poor servant,° thou hast lost!
Upon my right side still° I wore thy picture,
Palamon's on the left. Why so I know not,
75 I had no end in't else:° chance would have it so.
On the sinister° side the heart lies: Palamon
Had the best boding chance.°
Another cry, and shout within, and cornets.
This burst of clamor
Is sure th' end o' th' combat.

Enter Servant.

Servant. They said that Palamon had Arcite's body
80 Within an inch o' th' pyramid, that the cry
Was general "A Palamon!" But anon
Th' assistants° made a brave redemption,° and

63 **ward** pass of defense 63 **forfeit an offense** lose the opportunity of making an attack 69 **grace** favor 72 **Poor servant** i.e., Arcite 73 **still** always 75 **no end in't else** no purpose at all in it 76 **sinister** left 77 **the best boding chance** i.e., the most favorable omen 82 **assistants** i.e., Arcite's knights 82 **redemption** rescue

The two bold titlers° at this instant are
Hand-to-hand at it.

Emilia. Were° they metamorphosed
Both into one! O why? There were no woman 85
Worth so composed a man:° their single share,°
Their nobleness peculiar to them, gives
The prejudice of disparity, value's shortness,°
To any lady breathing.

Cornets. Cry within: "Arcite! Arcite!"

More exulting?
"Palamon" still?

Servant. Nay, now the sound is "Arcite!" 90

Emilia. I prithee lay attention to the cry.
Set both thine ears to th' business.

Cornets. A great shout and cry: "Arcite! Victory!"

Servant. The cry is
"Arcite!" and "Victory!" Hark! "Arcite! Victory!"
The combat's consummation is proclaimed
By the wind instruments.

Emilia. Half-sights° saw 95
That Arcite was no babe. God's lid,° his richness
And costliness° of spirit looked through him:° it
could
No more be hid in him than fire in flax,
Than humble banks can go to law° with waters
That drift° winds force to raging. I did think 100
Good Palamon would miscarry, yet I knew not
Why I did think so: our reasons are not prophets
When oft our fancies are. They are coming off.°
Alas, poor Palamon!

83 **titlers** claimants to the title 84 **Were** O that they were 86 **so composed a man** a man so compounded 86 **their single share** the share of virtue that each has singly 88 **The prejudice . . . shortness** i.e., the disadvantage of inequality, the state of inferiority 95 **Half-sights** glimpses 96 **lid** eyelid 97 **costliness** rareness 97 **looked through him** was apparent in him 99 **go to law** engage in conflict 100 **drift** driving 103 **coming off** leaving the place of tournament

Cornets. Enter Theseus, Hippolyta, Pirithous, Arcite as victor, and Attendants, &c.

105 *Theseus.* Lo, where our sister is in expectation,
Yet quaking and unsettled!° Fairest Emily,
The gods by their divine arbitrament
Have given you this knight: he is a good one
As ever struck at head. Give me your hands.
110 Receive you her, you him; be plighted with
A love that grows as you decay.

Arcite. Emily,
To buy you I have lost what's dearest to me
Save what is bought, and yet I purchase cheaply
As I do rate your value.

Theseus. O loved sister,
115 He speaks now of as brave a knight as e'er
Did spur a noble steed. Surely the gods
Would have him die a bachelor, lest his race
Should show i' th' world too godlike! His behavior
So charmed me that methought Alcides° was
120 To him a sow° of lead. If I could praise
Each part of him to th' all I have spoke,° your Arcite
Did° not lose by't, for he that was thus good
Encount'red yet his better. I have heard
Two emulous Philomels° beat the ear o' th' night
125 With their contentious throats, now one the higher,
Anon the other, then again the first,
And by and by outbreasted,° that the sense°
Could not be judge between 'em: so it fared
Good space between these kinsmen, till heavens did
130 Make hardly° one the winner. Wear the garland
With joy that you have won. For the subdued,

106 **unsettled** uncertain, still disturbed 119 **Alcides** Hercules 120 **sow** mass of solidified metal taken from a furnace 120–21 **If . . . spoke** if I were to praise his every quality in the same way as I have praised him in general terms 122 **Did** would 124 **Philomels** nightingales 127 **outbreasted** outsung 127 **that the sense** so that the hearing 130 **hardly** with difficulty

Give them our present justice,° since I know
Their lives but pinch° 'em. Let it here be done.
The scene's not for our seeing: go we hence
Right joyful, with some sorrow. [*To Arcite*] Arm
your prize:° 135
I know you will not loose her. Hippolyta,
I see one eye of yours conceives a tear
The which it will deliver. *Flourish.*

Emilia. Is this winning?
O all you heavenly powers, where is your mercy?
But that your wills have said it must be so, 140
And charge me live to comfort this unfriended,
This miserable prince, that cuts away
A life more worthy from him than all women,
I should, and would, die too.

Hippolyta. Infinite pity
That four such eyes should be so fixed on one 145
That two must needs be blind for't!°

Theseus. So it is. *Exeunt.*

Scene IV. [*The same.*]

Enter Palamon and his Knights pinioned, Jailer, Executioner, &c., Guard.

Palamon. There's many a man alive that hath outlived
The love o' th' people, yea i' th' self same state°
Stands many a father with his child: some comfort
We have by so considering. We expire,
And not without men's pity; to live still 5
Have their good wishes;° we prevent

132 **present justice** i.e., immediate execution 133 **pinch** irk 135 **Arm your prize** i.e., take Emilia to your arms 146 **That two must needs be blind for't** i.e., that one of the men must die V.iv.2 **state** condition 5–6 **to live still/Have their good wishes** have their good wishes that we should still live

The loathsome misery of age, beguile
The gout and rheum that in lag° hours attend
For gray approachers.° We come towards the gods
10 Young and unwappered,° not halting under crimes
Many and stale:° that sure shall please the gods
Sooner than such,° to give° us nectar with 'em,
For we are more clear° spirits. My dear kinsmen,
Whose lives for this poor comfort° are laid down,
You have sold 'em too too cheap.

15 *First Knight.* What ending could be
Of more content? O'er us the victors have
Fortune, whose title° is as momentary
As to us death is certain. A grain of honor
They not o'er-weigh us.

Second Knight. Let us bid farewell,
20 And with our patience anger tott'ring Fortune,
Who at her certain'st° reels.

Third Knight. Come, who begins?

Palamon. E'en he that led you to this banquet shall
Taste to you all.° [*To Jailer*] Ah, ha, my friend, my friend,
Your gentle daughter gave me freedom once:
25 You'll see't done now forever.° Pray, how does she?
I heard she was not well. Her kind of ill°
Gave me some sorrow.

Jailer. Sir, she's well restored,
And to be married shortly.

Palamon. By my short life,
I am most glad on't: 'tis the latest thing
30 I shall be glad of, prithee tell her so.

8 **lag** last 9 **gray approachers** gray-haired men approaching death 10 **unwappered** unwearied (perhaps with a suggestion of sexual excess) 11 **stale** of long standing 12 **such** i.e., men such as described 12 **to give** so that they will give 13 **clear** noble, unstained 14 **this poor comfort** (Palamon admits the puniness of his own consolation) 17 **title** i.e., favor 21 **at her certain'st** when she seems most stable 23 **Taste to you all** act as taster at a banquet for you 25 **You'll see't done now forever** i.e., you will see me win a final freedom 26 **kind of ill** i.e., madness

Commend me to her, and to piece° her portion
Tender her this. [*Gives him a purse.*]

First Knight. Nay, let's be offerers all.

Second Knight. Is it a maid?

Palamon. Verily I think so,
A right good creature, more to me° deserving
Than I can 'quite° or speak of.

All Knights. Commend us to her. 35
They give their purses.

Jailer. The gods requite you all, and make her thankful.

Palamon. Adieu; and let my life be now as short
As my leave-taking. *Lies on the block.*

First Knight. Lead, courageous cousin.

Second and Third Knights. We'll follow cheerfully.

A great noise within, crying "Run! Save! Hold!" Enter in haste a Messenger.

Messenger. Hold, hold, O hold, hold, hold!

Enter Pirithous in haste.

Pirithous. Hold, ho! It is a cursèd haste you made 40
If you have done° so quickly. Noble Palamon,
The gods will show their glory in a life°
That thou art yet to lead.

Palamon. Can that be,
When Venus I have said° is false? How do things fare?°

Pirithous. Arise, great sir, and give the tidings ear 45
That are most dearly° sweet and bitter.

31 **piece** contribute to 34 **to me** i.e., from me 35 **'quite** requite 41 **done** finished 42 **show their glory in a life** i.e., through your life (as their creature) their glory will be manifested 44 **I have said** i.e., as I have said 44 **How do things fare** what has happened 46 **dearly** intensely

Palamon. What
Hath waked us from our dream?°

Pirithous. List then. Your cousin,
Mounted upon a steed that Emily
Did first bestow on him, a black one, owing°
50 Not a hair-worth of white, which some will say
Weakens his price, and many will not buy
His goodness with this note°—which superstition
Here finds allowance°—on this horse is Arcite
Trotting the stones of Athens, which the calkins°
55 Did rather tell° than trample, for the horse
Would make his length a mile,° if't pleased his rider
To put pride in him. As he thus went counting
The flinty pavement, dancing as 'twere to th' music
His own hoofs made—for as they say from iron
60 Came music's origin—what envious flint,
Cold as old Saturn, and like him possessed
With fire malevolent, darted a spark,
Or what fierce sulphur else to this end made,
I comment not: the hot horse, hot as fire,
65 Took toy° at this, and fell to what disorder
His power could give his will, bounds, comes on end,
Forgets school-doing,° being therein trained
And of kind manage;° pig-like he whines
At the sharp rowel, which he frets at rather
70 Than any jot obeys; seeks all foul means
Of boist'rous and rough jadery to dis-seat
His lord, that kept it° bravely. When nought served,
When neither curb would crack, girth break, nor diff'ring° plunges
Dis-root his rider whence he grew, but that

47 **dream** i.e., of death 49 **owing** possessing 52 **with this note** because of this peculiarity 53 **Here finds allowance** is here confirmed 54 **calkins** (parts of a horseshoe turned down to prevent slipping) 55 **tell** count 56 **make his length a mile** take mile-long paces 65 **toy** fright, exception 67 **school-doing** training 68 **of kind manage** well disciplined 72 **it** i.e., his seat 73 **diff'ring** varying

He kept him 'tween his legs, on his hind hoofs 75
On end he stands,
That Arcite's legs being higher than his head
Seemed with strange art to hang; his victor's wreath
Even then fell off his head; and presently°
Backward the jade comes o'er, and his full poise° 80
Becomes the rider's load. Yet is he living,
But such a vessel 'tis that floats but for
The surge that next approaches. He much desires
To have some speech with you. Lo, he appears.

Enter Theseus, Hippolyta, Emilia, Arcite in a chair.

Palamon. O miserable end of our alliance! 85
The gods are mighty! Arcite, if thy heart,
Thy worthy, manly heart be yet unbroken,
Give me thy last words: I am Palamon,
One that yet loves thee dying.

Arcite. Take Emilia,
And with her all the world's joy. Reach° thy hand. 90
Farewell. I have told° my last hour. I was false,
Yet never treacherous.° Forgive me, cousin.
One kiss from fair Emilia. [*She kisses him.*] 'Tis done.
Take her. I die. [*Dies.*]

Palamon. Thy brave soul seek Elysium!

Emilia. I'll close thine eyes, prince. Blessed souls be with thee!° 95
Thou art a right good man, and while I live
This day° I give to tears.

Palamon. And I to honor.°

79 **presently** at once 80 **poise** weight 90 **Reach** i.e., give me 91 **told** counted, lived through 91–92 **false,/Yet never treacherous** (Arcite admits Palamon's greater right to Emilia in seeing her first, but declares he took no unfair advantage) 95 **Blessed souls be with thee** i.e., may you be with the blessed souls 97 **This day** i.e., the anniversaries of this day 97 **to honor** i.e., to honoring Arcite's memory

Theseus. In this place first you fought: e'en very here
I sund'red you. Acknowledge to the gods
100 Our thanks that you are living.°
His part is played, and though it were too short
He did it well. Your day is lengthened, and
The blissful dew of heaven does arrouse° you.
The powerful Venus well hath graced her altar,
105 And given you your love. Our master Mars
Hath vouched his oracle, and to Arcite gave
The grace of the contention.° So the deities
Have showed due justice. Bear this° hence.

Palamon. O cousin,
That we should things desire which do cost us
110 The loss of our desire!° That nought could buy
Dear love but loss of dear love!°

Theseus. Never Fortune
Did play a subtler game. The conquered triumphs,
The victor has the loss; yet in the passage°
The gods have been most equal.° Palamon,
115 Your kinsman hath confessed the right o' th' lady
Did lie in you, for you first saw her, and
Even then proclaimed your fancy. He restored her
As your stol'n jewel, and desired your spirit
To send him hence forgiven. The gods my justice
120 Take from my hand,° and they themselves become
The executioners. Lead your lady off,
And call your lovers° from the stage of death,°
Whom I adopt my friends. A day or two
Let us look sadly, and give grace unto
125 The funeral of Arcite, in whose end°

99–100 **Acknowledge . . . living** declare to the gods that we rejoice in your being alive (the emendation of "Our" to "Your" has been suggested) 103 **arrouse** sprinkle 107 **grace of the contention** i.e., good fortune in the contest 108 **this** i.e., Arcite's body 109–10 **That we . . . desire** i.e., alas that the winning of what we want takes away our desire for it 110–11 **That nought . . . dear love** i.e., that one love (Emilia) could be won only by losing another (Arcite) 113 **passage** course of events 114 **equal** just 120 **Take from my hand** i.e., take away from me 122 **lovers** i.e., his Knights 122 **stage of death** scaffold 125 **in whose end** at the conclusion of which

The visages of bridegrooms we'll put on
And smile with Palamon; for whom an hour,
But one hour since, I was as dearly sorry
As glad of Arcite; and am now as glad
As for him sorry. O you heavenly charmers,° 130
What things you make of us! For what we lack,
We laugh;° for what we have, are sorry;° still
Are children in some kind. Let us be thankful
For that which is, and with you leave° dispute
That are above our question. Let's go off, 135
And bear us like the time.° *Flourish. Exeunt.*

130 **you heavenly charmers** the Fates (who control us with their charms or magic) 131–32 **For what we lack,/We laugh** we feel pleasure at the thought of the thing we do not possess 132 **for what we have, are sorry** we are sad to have what we do possess 134 **leave** cease to 136 **bear us like the time** conduct ourselves appropriately to the occasion

EPILOGUE

I would now ask ye how ye like the play,
But, as it is with schoolboys, cannot say.°
I am cruel° fearful. Pray yet stay a while,
And let me look upon ye. No man smile?
5 Then it goes hard, I see. He that has
Loved a young handsome wench, then, show his face—
'Tis strange if none be here—and if he will
Against his conscience, let him hiss, and kill
Our market. 'Tis in vain, I see, to stay° ye.
10 Have at the worst can come,° then! Now what say ye?
And yet mistake me not: I am not bold;
We have no such cause. If the tale° we have told—
For 'tis no other—any way content ye,
For to that honest purpose it was meant ye,°
15 We have our end; and ye shall have ere long
I dare say many a better, to prolong
Your old loves to us. We, and all our might,
Rest at your service. Gentlemen, good night.
Flourish.

FINIS

Epilogue 2 **say** speak 3 **cruel** dreadfully 9 **stay** i.e., try to prevent 10 **Have at the worst can come** let us face the worst event possible 12 **tale** (alluding to the title of the source) 14 **meant ye** intended for you

Textual Note

There is no doubt that the text used by the printer of the quarto of 1634 had been in the hands of a prompter (presumably of the Blackfriars Theatre). The most obvious evidence of this is the appearance in the margin of three "warnings"—i.e., reminders that preparation must be made for an ensuing entry. These are noted below in the list of places where the present edition varies from the quarto, but it will be useful to bring them together here:

(1) On C3^{v} of the quarto, in the left margin opposite I.iii.58–64:

> 2. Hearses rea-/dy with Pala-/mon: and Arci-/ te: the 3./ Queenes./ Theseus*:* and/ his Lordes/ ready.

At this point the scene has more than thirty lines to run: the "warning" is of what will be required at the beginning of I.iv, which comes on C4^{r}.

(2) On C4^{v}, in the left margin opposite I.iv.26–27:

> 3. Hearses rea-/dy.

These hearses are for the bodies of the three kings slain at Thebes and will be brought on at the beginning of I.v twenty lines later, on the same page of the quarto.

(3) On G2^{v}, in the left margin opposite III.v.65–66:

> Chaire and/ stooles out.

These properties are required for Theseus and his company to sit on to watch the Schoolmaster's entertainment: the dialogue indicates that they sit some thirty lines later, at III.v.98.

Further evidence of theater use of the copy behind the quarto is in the appearance of actors' names in the entries. At IV.ii.69 the quarto stage direction reads *"Enter Messengers. Curtis."* (*"Messengers"* being clearly an error for *"Messenger"*), and the entry which opens V.iii reads *". . . and/ some Attendants, T. Tucke: Curtis."* The actors referred to can be identified as Curtis Greville, who was a hired man in the King's Company in 1626, probably having joined them the preceding year, and Thomas Tuckfield, whose name appears in a list of "Musitions and other necessary attendantes" of the King's Company in 1624.[1] From these dates it is clear that the actors' names were inserted on the occasion of a revival in the 1620's, not for the original performance of 1613.

Actors' names appearing in a text may be due to an author who has a particular member of the company in mind for a part, but this could not be the case with the two names in *The Two Noble Kinsmen*. For one thing, Greville and Tuckfield were not with the company when Shakespeare and Fletcher were writing the play; for another, the messenger of IV.ii and the attendants of V.iii are characterless parts: an author would have no views on who should play them, but a prompter might wish to remind himself of the actors' identities.

The quarto contains further indications of playhouse use. Act IV ends with the stage direction *"Florish. Exeunt."*, the *"Florish"* obviously being wrongly placed: it is needed for the entry of Theseus and the rest at the beginning of Act V. The same thing occurs at the end of V.ii. In these instances we can deduce that "Florish" was added in the margin between IV.iii and V.i and between V.ii and V.iii respectively, and the printer took it as going with the exits and not with the following entries. Then we have several marginal stage directions printed, like the "warnings" noted above, in roman type—one at the beginning of II.iv:

This short flo-/rish of Cor-/nets and/ Showtes with-/in.

[1] Gerald Eades Bentley, *The Jacobean and Caroline Stage*, II (Oxford, 1941), 451–52, 606–07.

and another opposite the heading *"Actus Tertius."*:

> Cornets in/ sundry places./ Noise and/ hallowing as/ people a May-/ing:

The marginal placing, the use of roman type, and the curious phrasing "This short florish" all suggest that here we have prompter's additions to the manuscript. A third instance of this is at III.v.134–37, where the text in the quarto is as follows:

	Per. Produce.	*Musicke Dance.*
Knocke for	*Intrate filij,* Come forth, and foot it,	
Schoole. Enter	*Ladies, if we have been merry*	
The Dance.	*And have pleased thee with a derry,*	

The italic stage direction can be taken as authorial. In the original manuscript we can assume there was a space after the one-word speech of Pirithous, and this could explain the omission of a speech heading before the next line, which is clearly the beginning of a speech by the Schoolmaster after the dance. But a prompter would see no clearly marked entry and would want one. Moreover, he might feel it necessary to indicate a signal to be given by the Schoolmaster, and therefore insert "Knocke for Schoole[master]"—i.e., the Schoolmaster should strike the floor of the stage with a staff. But at III.v.17 the agreed signal was to be his flinging up his cap: the author of the scene would not be likely to forget this so quickly, but a prompter might at first reading. Like the two previously noted stage directions, this one is in roman.

One other stage direction is marginal and in roman. This occurs at III.vi.93:

> They bow se-/verall wayes:/ then advance/ and stand.

An asterisk is inserted in III.vi.93 after Arcite has said "And me my love:" and before he continues "Is there ought else to say?" This is, I think, likely to be an authorial addition: it is literary in character, and the placing of the asterisk looks like an author's wish to indicate that the action must come between the two halves of Arcite's speech. But for the printer it would appear in the margin along with the prompter's additional stage directions and warnings, so he has used roman type for this as for those.

Even so, the evidence for the presence of the prompter's hand is fairly plentiful, and he may also have been responsible for all the indications of sound effects (horns, cornets, flourishes), not merely for those noted above. Yet it does not seem very likely that in 1634 the printer had in front of him a promptbook actually used in performance. Sir Walter Greg drew attention to the possibility that even "warnings" could appear in a manuscript which was merely annotated by a prompter before the promptbook itself was made.[2] And it is evident that the "warnings" here given are not complete: an executioner's block would be needed for V.iv, and a chair for Arcite at V.iv.86. Also, some of the entries are incomplete: Artesius and Attendants must be added at I.i.1 (though we can assume that the printer is responsible for the apparent omission of Pirithous); a Herald, Lords, Attendants, Palamon and Arcite must be added at I.iv.1; at III.v.1 the entry includes "2. *or* 3 *wenches*", but five are needed for the dance; at IV.i.102 the vague "*and others*", though possible in a prompt copy, may be an additional sign of authorial inexactitude.

Our text also contains certain things that might well have been eliminated in a prompt copy. At I.i.217 there is the stage direction "*Exeunt towards the Temple.*" This indicates that Hippolyta, Emilia, Pirithous and the Attendants begin to move toward the stage door that here represents the temple entrance, but Theseus has still an exchange with Pirithous (lines 219–24) before the procession has left the stage. This is clear enough to a reader, but a prompter would be likely to tidy it up. Then at II.i.51 there is the direction "*Enter Palamon and Arcite, above.*" The Jailer and his Daughter comment from below and then leave the stage. The quarto marks a general "*Exeunt.*" and then gives a new scene heading:

[2] *The Shakespeare First Folio* (Oxford, 1955), p. 141.

Scæna 2. *Enter Palamon, and Arcite in prison.*

The action is surely continuous, and in the present edition a new scene is not started at this point. The kinsmen need to remain above, as the later part of the scene will be more effective if they look down to the garden to see Emilia, as they do in Chaucer: moreover, the "leap the garden . . . and pitch between her arms" of II.i.277–78 strongly suggests that Arcite is above. The explanation of the condition of the text here is probably that II.i.1–59 are by Shakespeare and the rest of the scene by Fletcher: they had worked out in advance that Shakespeare would introduce the new characters (Jailer, Daughter, Wooer) and Fletcher would do the kinsmen's first encounter with Emilia. So the two sections of the scene would be separate: II.i.60 would start a new sheet of paper. In other words, this suggests that the printer in 1634 had in front of him either the holograph manuscript of Shakespeare and Fletcher or a transcript faithful to it. It should also be noted that the quarto is unusual in its indications of locality: in addition to the "*Temple*" and "*prison*" already noted, we have "*Enter Palamon as out of a Bush*" at III.i.30 and "*Enter Palamon from the Bush*" at III.vi.1. Such indications of locality are of course rare in seventeenth-century play texts: those in our play are similar to "*Enter Timon in the woods*" and "*Enter Timon from his Caue*" in the Folio text *Timon of Athens,* IV.iii.1 and V.i.30. *Timon* was almost certainly printed either from Shakespeare's own manuscript or from a faithful transcript of it.

Now it must be remembered that we know of performances of *The Two Noble Kinsmen* in 1613, probably in 1619, and around 1625.[3] The printer's copy in 1634 has some relation to the last of these (from the evidence of the two actors' names), but it is puzzling to think of the prompter on that occasion annotating the authors' original manuscript if a prompt copy for 1613 (and 1619) were available. It could of course have been lost or not immediately available. And we cannot be sure that all the

[3] See Introduction, p. xxxiv.

prompter's additions were made at the same time: the "warnings" and additional stage directions could have been inserted in 1613 and the actors' names in 1625. Nevertheless, there is a good case for believing that the quarto is directly based on the author's manuscript (or a faithful transcript of it) which the prompter had annotated before the making of a promptbook. When the play came to be printed, the company would be more likely to give such a manuscript to the publisher rather than the promptbook itself, which would be needed at the theater if the play were to be acted again.[4]

When the play was reprinted in the Beaumont and Fletcher Folio of 1679, the text was based on that of the quarto. This is firmly established not only by the statement in the Folio itself but by the frequent agreement between the texts in accidentals. Although the 1679 printing shows a considerable number of variants, they have no independent authority and are mainly corrections of misprints, new misprints, and casual changes in accidentals. For the present edition, therefore, the Folio readings have been treated in the same way as those of all subsequent texts: that is, they have been regarded as editorial emendations or errors, to be taken into account in emending the quarto text but not recorded where they have not been accepted by the present editor.

All substantive departures from the quarto are recorded below, with the reading of the present edition in italic followed by the quarto reading in roman. It will be seen that the prompter's "warnings" have been transposed into stage directions and inserted in square brackets at the appropriate places. The stage directions which have been noted above as almost certainly the prompter's are, however, printed in this edition in the same way as

[4] F. O. Waller in his article "Printer's Copy for *The Two Noble Kinsmen*," *Studies in Bibliography*, XI (1958), 61–84, has argued along these lines. This article incorporates material in Waller's unpublished Chicago dissertation of 1958, *A Critical, Old-spelling Edition of "The Two Noble Kinsmen"*: the fullest textual studies so far made of the play are to be found in this thesis and in Paul Bertram's *Shakespeare and The Two Noble Kinsmen* (New Brunswick, 1965). Bertram, however, takes the view that the printer in 1634 had before him a holograph Shakespeare manuscript which had been used as a prompt book.

other stage directions (which may of course be either author's or prompter's).

It may be noted that, unlike most of his predecessors, the present editor accepts Skeat's emendation "harebells" at I.i.9, and that he is the first to take the quarto speech heading *"All"* at IV.i.146 as part of the Jailer's Daughter's speech.

In this edition italic type is used for speech headings and stage directions, as generally in the quarto, and roman type is used for all dialogue and songs (in place of the quarto's italic for proper names in the dialogue and for the songs). Punctuation and spelling have been modernized, obvious typographical errors have been silently corrected, and the quarto's Latin headings for acts and scenes are given in English. The quarto's "nev'r," "ev'r," "ev'n" spellings are here rendered as "ne'er," "e'er," "e'en," whenever the meter seems to require a monosyllable; elsewhere the full spellings of these words are used. When a quarto reading exists in two states, corrected and uncorrected, the list below indicates the uncorrected state by a raised "a" after the reading given, the corrected state by a raised "b."

In a number of places the quarto prints lines as prose which there seems to be good reason to take as blank verse. Decisions in such cases are always difficult, but the present edition follows several of its predecessors in printing as verse where a blank verse rhythm seems to underlie, and sometimes clearly to emerge from, the fairly free dialogue pattern.

In conformity with the practice of this series, localities have been inserted in scene headings, but these and all other editorial additions to the quarto are given in square brackets.

Prologue 19 *writer* wrighter 25 *water, do* water. Do 26 *tack* take 29 *travail* travell

I.i. s.d. *Pirithous* Theseus 9 *harebells* her bels 16 *angel* angle 20 *chough hoar* Clough hee 59 *lord. The day* Lord the day 61 *groom.* Groome, 68 *Nemean* Nenuan 83 *'stilled* stilde (Folio "stil'd") 90 *thy* the 99 *blood-sized* blood cizd 112 *glassy* glasse 125 *sister* sifter 138 *move* mooves 155 *Rinsing* Wrinching 210 *soldier, as before.* Soldier (as before) 211 *Aulis* Anly 217 s.d. *Hippolyta . . . towards* Exeunt towards

I.ii.65 *power there's nothing; almost puts* power: there's nothing, almost puts 70 *glory; one* glory on;[b] glory on[a]

I.iii.22 *brine* brine, 31 *one* ore 54 *eleven* a eleven 54 *Flavina* Flauia 58–64 (note in quarto margin: "2. Hearses rea-/dy with Palamon: and Arci-/te: the 3./ Queenes./ Theseus: and/ his Lordes/ ready.") 79 *every innocent* fury-innocent 82 *dividual* individuall

I.iv.18 *smeared* smeard[b] succard[a] 22 *We 'lieve* We leave 26–27 (note in quarto margin: "3. Hearses rea-/dy.") 40 *friends' behests* friends, beheastes 41 *Love's provocations* Loves, provocations 45 *O'er-wrestling* Or wrastling 49 *'fore* for

II.i.1 *little . . . live:* little, . . . live, 18–19 *that now. So* that. Now, so 51 s.d. (in quarto, after "night" in line 49) 59 (in quarto, new scene heading: "Scæna 2. Enter Palamon, and Arcite in prison.") 62 *war. Yet* warre yet, 80 *wore* were 81 *Ravished* Bravishd 126 *could.* could, 177 (quarto makes this the last line of Arcite's speech) 209 *mere* neere 216 *have.* have, 261 *be,* be. 262 *Arcite:* Arcite, 277 s.d. (and throughout rest of scene) *Jailer* Keeper 321 *life?* life.

II.ii (quarto marks as "Scæna 3.") 39 *ye* yet 51 *means.* meanes 51 *says* sees 73 *him!* him

II.iii (quarto marks as "Scæna 4.")

II.iv s.d. *Short . . . within.* This short . . . within (in margin) 19 *I believe* Beleeve,

II.v (quarto marks as "Scæna 6.")

III.i s.d. *Cornets . . . a-Maying* (in quarto, in margin) 2 *laund* land 2 *rite* Right 10 *place* pace 36 *looked, the void'st* lookd the voydes 94 *only, sir. Your* onely, Sir your 95 *Wind horns off* Winde hornes of Cornets 97 *musit* Musicke 107 *not.* nor;

III.ii.1 *brake* Beake 7 *reck* wreake 19 *fed* feed 28 *brine* bine

III.iii.23 *them* then 50 *armor?* Armour.

III.iv.9 *Spoon* Vpon 10 *tack* take

III.v (quarto marks as "Scæna 6.") s.d. *Bavian* Baum five [italic] 2. or 3. 8 *jean* jave 47 *once! You can tell, Arcas,* once, you can tell Arcas 65–67 (note in quarto margin: "Chaire and/stooles out.") 67 *till we* till 91 *Wind horns* (in quarto after "I'll lead") 93 *Exeunt . . . Schoolmaster* (in quarto, after "boys," line 92) 97 *Theseus* Per. 135 s.d. *Knock* Knocke for Schoole (in margin) 135 (quarto omits speech heading) 137 *ye* thee 140 *thee* three 155 *Wind horns* (in quarto, after "made," line 156)

III.vi (quarto marks as "Scæna 7.") 28 *man. When* man, when 39 *spared. Your* spard, your 68 *I warrant* Ile warrant 86 *strait* streight 111 *safety,* safely 146 *thy* this 175 *us;* us, 176 *valiant,* valiant; 243 *prune* proyne 290 *again, it* againe it

IV.i.45–46 *Wooer. No, sir . . . 'Tis—* Wooer, [italic] No Sir not well. / Woo. [speech heading] Tis 48 *have told* told 84 *wreath* wreake 110 *rearly* rarely 120 *Far* For 141 *Second Friend* 1. Fr. 145 *cheerly all! O, O, O* cheerely./ All. [speech heading] Owgh, owgh, owgh 149 *Tack* take

IV.ii.16 *Jove* Love 37 *pardon, Palamon:* pardon: Palamon, 54 s.d. *Enter a Gentleman* Enter Emil. and Gent. 69 s.d. *Enter a Messenger* Enter Messengers. Curtis 76 *first* fitst 81 *fire* faire 86–87 *baldric, . . . with:* Bauldricke; . . . with, 104 *tods* tops 109 *court* corect

IV.iii.8 s.d. (in quarto, after "business," line 8) 32 *i' th' other* i'th/Thother 90 *carve* crave

V.i.s.d. *Flourish* (in quarto, precedes *"Exeunt."* of IV.iii) 7 s.d. *Flourish of cornets* (in quarto, at line 5) 50 *whose approach* (first added by Seward in 1750: the words, or something like them, seem necessary) 54 *armipotent* armenypotent 68 *design march boldly*. designe; march boldly, 91 *his;* his 118–21 *Brief, I . . . done no companion;/ To . . . not a defier;/ To . . . rejoicer.* briefe I . . . done; no Companion/ To . . . not; a defyer/ To . . . cannot; a Rejoycer, 130 (quarto inserts speech heading "Pal.") 136 *They bow* (in quarto, after line 134) 151 *'pointed* pointed 152 *him; out of two* him out of two, 154 *election. Of mine eyes* election of mine eyes,

V.ii.34 *Videlicet, the way of flesh* (quarto has "Videlicet" in roman and "way of flesh" in italic, doubtless through a casual error) 39 *humor* honour 53 *tune* turne

V.iii s.d. *Flourish* (in quarto, precedes *"Exeunt"* of V.ii) *Attendants* (quarto adds: "T. Tucke: Curtis.") 13 *well, penciled* well pencild 54 *him* them 66 s.d. *Cornets . . . "A Palamon!"* (in quarto, at line 64) *Enter a Servant* (may be erroneous, as there were attendants on stage, and the servant brings no news) 75 *in't else:* in't; else 77 s.d. (in quarto, at line 75) 92 s.d. (in quarto, at line 91) 121 *to th' all I* to'th all; I

V.iv.1 (quarto omits speech heading) 5–6 *pity; to live still . . . wishes;* pitty. To live still, . . . wishes, 39 *Second and Third Knights* 1. 2. K 46 *dearly* early 76 *On end he stands* (in quarto, printed at the end of the line, perhaps indicating that it was preceded by some illegible words in the manuscript 78 *victor's* victoros 86–87 *mighty! . . . unbroken,* mightie . . . unbroken: 106 *Hath* Hast 132 *sorry; still* sorry still,

A Note on the Source of *The Two Noble Kinsmen*

The play's source, we have seen, is *The Knight's Tale,* which was most easily available to the collaborators in Speght's edition of Chaucer published in 1598 (reprinted three times by 1602). In the dramatization a considerable number of changes were made. We may notice them under several heads:

(1) The action throughout is compressed. In Chaucer there is a time lapse between the first seeing of Emilia by the kinsmen and the release of Arcite. Then Arcite spends some years in Thebes before returning to Athens to see Emilia again. Meanwhile Palamon has seven years in prison. When Theseus has arranged the tournament, the kinsmen are to return to Athens in a year's time. Arcite takes some time to die after the horse has thrown him, and it is a matter of years before Emilia brings herself to marry Palamon. In the play we are not told how long Palamon and Arcite are in prison, but there is no suggestion that it is a great while. Clearly Palamon escapes soon after Arcite has entered Emilia's service. The time lapse before the tournament is a single month. Arcite dies almost immediately, and Emilia is to marry Palamon, it appears, the next day.

These changes are partly to give an effect of tighter structure to what is in Chaucer a diffuse narrative, but they also increase the sense of divine manipulation. The kinsmen in II.i look forward to a slow lifetime in prison: instead, they are whirled through a series of events, and at the end of the play Emilia is passed from arm to arm in a manner that suggests no cosmic concern for her dignity.

(2) There are also changes for the sake of obvious dramatic effectiveness. In the poem Theseus' wedding is not interrupted by the mission of the Queens. There are not three Queens but a crowd of queens and duchesses. Emilia has no attendant in the garden with whom she can talk informally and lightly. Palamon is not removed from the garden-room after Arcite's departure. At the tournament each of the kinsmen is to be accompanied by a hundred knights. The invocations to the gods are in the order Venus, Diana, Mars, which has not the climactic effect secured in the play by Emilia's prayer coming last. The falling of the single rose from the tree brings the whole scene to a striking (and disturbing) conclusion.

(3) Other changes increase this sense of disturbance. Most obvious among these is the decree of Theseus that the knights defeated in the tournament shall die. Of course, this allows the theatrically effective saving of Palamon from the block, and it puts more at stake than the disposal of Emilia's person. Shakespeare may have thought of this change because in *Pericles* the unsuccessful suitors of Antiochus' daughter were similarly vowed to death. In any event, it is an element in the play that links it with the dangers and actual deaths that are found in the preceding "romances." Moreover, there is nothing in the invocation of Venus in *The Knight's Tale* that resembles the words on the goddess' power that Palamon speaks. He hails her as

> sovereign queen of secrets, . . .
> that canst make
> A cripple flourish with his crutch, and cure him
> Before Apollo; that may'st force the king
> To be his subject's vassal, and induce
> Stale Gravity to dance: the pollèd bachelor
> Whose youth like wanton boys through bonfires
> Have skipped thy flame, at seventy thou canst catch
> And make him, to the scorn of his hoarse throat,
> Abuse young lays of love.
>
> (V.i.77, 81–9)

The images of the cripple grotesquely cured, of authority submissive and dancing, of old age straining its throat with a love song, contribute powerfully to that harsh strain in Shakespeare's section of the play that has been noted in the Introduction. And then we find Palamon seeking favor by boasting of his own credulity, and doing it in terms that, for an audience, are surely meant to be repellent:

> I knew a man
> Of eighty winters, this I told them, who
> A lass of fourteen brided. 'Twas thy power
> To put life into dust: the aged cramp
> Had screwed his square foot round,
> The gout had knit his fingers into knots,
> Torturing convulsions from his globy eyes
> Had almost drawn their spheres, that what was life
> In him seemed torture. This anatomy
> Had by his young fair fere a boy, and I
> Believed it was his, for she swore it was,
> And who would not believe her?
> (V.i.107–18)

We may think back to Antony's concern with his gray hairs, to Leontes' finding wrinkles in what he thinks is Hermione's statue, but the degree of frankness is new. Palamon, the servant of Venus, puts himself side by side with the other victims he describes.*

(4) Nothing in Chaucer corresponds to the Jailer's Daughter plot. We are simply told that Palamon escaped with the help of a friend. In the Introduction (pp. xxxii–xxxiii) we have seen how Shakespeare and Fletcher use the subplot to affect the audience's response to the story of the knights and their love.

(5) In Chaucer the gods are at odds with each other, and the quarrel is settled by the ingenuity of Saturn, so

* In his introduction to the Signet edition of Shakespeare's *Sonnets* (1964), W. H. Auden has commented on this passage's choice of "humiliating or horrid" examples of the power of Venus and on "the intensity of the disgust at masculine sexual vanity."

that all promises can be kept. In the play we are rather made to feel that a single power speaks through the gods, that the matter is predetermined, that all that the gods do is to give hints of a future which neither prayer nor divine intervention can modify.

In a few places the play includes some quite incidental echoes of Chaucer. Thus Arcas, one of the Countrymen named at II.ii.37 and III.v.47, is the name of the son of Callisto, who, as "Calystope," is referred to in *The Knight's Tale,* line 1198. The Schoolmaster mentions the story of Meleager and Atalanta at III.v.18: Chaucer mentions it at *The Knight's Tale,* lines 1212–13. In the play the tournament is held in the place where Theseus found the knights fighting (III.vi.293): in *The Knight's Tale,* lines 1999–2006, we learn that it is Arcite's funeral pyre that is to be erected in that place. The consolation that Palamon offers to his friends as they are about to submit themselves to the block (V.iv.1–13), although altogether sharper in its comments on the nature of life, bears an obvious relation to the arguments that Theseus uses in *The Knight's Tale,* lines 2189–98, in order to persuade Palamon and Emilia to give up their mourning for Arcite and enter into marriage. Such points of casual resemblance between play and poem, with the dramatists freely manipulating the words and images they found in Chaucer, show the intimacy of their acquaintance with the source.

The Knight's Tale had been twice dramatized before 1613. In 1566 Richard Edwardes' *Palamon and Arcite* was acted at Christ Church, Oxford, before Elizabeth, and Henslowe's *Diary* registers a *Palamon and Arcite* acted in 1594, probably as a new play. Neither of these is extant, but there is no reason to believe that they had any connection with *The Two Noble Kinsmen.*

In the Introduction (pp. xxviii–xxxii) we have seen that Shakespeare and Fletcher were dependent also on their memories of several earlier Shakespeare plays, ranging from *The Two Gentlemen of Verona* to the late "romances," and that this has helped to make the play into something very different from a straightforward dramatization of Chaucer.

Commentaries

GERALD EADES BENTLEY

Shakespeare and the Blackfriars Theatre

It is necessary at the outset in a discussion of this sort to place Shakespeare in what seems to me his proper context—a context which none but the Baconians and Oxfordians deny, but which most scholars and critics tend to ignore. That context is the London commercial theatre and the organized professional acting troupe.

Shakespeare was more completely and continuously involved with theatres and acting companies than any other Elizabethan dramatist whose life we know. Most Elizabethan dramatists had only their writing connection with the theatres, but Shakespeare belonged to the small group which both wrote and acted. In this small group of actor-dramatists, the best-known names are those of Heywood, Rowley, Field and Shakespeare. Of this thoroughly professionalized band, Shakespeare is the one most closely bound to his company and his theatre, for he is the only one of the four who did not shift about from company to company but maintained his close association with a single acting troupe for more than twenty years. Besides this, he was bound to theatres and actors

From *Shakespeare Survey I* (1948), pp. 38–50. Reprinted by permission of the author and the editor.

in still another fashion which makes him unique among all Elizabethan dramatists: he is the only dramatist we know who owned stock in theatre buildings over an extended period. His income was derived from acting, from writing plays, from shares in dramatic enterprises, and from theatre rents. From the beginning to the end of his writing career we must see him in a theatrical context if we are not to do violence to the recorded facts. At the beginning is our first reference to him in Greene's allusion to the "Tygers hart wrapt in a Players hyde"; at the end are his own last words, so far as we know them, in his will. This will is mostly concerned with Stratford affairs, but when he does turn to the years of his London life and his many London associates, he singles out only three for a last remembrance. These men are John Heminges, Henry Condell, and Richard Burbage—all three actors, all three fellow-sharers in the acting company of the King's men, all three fellow-stockholders in the Globe and the Blackfriars. If Shakespeare's proper context is not the London commercial theatres and the professional troupes, then evidence has no meaning, and one man's irresponsible fancies are as good as another's.

Now in spite of all the evidence that Shakespeare's dominant preoccupation throughout his creative life was the theatre, most scholars and critics of the last 150 years have written of him as the professional poet and not as the professional playwright. For the most part he has been studied as Spenser and Milton and Keats are studied. For a century and a half the great majority of studies of Shakespeare's genius and development have been concerned with literary influences and biographical influences and not with theatrical influences.[1] We have studied his

[1] *The Cambridge Bibliography of English Literature* will serve as an example. The bibliography of Shakespeare fills 136 columns, of which one half-column is devoted to "The Influence of Theatrical Conditions." This is not to say, of course, that there have been no proper studies of the theatres and acting companies of Shakespeare's time. There are many. But there are comparatively few books and articles devoted to the examination of Shakespeare's work in the light of this knowledge or to a consideration of the specific influence such matters had on his methods and development.

sources and his text, his indebtedness to Ovid and Holinshed and Montaigne and Plutarch. Even in biographical studies the preference has always been for the nontheatrical aspects of Shakespeare's life—his boyhood in the woods and fields about Stratford, his marriage and his wife, the death of his son Hamnet, his relations with Southampton and Essex, his supposed breakdown, his retirement to Stratford. Now any or all of these facts, or alleged facts, no doubt had an influence on the great creations of Shakespeare. I do not suggest that our study of them should be discontinued. But given the verified documentary evidence which we have, is it not dubious practice to devote a large part of our investigations to the more or less problematical influences in Shakespeare's career and to devote a very small part of our efforts to that enormously significant influence which dominated the majority of his waking hours for the twenty-odd years of his creative maturity? A dozen or more unquestioned documents show that Shakespeare's daily concern was the enterprise of the Lord Chamberlain-King's company. Shakespeare had obviously read Ovid and Holinshed and Lord North's *Plutarch;* surely he must have mourned for the untimely death of his only son; but none of these can have occupied his mind for so long as his daily association with the enterprise of the Lord Chamberlain-King's men. Of the factors in his life and development which we can now identify, this was surely the most important.

Now what are the events in his long and absorbing association with this troupe which we can expect to have influenced his work? One of the first must have been the protracted plague closings of 1593 and 1594, for out of this disaster to all London players the Lord Chamberlain's company apparently rose.[2] Another must have been the assembling of the players and the drawing up of the agreement for the formal organization of the Lord Chamberlain's company. The record suggests that Shakespeare was one of the leaders in this organization, for when

[2] E. K. Chambers, *The Elizabethan Stage,* II, 192–93 and IV, 348–49; *William Shakespeare,* I, 27–56.

the new company performed before the court in the Christmas season of 1594–95, payment was made to Richard Burbage, the principal actor, Will Kemp, the principal comedian, and William Shakespeare.[3] How did the great possibilities offered by this new troupe, destined to become the most famous and most successful in the history of the English theatre, affect the writing of its chief dramatist?

In the winter of 1598–99 occurred another event which must have been of absorbing interest for all members of the company. This was of course the building of the Globe on the Bankside. Here was a theatre built for the occupancy of a particular company, and six of the seven owners were actors in the company. Assuredly it was built, so far as available funds would allow, to the specific requirements of the productions of the Lord Chamberlain's men. What facilities did Shakespeare get which he had not had before? How did he alter his composition to take advantage of the new possibilities? Can there be any doubt that as a successful man of the theatre he did so? Yet I know of no study which attempts to assess this vital new factor in relation to Shakespeare's development.

The next event which must have been of great importance for Shakespeare's company was its involvement in the Essex rebellion. This exceptional case has received the full attention of critics and scholars because of its supposed relation to a performance of Shakespeare's *Richard II*. Actually, however, the Essex rebellion, much though it must have excited the company for a few months, was the least influential of all these factors affecting the company's activities and Shakespeare's development. Apparently the company's innocence was established without much difficulty.[4] There is no indication that their later performances or Shakespeare's later writing were affected by the experience. Though the events were sensational, and though they must have caused great anxiety for a time, they cannot be thought of as events of long-term significance in the history of this group of men

3 *The Elizabethan Stage*, IV, 164.
4 *William Shakespeare*, I, 353–55; *The Elizabethan Stage*, II, 204–07.

who were so important and influential in Shakespeare's career and development.

Of much more importance in the affairs of the company was their attainment of the patronage of James I less than two months after the death of Elizabeth.[5] This patronage and the King's livery certainly became one of the important factors in creating the great prestige of the company. In the ten years before they became the King's company, their known performances at court average about three a year; in the ten years after they attained their new service their known performances at court average about thirteen a year, more than those of all other London companies combined.[6] They were officially the premier company in London; a good part of their time must have been devoted to the preparation of command performances. Surely this new status of the troupe must have been a steady and pervasive influence in the development of its principal dramatist, William Shakespeare.

The final event which I wish to mention in the affairs of the King's company was perhaps the most important of all. There is no doubt that it made a great change in the activities of the company, and I do not see how it can have failed to be a principal influence in Shakespeare's development as a dramatist. This event was the acquisition of the famous private theatre in Blackfriars. No adult company in London had ever before performed regularly in a private theatre. For thirty years the private theatres with their superior audiences, their concerts, their comfortable accommodations, their traffic in sophisticated drama and the latest literary fads, had been the exclusive homes of the boy companies, the pets of Society. Now for the first time a troupe of those rogues and vagabonds, the common players, had the temerity to present themselves to the sophisticates of London in a repertory at the town's most exclusive theatre. I suspect that this was one of the turning points in Tudor and Stuart dramatic history. Beaumont and Jonson and Fletcher had

[5] *The Elizabethan Stage,* II, 208–09.
[6] *Ibid.,* IV, 108–30.

begun to make the craft of the playwright more socially respectable. The increasing patronage of the drama by the royal family, and the growing splendor and frequency of the court masques which were written by ordinary playwrights and performed in part by common players, were raising the prestige of the drama and the theatre from its Elizabethan to its Caroline state. The acquisition of the Blackfriars in 1608 by the King's company and the full exploitation of the new playhouse must have been the most conspicuous evidence to Londoners of the changing state of affairs. Surely it is impossible that the King's men and their principal dramatist, William Shakespeare, could have been unaware of this situation. Surely they must have bent all their efforts in the selection and performance of old plays and in the commissioning and writing of new ones to the full exploitation of this unprecedented opportunity. The new state of affairs must have been apparent in much that they did, and it must have influenced decidedly the dramatic compositions of Shakespeare.

So far, it has been my contention that all we know of William Shakespeare has shown him to be above all else a man of the theatre, that during the twenty years of his creative maturity most of his time was spent in closest association with members of the Lord Chamberlain-King's company and in thought about their needs and their interests, and that therefore in the affairs of this company we should seek one of the principal influences in his creative life. I have mentioned six events which (so far as we can tell through the mists of 350 years) seem to have been important in the affairs of that theatrical organization. These events are not all of equal importance, but each of them, except possibly the Essex rebellion, must have had a marked effect on the activities of Shakespeare's company and therefore on the dramatic creations of Shakespeare himself. Each one, it seems to me, deserves more study that it has received in its relation to the development of Shakespeare's work.

Let me invite your attention now to a fuller consideration of one of the most important of these events in the history of the Lord Chamberlain-King's company, namely the acquisition of the Blackfriars Theatre. What did this event mean in the history of the company, and how did it affect the writing of William Shakespeare?

Probably we should note first the time at which the Blackfriars would have begun to influence the company and the writing of Shakespeare. All the dramatic histories say that the King's men took over the Blackfriars Theatre in 1608, and this is true in a legal sense, for on 9 August 1608 leases were executed conveying the Blackfriars Playhouse to seven lessees: Cuthbert Burbage, Thomas Evans, and five members of the King's company—John Heminges, William Sly, Henry Condell, Richard Burbage, and William Shakespeare.[7] The few scholars who have examined in detail the history of the King's company have noted, however, that Shakespeare and his fellows probably did not begin to act at the Blackfriars in August of 1608. The plague was rife in London at that time; fifty plague deaths had been recorded for the week ending 28 July, and for a year and a half, or until December 1609, the bills of mortality show an abnormally high rate from the plague.[8] Though specific records about the closing of the theatres are not extant, we have definite statements that they were closed for part of this period, and comparison with other years suggests that there must have been very little if any public acting allowed in London between the first of August 1608 and the middle of December 1609. Therefore, it has occasionally been said, the Blackfriars was not used by the King's men much before 1610, and no influence on their plays and their productions can be sought before that year.

This conclusion of little or no influence before 1610 is, I think, a false one. It is based on the erroneous assumption that the actors and playwrights of the King's company would have known nothing about the peculiarities of the Blackfriars and that they would have had no plays

[7] *The Elizabethan Stage*, II, 509–10. Technically Richard Burbage leased one-seventh of the theatre to each of the other six.

[8] *Ibid.*, IV, 351.

prepared especially for that theatre until after they had begun performing in it. Actors are never so stupid or so insular as this in any time. The King's men, we may be sure, were well aware of the Blackfriars and the type of performance it required, or specialized in, long before they came to lease the theatre. There must be many evidences of this, but three in particular come readily to mind.

Seven years before, in 1601, the King's men had been involved in the War of the Theatres, which was in part a row between the public theatres and the private theatres. The chief attack on the public theatres and adult actors was made in Jonson's *Poetaster,* performed at the Blackfriars. Certain actors of the Lord Chamberlain's company, and possibly Shakespeare himself, were ridiculed in this Blackfriars play. The reply, *Satiromastix,* was written by Thomas Dekker and performed by Shakespeare's company at the Globe.[9] Certainly in 1601 at least, the company was well aware of the goings on at Blackfriars.

A second piece of evidence pointing to their knowledge of the peculiar requirements of the Blackfriars is the case of Marston's *Malcontent*. Marston wrote this play for the boys at the Blackfriars, who performed it in that theatre in 1604. The King's men stole the play, as they admitted, and performed it at the Globe; the third edition, also 1604, shows the alterations they commissioned John Webster to make in order to adapt a Blackfriars script to a Globe performance, and in the induction to the play Richard Burbage, speaking in his own person, points out one or two of the differences between Blackfriars requirements and Globe requirements.[10]

Finally, and most familiar of all evidence that the King's men were quite alive to what went on at Blackfriars, is the "little eyases" passage in *Hamlet* and Shakespeare's rueful admission that, for a time at any rate, the competition of the Blackfriars was too much for the company at the Globe.

[9] See J. H. Penniman, *The War of the Theatres,* and R. A. Small, *The Stage Quarrel.*
[10] F. L. Lucas, *The Works of John Webster,* III, 294–309.

Clearly the King's men did not have to wait until their performances of 1610 at the Blackfriars to know how their plays needed to be changed to fit them to that theatre and its select audience. They had known for several years what the general characteristics of Blackfriars performances were. Indeed, the leading member of the company, Richard Burbage, had a double reason for being familiar with all the peculiarities of the Blackfriars, for since his father's death in 1597 he had been the owner of the theatre and the landlord of the boy company that made it famous.[11] We can be perfectly sure, then, that from the day of the first proposal that the King's men take over the Blackfriars they had talked among themselves about what they would do with it and had discussed what kinds of plays they would have to have written to exploit it. It is all too often forgotten that in all such discussions among the members of the King's company William Shakespeare would have had an important part. He had more kinds of connections with the company than any other man: he was actor, shareholder, patented member, principal playwright, and one of the housekeepers of the Globe; even Burbage did not serve so many functions in the company. Few men in theatrical history have been so completely and inextricably bound up with the affairs of an acting troupe.

When would the King's men have begun planning for their performances at the Blackfriars? We cannot, of course, set the exact date, but we can approximate it. There is one faint suggestion that consideration of the project may have started very early indeed. Richard Burbage said that Henry Evans, who had leased the theatre from him for the Children of the Queen's Revels, began talking to him about the surrender of his lease in 1603 or 1604.[12] These early discussions evidently came to nothing, for we know that the boys continued in the theatre for three or four years longer. Burbage's statement

11 J. Q. Adams, *Shakespearean Playhouses*, pp. 199–223.

12 "The Answers of Heminges and Burbage to Edward Kirkham," 1612, printed by F. G. Fleay, *A Chronicle History of the London Stage*, p. 235.

about Evans does suggest the interesting possibility that the King's men may have dallied with the project of leasing the Blackfriars Theatre as early as 1603 or 1604. This, however, is only the faintest of possibilities. The Blackfriars was tentatively in the market then, but all we know is that Burbage had to consider for a short time the possibility of getting other tenants for his theatre. Whether the King's men came to his mind and theirs as possible tenants, we do not know.

We can be sure that active planning for performances at the Blackfriars did get under way when Burbage, who was both the leading actor of the King's men and owner of the Blackfriars Theatre, knew for certain that the boy actors would give up their lease and that arrangements for a syndicate of King's men to take over the theatre could be made. Conferences among these men—the Burbages, Heminges, Condell, Shakespeare, and Sly—and probably preliminary financial arrangements would have been going on before a scrivener was called in to draw up a rough draft of the lease. Such preliminaries, which must come before a lease can be formally signed, often consume months. We know that the leases were formally executed on 9 August 1608;[13] therefore discussions in June and July or even in April and May are likely enough. We know that the Blackfriars Theatre was available as early as March 1608, for in a letter dated 11 March 1608 Sir Thomas Lake officially notified Lord Salisbury that the company of the Children of Blackfriars must be suppressed and that the King had vowed that they should never act again even if they had to beg their bread. General confirmation of this fact is found in a letter written two weeks later by the French ambassador.[14] Thus it is evident that in March of 1608 Richard Burbage knew his theatre was without a tenant. March to July 1608, then, are the months for discussions among the King's men of prospective performances at the Blackfriars.

What did this little group of Shakespeare and his

13 *William Shakespeare,* II, 62–63.
14 *The Elizabethan Stage,* II, 53–54.

intimate associates of the last fourteen years work out during their discussions in the months of March to July 1608?

One of the things they must have considered was alterations of their style of acting. As Granville-Barker has pointed out,[15] the acting in the new Blackfriars before a sophisticated audience would have to be more quiet than in the large open-air Globe before the groundlings. It would be easier to emphasize points in the quiet candlelit surroundings, and "sentiment would become as telling as passion." There must also have been extended discussions of what to do about the repertory: which of the company's plays would be suitable for the elegant new theatre and which should be kept for the old audience at the Globe? Some of their decisions are fairly obvious. *Mucedorus,* which Rafe in *The Knight of the Burning Pestle* says he had played before the Wardens of his company and which went through fifteen editions before the Restoration, was clearly one of the Globe plays which might be laughed at by a Blackfriars audience. Similarly, *The Merry Devil of Edmonton* was not a good Blackfriars prospect. Certain other plays in the repertory might be expected to please at the Blackfriars; Marston's *Malcontent,* for instance, could easily be changed back to its original Blackfriars form, and Jonson's *Every Man in His Humour* and *Every Man out of His Humour*, though nine and ten years old, had been played by the company at court in the last three years and ought to be suitable for the Blackfriars.

These discussions of the old repertory, though no doubt important to the company then, are fruitless for us now. I know of no evidence as to their decisions. More important are the proposals for new plays for the Blackfriars, and I think we do have some evidence as to what these decisions were. The experienced members of the King's company were familiar with the fact so commonly recorded in the annals of the Jacobean theatre that new plays were in constant demand. With the acquisition of the new theatre they had an opportunity to claim for their

15 *Prefaces to Shakespeare,* 2nd ser., pp. 249–50.

own the most profitable audience in London. We know from the later Jacobean and Caroline records that this is just what they did.[16] It seems likely that one of the foundations of their later unquestioned dominance of the audiences of the gentry was their decision about plays and playwrights made in their discussions of March to July 1608.

One of their decisions, I suggest, was to get Jonson to write Blackfriars plays for them. He was a likely choice for three reasons. First, because he was developing a following among the courtly audience (always prominent at the Blackfriars) by his great court masques. At this time he had already written his six early entertainments for King James—those at the Coronation, at the Opening of Parliament, at Althorp, at Highgate, and the two at Theobalds. He had written for performance at Whitehall *The Masque of Blackness, The Masque of Beauty, Hymenaei,* and the famous *Lord Haddington's Masque*. The sensational success of these courtly entertainments made Jonson a most promising choice to write plays for the courtly audience which the King's men did succeed in attracting to Blackfriars.

A second reason which would have led the King's men to Jonson as a writer for their new theatre was his great reputation among the literati and critics. In this decade from 1601 to 1610 the literary allusions to him are numerous, more numerous than to Shakespeare himself. The poems to Jonson and the long prose passages about him in this time are far more frequent than to Shakespeare; quotations from his work occur oftener, and I find three times as many literary and social references to performances of his plays and masques as to Shakespeare's. Poems about him or references to his work are written in these years by John Donne, Sir John Roe, Sir Dudley Carleton, the Venetian ambassador, John Chamberlain, Sir Thomas Lake, Sir George Buc, Sir Thomas Salusbury.[17] This is just the kind of audience which

16 See Bentley, *The Jacobean and Caroline Stage,* Vol. I, chap. I *passim*; II, 673–81.

17 See Bentley, *Shakespeare and Jonson,* I, 38–41, 65–67, 73–79, 87–90, and Bradley and Adams, *The Jonson Allusion-Book, passim.*

might be attracted to the Blackfriars, and which, eventually, the King's men did attract there.

There was a third reason which would have made Jonson seem to the King's men a very likely bet for their new theatre: he had already had experience in writing plays for this theatre when it was occupied by boys. Before the conferences of the King's men about their new project he had already had performed at Blackfriars *Cynthia's Revels, The Poetaster, The Case Is Altered,* and *Eastward Ho.* Possibly just before the time of the conferences of the King's men he had been writing for the Blackfriars another play, *Epicoene,* for he says in the Folio of 1616 that the play was performed by the Children of Blackfriars, but the date he gives for performance comes after their expulsion from the Blackfriars Theatre. Not only had Jonson had the valuable experience of writing four or five plays for the Blackfriars, but the Induction to *Cynthia's Revels* and his personal statements about boys of the company, like Nathan Field and Salathiel, or Solomon, Pavy,[18] strongly suggest that he had directed them in their rehearsals. What valuable experience for the King's men planning their first performance in this new theatre!

Now all these qualifications of Jonson as a prospect for the King's men are, in sober fact, only speculations. Perhaps they simply show that if *I* had been participating in the conferences about the Blackfriars I should have argued long and lustily for Ben Jonson. Alas, I was not there! What evidence is there that they really did agree to secure his services for the company? The evidence is that before these conferences he had written only four plays for the Lord Chamberlain's or King's company—three, nine, and ten years before—nothing for the company in the years 1605–08. After these conferences, he wrote all his remaining plays for the company, with the exception of *Bartholomew Fair* six years later, a play which he gave to his good friend and protégé Nathan Field for the Lady Elizabeth's company at the Hope, and *A Tale of a Tub,* twenty-five years later, which he gave to Queen Henri-

18 See "A Good Name Lost," *Times Literary Supplement* (30 May 1942), p. 276.

etta's men. Jonson's first play after the reopening of Blackfriars was *The Alchemist;* it was written for the King's men, and numerous allusions show clearly that it was written for Blackfriars. So were *Catiline, The Devil Is an Ass, The Staple of News, The New Inn,* and *The Magnetic Lady*. Of course we lack the final proof of recorded reference to a definite agreement, but the evidence is such as to suggest that one of the decisions reached by the King's men in the reorganization of their enterprise to exploit the great advantages of their new theatre was to secure the services of Ben Jonson to write plays for the literate and courtly audience at Blackfriars.

Another decision, which I suggest the King's men made at these conferences, was to secure for their new theatre the services of the rising young collaborators, Francis Beaumont and John Fletcher. These gentlemen were younger than Jonson by about ten years, and as yet their reputations were distinctly inferior to his, but they had already displayed those talents which were to make their plays the stage favorites at Blackfriars for the next thirty-four years,[19] and were to cause Dryden to say sixty years later that "their plays are now the most pleasant and frequent entertainments of the stage."

One of the great assets of Beaumont and Fletcher was social. In the years immediately before and after 1608, the London theatre audience was developing the social cleavage which is such a marked characteristic of the Jacobean and Caroline drama and stage. In Elizabeth's time the London theatre was a universal one, in which a single audience at the Globe could embrace Lord Monteagle, Sir Charles Percy, city merchants, lawyers, Inns of Court students, apprentices, servants, beggars, pickpockets, and prostitutes. The later Jacobean and Caroline audience was a dual one. The gentry, the court, the professional classes, and the Inns of Court men went to the Blackfriars, the Phoenix, and later to the Salisbury Court; the London masses went to the larger and noisier Red Bull and Fortune and Globe. This new state of affairs was just developing when the King's men had their confer-

[19] *The Jacobean and Caroline Stage,* I, 29 and 109–14.

ences about the Blackfriars in 1608. They evidently saw what was coming, however, for in the next few years they understood and exploited the situation more effectively than any other troupe in London. Indeed, the very acquisition of the Blackfriars and its operation in conjunction with the Globe was a device which had never been tried before in London and which is the clearest evidence that the King's men knew just what was happening.

Under these circumstances, then, the social status of Beaumont and Fletcher was an asset for the company in their new house. Francis Beaumont came of an ancient and distinguished Leicestershire family, with many connections among the nobility. John Fletcher was the son of a Lord Bishop of London and one-time favorite of Elizabeth. To a Blackfriars audience the social standing of these two young men would have been more acceptable than that of any other dramatist writing in London in 1608.

Another asset which made Beaumont and Fletcher valuable for the new enterprise of the King's men was their private theatre experience. So far as we can make out now, all their plays before this time had been written for private theatres and most of them for the Blackfriars. *The Woman Hater* had been prepared for the private theatre in St. Paul's, but *The Knight of the Burning Pestle, The Scornful Lady,* and *The Faithful Shepherdess* were Blackfriars plays. I think we can add to this list *Cupid's Revenge*. This play has been variously dated, but two forthcoming articles by James Savage[20] seem to me to offer convincing evidence that the play was prepared for Blackfriars about 1607 and that it displays a crude preliminary working out of much of the material which made *Philaster* one of the great hits of its time and one of the most influential plays of the seventeenth century. In any event, Beaumont and Fletcher were among the most experienced Blackfriars playwrights available in 1608. It is true that in 1608 none of their plays had been a great success; indeed the two best, *The Knight of the*

20 "The Date of Beaumont and Fletcher's *Cupid's Revenge*" and "Beaumont and Fletcher's *Philaster* and Sidney's *Arcadia*."

Burning Pestle and *The Faithful Shepherdess,* are known to have been unsuccessful at first. The King's men, however, were experienced in the ways of the theatre; it does not seem rash to assume that at least one of them knew enough about audiences and about dramatic talents to see that these young men were writers of brilliant promise—especially since that one was William Shakespeare.

Beaumont and Fletcher, then, because of their experience and social standing were very desirable dramatists for the King's men to acquire in 1608 for their new private theatre. What is the evidence that they did acquire them? The evidence is that all the Beaumont and Fletcher plays of the next few years are King's men's plays, several of them famous hits—*Philaster, The Maid's Tragedy, A King and No King, The Captain, The Two Noble Kinsmen, Bonduca, Monsieur Thomas, Valentinian.* The dating of many of the Beaumont and Fletcher plays is very uncertain because of their late publication, and it may be that two or three of the later plays were written for other companies, but at least forty-five plays by Beaumont and Fletcher were the property of the Jacobean and Caroline King's men.[21] None of their plays before 1608, when Blackfriars was acquired, was, so far as we can find, written for the King's men. It seems a reasonable assumption, therefore, that another of the policies agreed upon at the conferences of 1608 was to secure the services of Beaumont and Fletcher for the company in its new enterprise at the Blackfriars.

The third of these three important changes in policy which I think the King's men agreed upon at their conferences about the new Blackfriars enterprise in 1608, is the most interesting of all to us, but it was the easiest and most obvious for them. Indeed, it may well have been assumed almost without discussion. It was, of course, that William Shakespeare should write henceforth with the Blackfriars in mind and not the Globe.

Why was this decision an easy and obvious one? The company could assume, of course, that he would continue to write for them, since he was a shareholder and a

21 *The Jacobean and Caroline Stage,* I, 109–15.

patented member of the company and a housekeeper in both their theatres. Since the formation of the company, fourteen years before, all his plays had been written for performance by them, always, in the last ten years, for performance at the Globe. All his professional associations as well as his financial ones were with this company, and probably no one in the group even considered his defection. Burbage, Shakespeare, Heminges, and Condell were the real nucleus of the organization.

This new enterprise at the Blackfriars was a very risky business. As we have noted, no adult company had ever tried to run a private theatre before. The King's men not only proposed to make a heavy investment in this new departure, but they intended to continue running their old public theatre at the same time. Every possible precaution against failure needed to be taken. One such precaution would be the devotion of Shakespeare's full-time energies to the Blackfriars instead of the Globe. They could trust Shakespeare; he knew their potentialities and their shortcomings as no other dramatist did—indeed, few dramatists in the history of the English theatre have ever had such a long and intimate association with an acting company as William Shakespeare had had with these men. If anybody knew what Burbage and Heminges and Condell and Robert Armyn and Richard Cowley could do on the stage and what they should not be asked to do, that man was William Shakespeare. He could make them a success at the Blackfriars as they had been at the Globe if any one could.

Another reason for the transfer of Shakespeare's efforts was the fact that the Globe could be left to take care of itself with an old repertory as the Blackfriars could not. For one thing, there was no old repertory for the Blackfriars, since the departing boys appear to have held on to their old plays. For another thing, it was the Blackfriars audience which showed the greater avidity for new plays; the public theatre audiences were much more faithful to old favorites. They were still playing *Friar Bacon and Friar Bungay* at the Fortune in 1630 and Marlowe's *Edward II* at the Red Bull in 1620 and *Dr. Faustus* at the Fortune in 1621 and *Richard II* and *Pericles* at the Globe in 1631.[22] In the archives of the Globe at this time there must have been a repertory of more than a hundred plays, including at least twenty-five of Shakespeare's. Moreover, certain plays written for the Globe in the last few years, like Wilkins's *Miseries of Enforced Marriage* and the anonymous *Yorkshire Tragedy* and *The Fair Maid of Bristol* and *The London Prodigal,* had provided playwrights who might be expected to entertain a Globe audience with more of the same fare, but who could scarcely come up to the requirements of sophistication at Blackfriars. Altogether, then, the Globe repertory had much less need of Shakespeare's efforts in 1608 than did the Blackfriars repertory.

Why should Shakespeare have wanted to write for the Blackfriars, or at least have agreed to do so? The most compelling of the apparent reasons is that he had money invested in the project and stood to lose by its failure and gain by its success. He was one of the seven lessees of the new theatre; he had paid down an unknown sum and had agreed to pay £5. 14*s.* 4*d.* per year in rent.[23] He had at least a financial reason for doing everything he could to establish the success of the Blackfriars venture, and what Shakespeare could do most effectively was to write plays which would insure the company's popularity with the audience in its new private theatre.

A third reason for this postulated decision of the King's men in 1608 to have Shakespeare devote his entire attention to the Blackfriars and abandon the Globe was that the King's men saw that the real future of the theatrical profession in London lay with the court and the court party in the private theatres. Their receipts for performances at court showed them this very clearly. In the last nine years of Elizabeth, 1594–1602, they had received from court performances an average of £35 a year; in the first five years of the reign of the new king, 1603–07, they had averaged £131 per year in addition to their new

22 *Ibid.*, I, 156, 174, 157, 24, 129.
23 *Shakespearean Playhouses*, pp. 224–25.

allowances for liveries as servants of the King.[24] The Blackfriars and not the Globe was the theatre where they could entertain this courtly audience with commercial performances. There is no doubt that in the next few years after 1608 the Blackfriars did become the principal theatre of the company. In 1612 Edward Kirkham said they took £1,000 a winter more at the Blackfriars than they had formerly taken at the Globe.[25] When Sir Henry Herbert listed receipts from the two theatres early in the reign of King Charles, the receipts for single performances at the Globe averaged £6. 13*s.* 8*d.*; those for single performances at the Blackfriars averaged £15. 15*s.*, or about two and one-half times as much.[26] In 1634 an Oxford don who wrote up the company simply called them the company of the Blackfriars and did not mention the Globe at all;[27] when the plays of the company were published in the Jacobean and Caroline period, the Blackfriars was mentioned as their theatre more than four times as often as the Globe was.[28] Such evidence proves that the Blackfriars certainly did become the principal theatre of the King's men. I am suggesting that in the conferences of 1608 the King's men had some intimation that it would, and accordingly they persuaded William Shakespeare to devote his attention to that theatre in the future instead of to the Globe.

So much for the reasons that Shakespeare might be expected to change the planning of his plays in 1608. What is the evidence that he did? The evidence, it seems to me, is to be seen in *Cymbeline, The Winter's Tale, The Tempest,* and *The Two Noble Kinsmen,* and probably it was to be seen also in the lost play, *Cardenio.* The variations which these plays show from the Shakespearian norm have long been a subject for critical comment. The first three of them in particular, since they are the only ones which have been universally accepted as part of the

24 *The Elizabethan Stage,* IV, 164–75.
25 C. W. Wallace, *University of Nebraska Studies,* VIII (1908), 36–37, n. 6.
26 *The Jacobean and Caroline Stage,* I, 23–24.
27 *Ibid.,* I, 26, n. 5.
28 *Ibid.,* I, 30, n. 1.

Shakespeare canon, have commonly been discussed as a distinct genre. Widely as critics and scholars have disagreed over the reasons for their peculiar characteristics, those peculiarities have generally been recognized, whether the plays are called Shakespeare's Romances, or Shakespeare's Tragi-Comedies, or his Romantic Tragi-Comedies, or simply the plays of the fourth period. No competent critic who has read carefully through the Shakespeare canon has failed to notice that there is something different about *Cymbeline, The Winter's Tale, The Tempest,* and *The Two Noble Kinsmen.*

When critics and scholars have tried to explain this difference between the plays of the last period and Shakespeare's earlier work, they have set up a variety of hypotheses. Most of these hypotheses have in common only the trait which I noted at the beginning of this paper—namely, they agree in considering Shakespeare as the professional poet and not the professional playwright. They turn to Shakespeare's sources, or to his inspiration, or to his personal affairs, or to the bucolic environment of his Stratford retirement, but not to the theatre which was his daily preoccupation for more than twenty years. Dowden called this late group in the Shakespeare canon "On the Heights," because he thought the plays reflected Shakespeare's new-found serenity. Such a fine optimism had, perhaps, something to recommend it to the imaginations of the Victorians, but to modern scholars it seems to throw more light on Dowden's mind than on Shakespeare's development. Dowden's explanation seemed utterly fatuous to Lytton Strachey, who thought that the plays of "Shakespeare's Final Period" were written by a Shakespeare far from serene, who was really "half enchanted by visions of beauty and loveliness and half bored to death." Violently as Dowden and Strachey differ, they agree in seeking subjective interpretations.

Best known of the old explanations of the peculiarities of the plays of this last period is probably Thorndike's:[29] the contention that the great success of *Philaster* caused

29 Ashley H. Thorndike, *The Influence of Beaumont and Fletcher on Shakespeare.*

Shakespeare to imitate it in *Cymbeline* and to a lesser extent in *The Winter's Tale* and *The Tempest*. In spite of the great horror of the Shakespeare idolaters at the thought of the master imitating superficial young whipper-snappers like Beaumont and Fletcher, no one can read the two plays together without noting the striking similarities between them. The difficulty is that although the approximate dates of the two plays are clear enough, their *precise* dates are so close together and so uncertain that neither Thorndike nor any subsequent scholar has been able to prove that *Philaster* came before *Cymbeline,* and the Shakespeare idolaters have been equally unable to prove that *Cymbeline* came before *Philaster*.

I suggest that the really important point is not the priority of either play. The significant and revealing facts are that both were written for the King's company; both were written, or at least completed, after the important decision made by the leaders of the troupe in the spring of 1608 to commission new plays for Blackfriars, and both were prepared to be acted in the private theatre in Blackfriars before the sophisticated audience attracted to that house. It is their common purpose and environment, not imitation of one by the other, which makes them similar. Both *Philaster* and *Cymbeline* are somewhat like Beaumont and Fletcher's earlier plays, especially *Cupid's Revenge,* because Beaumont and Fletcher's earlier plays had all been written for private theatres and all but one for Blackfriars. Both *Philaster* and *Cymbeline* are unlike Shakespeare's earlier plays because none of those plays had been written for private theatres. The subsequent plays of both Beaumont and Fletcher and Shakespeare resemble *Philaster* and *Cymbeline* because they too were written to be performed by the King's men before the sophisticated and courtly audience in the private theatre at Blackfriars.

So much I think we can say with some assurance. This explanation of the character of Shakespeare's last plays is in accord with the known facts of theatrical history; it accords with the biographical evidence of Shakespeare's long and close association with all the enterprises of the

Lord Chamberlain's-King's men for twenty years; it is in accord with his fabulously acute sense of the theatre and the problems of the actor; and it does no violence to his artistic integrity or to his poetic genius.

May I add one further point much more in the realm of speculation? Since John Fletcher became a playwright for the King's men at this time and continued so for the remaining seventeen years of his life, and since the activities of the King's men had been one of Shakespeare's chief preoccupations for many years, is it not likely that the association between Fletcher and Shakespeare from 1608 to 1614 was closer than has usually been thought? Shakespeare was nearing retirement; after 1608 he wrote plays less frequently than before; Fletcher became his successor as chief dramatist for the King's company. In these years they collaborated in *The Two Noble Kinsmen, Henry VIII,* and probably in *Cardenio.* Is it too fantastic to suppose that Shakespeare was at least an adviser in the preparation of *Philaster, A King and No King,* and *The Maid's Tragedy* for his fellows? Is it even more fantastic to think that Shakespeare, the old public theatre playwright, preparing his first and crucial play for a private theatre, might have asked advice—or even taken it—from the two young dramatists who had written plays for this theatre and audience four or five times before?

Perhaps this is going too far. I do not wish to close on a note of speculation. My basic contention is that Shakespeare was, before all else, a man of the theatre and a devoted member of the King's company. One of the most important events in the history of that company was its acquisition of the Blackfriars Playhouse in 1608 and its subsequent brilliantly successful exploitation of its stage and audience. The company was experienced and theatre-wise; the most elementary theatrical foresight demanded that in 1608 they prepare new and different plays for a new and different theatre and audience. Shakespeare was their loved and trusted fellow. How could they fail to ask him for new Blackfriars plays, and how could he fail them? All the facts at our command seem to me to demonstrate that he did not fail them. He turned from his old and tested methods and produced a new kind of play for the new theatre and audience. Somewhat unsurely at first he wrote *Cymbeline* for them, then, with greater dexterity in his new medium, *The Winter's Tale,* and finally, triumphant in his old mastery, *The Tempest.*

THEODORE SPENCER

The Two Noble Kinsmen

For about a hundred years critical opinion has been divided as to whether Shakespeare did or did not write a large part of *The Two Noble Kinsmen.* The play was entered on the Stationers' Register in 1634 as "by John Fletcher and William Shakespeare," and the quarto was printed in the same year with their names on the title page. But the play does not occur in any of the Shakespeare folios, and though Fletcher's style is unmistakably present, in the so-called Shakespearean scenes there are characteristics which to many readers have seemed un-Shakespearean. Professor Tucker Brooke sums up the negative case: "When we consider individually the parts of *The Two Noble Kinsmen* which have been ascribed to Shakespeare, we find invariably that each act, scene or verse falls just short of what it should be. Always there is the strong Shakespearean reminiscence, but nowhere the full and perfect reality that we could swear to."[1] Consequently other authors, especially Massinger, have been suggested for these scenes, and the play is ordinarily omitted from Shakespeare's collected works.[2]

From *Modern Philology,* XXXVI (1939), 255–76. Reprinted by permission of The University of Chicago Press.

[1] The *Shakespeare Apocrypha* (Oxford, 1908), p. xliii.

[2] There is a good summary of the history of the criticism of *The Two Noble Kinsmen* by Henry D. Gray. "Beaumont and *The Two Noble Kinsmen,*" *PQ,* II (1923), 112–31. Mr. Gray's own theory is, however, one of the most fantastic of the lot. He suggests that Fletcher timorously began the play alone, then got stuck and asked for Beaumont's help. Beaumont saw a chance of giving wider publicity to his recent *Masque of the Temple and Gray's Inn,* and started to assist Fletcher by inserting some of the characters from it in the third act; he also wrote a first draft of most of the other scenes. Before he finished, however, he got married and went to live in Kent, out of reach. Fletcher, in despair, and feeling quite unable to write the play alone, turned to Shakespeare. Shakespeare agreed to help, rewrote most of Act III, scene i, and brightened up the characters of Palamon and Arcite. But he too left town before he finished, going home to Stratford for good, and the play remained largely as Beaumont had drafted it.

But there is opinion of equal weight on the other side, and it is, I believe, now generally agreed that Shakespeare wrote Act I, scenes i–iii; Act III, scene i; Act V, except scene ii, and possibly more, and that he was equally responsible with Fletcher for the characterization and the plotting. To my mind the matter is clinched by a remarkably able and interesting article by Mr. Alfred Hart,[3] which analyzes the language of the Shakespearean scenes in the play in great detail, and by showing how closely it resembles that of Shakespeare's other plays, makes Shakespeare's authorship entirely convincing.

That the play was written in 1613 there can also be little doubt: the inclusion of the characters from Beaumont's masque of that date is strong evidence. As Professor Kittredge says, it "may be put immediately after *Henry VIII*."[4] Shakespeare's share in it, therefore, is the last thing he wrote, and it may be of considerable interest to study the play in the light of that fact. We may be able, as a result, to understand more clearly Shakespeare's latest style; we may be able to reach some conclusions as to why he ended his dramatic career when he did; and we may get a clearer picture not only of Jacobean drama at the end of Shakespeare's career, but of the different ways human experience can be represented on the stage.

II

The story of Palamon and Arcite, whether told by Boccaccio, Chaucer, or Shakespeare and Fletcher, is intrinsically feeble, superficial, and undramatic. For there is no real difference between Palamon and Arcite; they are both noble individuals, and the only reasons Palamon, rather than Arcite, wins the lady whom they both love are (*a*) that he saw her first and (*b*) that he had the sense to pray for success to Venus rather than to Mars. These reasons, to be sure, may have been more forceful in Chaucer's day, when the courtly ideal of love still had

[3] "Shakespeare and the Vocabulary of *The Two Noble Kinsmen*," *RES*, X (1934), 274–87.

[4] *Complete Works of William Shakespeare* (Boston, 1936), p. 1409.

some literary vitality, than they were in Shakespeare's, but even in Chaucer they are entirely external; they have nothing to do with character; when Palamon finally wins the lady, he does so by the help of a supernatural trick, not because he is the better man. Granted the outline of the story, anyone who tells it is forced to make the two heroes colorless and indistinguishable: should he do anything else, the story disappears. The same albinism extends to Emily, the heroine. She has no will of her own; if she should express a preference for either Arcite or Palamon, it would ruin the plot, which is based entirely on external motivation, and as a result she can be only a passive, if beautiful, doll, a shop-window dummy, forced to take whichever husband the gods decide. The whole thing is two-dimensional and unreal, a piece of tapestry, not, like the story of Troilus and Cressida, an active conflict.

Chaucer, however, makes it very appealing, and after reading *The Knight's Tale,* subdued by its grace and charm, we can see why an Elizabethan dramatist might think the story suitable for the stage. The opportunity, of which Chaucer takes such admirable advantage, for set speeches; the apparent, though superficial, conflict between the two heroes; the extension of their personal quarrel into a quarrel that involves the gods—all these things look like good dramatic material. Actually, of course, they are not, and I imagine that both Shakespeare and Fletcher, once they got started on their dramatization, realized that they were faced with a tough problem. They solved it very differently, and—as far as the immediate result was concerned, i.e., the writing of an effective play—Fletcher succeeded, and Shakespeare failed. The failure, to us, is more interesting than the success, but we must not be fooled by our idolatry of Shakespeare into taking credit away from Fletcher. The artificiality and spurious dramatic validity of the story offered a good opportunity for his accomplished and unscrupulous talent, and within his usual limits he made an expert job of it. The Fletcherian parts of the play are first-rate theater; their contrasts and conflicts make an immediate and successful impression. The Shakespearean parts, on the other hand, are static and, though with splendor, stiff. They are slow, and dense, compared with Fletcher's easy liquescence. They have a deliberate yet vague grandeur, a remote and half-exhausted exaltation; they are expressed through a clotted rhetoric that is the poetry of a man who has finished with action. Their style is the style of old age, and the imagery is an old man's imagery. Nevertheless, there is underneath a nobility, a control, a mastery of words, however fatigued, which make Fletcher's cleverness look cheap.[5] That mastery, and its peculiarity, its poetic success and its dramatic failure, its relation to Shakespeare's work as a whole, are worth careful study.

The play begins with an uninteresting prologue of a very conventional variety, a piece of hack writing (whoever wrote it) without significance. But the first scene of the first act, a scene which is unquestionably by Shakespeare, starts in a fashion as characteristic of Shakespeare's part in this play as it is uncharacteristic of nearly all his previous writing. It starts with a pageant: Hymen and a nymph symbolically attend the majestic entrance of Theseus, Hippolyta, and Emilia. It is processional, static, dignified, in the manner of a masque: the exact opposite to the opening of *The Tempest*, where all is action and excitement. It is the kind of thing that in an earlier play Shakespeare would have saved for a later scene, after the interest of the audience had been aroused by a personality or a conflict. And the entrance of these three chief characters is followed not by speech, but by a song:

> Roses, their sharp spines being gone,
> Not royal in their smells alone,
> But in their hue;
> Maiden pinks, of odor faint,
> Daisies smell-less, yet most quaint
> And sweet thyme true—

[5] De Quincey (*Works*, ed. Black [1862], X, 49), in his essay on rhetoric, wrote of Shakespeare's part of the play as follows: "The first and the last acts of *The Two Noble Kinsmen*, which in point of composition, is perhaps the most superb work in the language . . . had been the most gorgeous rhetoric, had they not happened to be something far better."

It is a song about flowers, echoing the subject matter of Perdita's flower speeches in the fourth act of *The Winter's Tale,* and with a reminiscence, it seems, of the tone of *The Phoenix and the Turtle:*

> The crow, the sland'rous cuckoo, nor
> The boding raven, nor chough hoar,
> Nor chatt'ring pie
> May on our bridehouse perch or sing,
> Or with them any discord bring,
> But from it fly!

Even when the song is over, and the semiritualistic, removed, pageant-like tone is established, the action does not begin vigorously: it still moves slowly, in a kind of dramatic pavane: "Enter three *Queens,* in black, with veils stain'd, with imperial crowns. The first *Queen* falls down at the foot of *Theseus;* the second falls down at the foot of *Hippolyta;* the third before *Emilia.*" And the three queens, thus disposed about the stage in a formal design, begin the dialogue rhythmically, almost in a chant:

> 1. *Queen:* For pity's sake and true gentility's,
> Hear and respect me!
> 2. *Queen:* For your mother's sake,
> And as you wish your womb may thrive with fair ones,
> Hear and respect me!
> 3. *Queen:* Now for the love of him whom Jove hath mark'd
> The honor of your bed, and for the sake
> Of clear virginity, be advocate
> For us and our distresses!

Theseus, Hippolyta, and Emilia reply in turn, with the same formal grace, in slow rhythms, the courtly echoes of dramatic action.

The queens request Theseus to do justice to their dead lords, and Theseus, interrupted in his wedding ceremony, is "transported" by their words, being carried out of the action back into the past. His speech to the first queen (ll. 54 ff.) illustrates one of the kinds of rhythm which seems to be natural to Shakespeare at the close of his career. The thought almost invariably stops, not at the end, but in the middle of the line, there is a striking reliance on strong verbs for descriptive effect, and the slow lines move like figures in heavy garments:

> King Capaneus was your lord. The day
> That he should marry you, at such a season
> As now it is with me, I met your groom
> By Mars's altar. You were that time fair;
> Not Juno's mantle fairer than your tresses,
> Nor in more bounty spread. Your wheaten wreath
> Was then nor thresh'd nor blasted; Fortune at you
> Dimpled her cheek with smiles. Hercules our kinsman
> (Then weaker than your eyes) laid by his club;
> He tumbled down upon his Nemean hide,
> And swore his sinews thaw'd. O grief and time,
> Fearful consumers, you will all devour!

As usual with Shakespeare, the situation is generalized at the end. But the speech does not advance the action in any way: it is more like the comment of a chorus than the speech of a protagonist, it is melancholy and dreamlike. Theseus' reflections about the ravages made by grief and time on the queen's once beautiful face disturb him, and he turns aside—"Troubled I am"—abstracted by his thoughts of evanescence and decay.

The ritualistic movement proceeds, and the second queen appeals for help to Hippolyta. Her speech, too, has a tone which is characteristic of Shakespeare's final style. It is not, like the tone of Theseus' speech, the tone of remembrance, or of reverie, though it is related to that, being also "nonactive"; it is rather the tone of invocation, of apostrophe, of worship. It is again "removed," the tone of a looker-on, not a participant: appropriate as it is to the particular situation, it is also, one feels, appropriate to Shakespeare's own feeling about human experience at this last period in his life. Everyone who has written poetry knows that there are times when the tension of the immediate practical problem of composition is half-consciously resolved by a relapse or release into a semihypnotic incantation. The immature poet will fall into an incantation borrowed from someone else; the poet who is ripe and rich in technical experience discovers in words the beat of his own emotional vibration, and will produce, when set in his maturity at a particular job, the incantation, the tone, and the order which belong only to him. These may be different at different periods of his career, but to a sensitive reader they are unmistakable. And there are, in the Shakespearean parts of *The Two Noble Kinsmen,* an unmistakable incantation, tone, and order: the incantation which accepts illusion, the tone which has forgotten tragedy, and an order melted at the edges into a larger unity of acceptance and wonder. They appear again, in a tired fashion, in the long speech which Palamon makes to Venus in the first scene of the fifth act; in that speech, as in the speech of the second queen to Hippolyta, there is something trancelike and remote. In both speeches we feel a continuation of the mood of Miranda's "O brave, new world," and the rhythm of the queen's words is an adagio rhythm, haunting, invocatory, spoken, as it were, behind a veil.

As rhetoric, the speech is superb. It consists of a twenty-three-line sentence, the first nine lines invariably running over, to break in the middle, leading in the tenth line to a variation, with the pause at the end of the line for once, which alters the flow and hence commands attention. And yet, in spite of its excellence, the writing is tired, the muscles behind it seem slack and old, and, like the speech of Theseus I have already quoted, it ends unconvincingly.

Honored Hippolyta,
Most dreaded Amazonian, that hast slain
The scythe-tusk'd boar; that with thy arm, as strong
As it is white, was near to make the male
To thy sex captive, but that this thy lord—
Born to uphold creation in that honor
First Nature styl'd it in—shrunk thee into
The bound thou wast o'erflowing, at once subduing

Thy force and thy affection; soldieress
That equally canst poise sternness with pity:
Who now, I know, hast much more power on him
Than ever he had on thee; who ow'st his strength,
And his love too, who is a servant for
The tenor of thy speech; dear glass of ladies,
Bid him that we, whom flaming War doth scorch,
Under the shadow of his sword may cool us;
Require him he advance it o'er our heads;
Speak't in a woman's key, like such a woman
As any of us three; weep ere you fail;
Lend us a knee;
But touch the ground for us no longer time
Than a dove's motion when the head's plucked off;
Tell him, if he i' th' blood-siz'd field lay swol'n,
Showing the sun his teeth, grinning at the moon,
What you would do.

To this prayer Hippolyta offers a consoling answer, and then the third queen turns to Emilia, with the same studied, elaborate, and removed kind of expression used by the other queens. Emilia replies at some length; her speeches are deliberately longer than those of Theseus and Hippolyta so that, being the heroine of the play, she may appear more prominent at the opening. When she has finished, Theseus starts abruptly out of his trance, and in a peremptory tone orders the wedding procession to proceed:

Forward to th' temple! Leave not out a jot
O' th' sacred ceremony.

But the queens delay him still further, in their eloquent speeches begging him to bury their slain husbands. At first Theseus continues to hold out against them:

Why, good ladies,
This is a service, whereto I am going,
Greater than any war. It more imports me
Than all the actions that I have foregone
Or futurely can cope.

But they persuade him still. The rhythm of the first queen's speech on this occasion is again the rhythm of invocation, although she speaks in a different tone, and from a different angle than before. She still, however, describes experience contemplated from a distance; as, in a sense, the writing of Fletcher describes experience contemplated from a distance. But, as we shall see, the distance from which Fletcher contemplates is very different in altitude, and in direction, from Shakespeare's:

1. *Queen:* The more proclaiming
Our suit shall be neglected. When her arms,
Able to lock Jove from a synod, shall
By warranting moonlight corslet thee—O, when
Her twinning cherries shall their sweetness fall
Upon thy tasteful lips, what wilt thou think
Of rotten kings or blubber'd queens? What care
For what thou feel'st not? What thou feel'st being able
To make Mars spurn his drum. O, if thou couch
But one night with her, every hour in't will
Take hostage of thee for a hundred, and
Thou shalt remember nothing more than what
That banquet bids thee to![6]

Finally, Theseus succumbs; he will postpone his marriage and revenge the queens, and he ends by saying—it is the third example in this scene of an un-electrified platitude:

As we are men,
Thus should we do. Being sensually subdu'd,
We lose our human title. Good cheer, ladies!
Now turn we towards your comforts.

6 This speech illustrates a peculiarity of the Shakespearean parts of the play: the number of invocatory "O's." In this first scene, of 234 lines, there are 12 of such "O's"—a minor reflection of the general tone. In a typical Fletcher scene, II, ii, of 277 lines, there are only 4 invocatory "O's."

III

I have discussed the opening scene of this play at length because it has several striking characteristics. In the first place, it represents a great elaboration, on Shakespeare's part, of his source. Chaucer describes the supplication of the queens and Theseus' determination to help them in about eighty lines; there is no suggestion that they are appealing to Theseus on his marriage day, and there is no suggestion of the conflict in his mind between love and war. Chaucer is too anxious to get started on the story of Palamon and Arcite to waste time on any but the most necessary of preliminaries. Yet Shakespeare makes a great deal of the preliminaries: each of the queens speaks, each of the main characters responds, and there is an obvious, if incomplete, expression of a conflict in values. The value of war and the value of love, the standard of action and the standard of emotion, which, as Mr. Wilson Knight has observed, play so large a part in Shakespeare's work, are here, in the mind of Theseus, deliberately presented, and yet, dramatically speaking, they are the ghosts of themselves. For Theseus' queerly abstracted conflict between the joys of marriage and his responsibility to the queens has no real bearing on the course of the main events in the play, and the decisions he comes to are abrupt, apart from the action—if we can call it "action." It is as if Shakespeare had written the scene half automatically, recalling the kind of conflict which he had described earlier with passion and penetration, but which he was now using as merely the most convenient means for dramatic exposition; a remembered technique, with the emotional content forgotten. Technically, as I have tried to suggest, the scene is admirable. The first queen is set against Theseus, the second queen is set against Hippolyta, the third queen is set against Emilia: each responds to each, in a mounting rhythm, in a verbal counterpoint, like voices in a chorale; it is planned, deliberate and controlled. But it is not the technique of *Julius Caesar* or of *Lear*. If we imagine the scene on the stage, we see gesture rather than action. Drama has returned to its womb, and has once more become ritual. It is the dramatic writing of a man to whom action has lost importance, but who is trying to recapture, for the immediate necessity of writing a money-making play, the devices and the lost enthusiasm of a forgotten intensity. It is the writing of a man who has come out on the other side of human experience, and who, looking back, can no longer be interested in what he has once seen so vividly and so passionately felt. The figures still struggling in the *selva oscura* are the figures of a pageant or a dream.

IV

Fletcher's share in the play is very different. The emotional tone is not that of a man who has been *through* experience: it is the tone of a man who has never got there. His rhythms are the rhythms, not of remote or incandescent contemplation, but of the easy lullaby of sentiment. We are not abstracted or lifted up; there is no incantation. Instead we are soothed, smoothed, softened. And yet, theatrically speaking, it is a great success; and only when we reflect do we realize that we are in so much smaller a dimension. Act II, scene ii, is a good example of Fletcher's ability.

Arcite and Palamon are in prison, having been captured by Theseus in his avenging war against Creon. They enter on the upper stage and begin discussing their situation. They are in prison for life, and all activity is over. "Here we are," says Arcite,

> And here the graces of our youth must wither
> Like a too timely spring. Here age must find us,
> And, which is heaviest, Palamon, unmarried.
> The sweet embraces of a loving wife,
> Loaden with kisses, arm'd with thousand Cupids,
> Shall never clasp our necks; no issue know us;
> No figures of ourselves shall we ev'r see
> To glad our age, and like young eagles teach 'em
> Boldly to gaze against bright arms, and say
> "Remember what your fathers were, and conquer!"

The technique and the tone are typically Fletcherian: the great majority of the lines end with an extra syllable; there are few of those heavy pauses in the middle of the lines which produce in Shakespeare's latest style so rich and full an effect; all is languorous and gentle. The tone, like Shakespeare's tone, might be called remote. Yet it is remote in a very different sense. If we compare what Arcite says about "The sweet embraces of a loving wife" with what Theseus has said earlier to the first queen (I, i, 59 ff.), we realize that what weakens Fletcher's writing is that he is describing something that has never happened. It is one of his favorite emotional tricks to project us into a fanciful future, and then to melt us by telling us what may go on there in relation to the character who is speaking. For example, in *Henry VIII* (III, i, 431 ff.) Wolsey speaks to Cromwell:

> And when I am forgotten, as I shall be,
> And sleep in dull cold marble, where no mention
> Of me more must be heard of, say I taught thee—
> Say Wolsey, that once trod the ways of glory
> And sounded all the depths and shoals of honor,
> Found thee a way (out of his wrack) to rise in—

There are a thousand examples of this kind of writing in Fletcher's plays; this emotional tone is perhaps the surest mark of his style, and the falling lines, with their lingering feminine endings, fit it very appropriately. But, as far as I am aware, it never occurs in Shakespeare; Shakespeare has too strong a sense of reality. To tease our feelings by summoning up melancholy pictures of how people are going to behave when a character is dead, or to lament the loss of imaginary blessings, are not devices which occur to his more robust and unsentimental temperament. Fletcher, on the other hand, could not write an emotional scene without using them. They make an immediate effect on the audience, and we are moved by a vague feeling of rather complacent pity as we listen. Such scenes seem to have caught the Elizabethan ear at once, and to have held the affection of audiences for nearly a century. The emotion is so much easier than Shakespeare's; it is no trouble to understand because there is no mental toughness or gristle combined with it. Fletcher's share in *The Two Noble Kinsmen* is, as I have said, much better theater than Shakespeare's.[7]

The rest of this particular scene is very cleverly written. Palamon and Arcite console themselves for the prospect of their long imprisonment by thinking that they will at least have each other, and they work themselves up to vows of mutual affection:

> *Palamon:* Is there record of any two that lov'd
> Better than we do, Arcite?
> *Arcite:* Sure, there cannot.
> *Palamon:* I do not think it possible our friendship
> Should ever leave us.
> *Arcite:* Till our deaths, it cannot.

[7] Once we become aware of this emotional habit of Fletcher's we can detect his hand where we might otherwise be uncertain. For example, the beginning of Act III, scene i, is unquestionably Shakespeare's; style, meter, tone, and vocabulary are firmly his. Yet all these begin to weaken as the scene progresses. We move from incantation to action, and Fletcher's hand becomes unmistakable. Palamon (ll. 72 ff.) asks Arcite to fight with him for Emily, and the first thing he does is to project himself into an imaginary future, producing in the rhythm of the lines and in the minds of the audience that sentimental, unreal, and melting sensation which I have just tried to describe.

> Give me a sword . . .
> and do but say
> That Emily is thine, I will forgive
> That trespass thou hast done me, yea, my life,
> If then thou carry't; and brave souls in shades,
> That have died manly, which will seek of me
> Some news from earth, they shall get none but this—
> That thou art brave and noble.

Another sure sign of Fletcher's hand in the end of this scene is the way Palamon and Arcite use each other's names when they address each other:

> *Palamon:* O you heavens, dares any
> So noble bear a guilty business? None
> But only Arcite; therefore none but Arcite
> In this kind is so bold.
> *Arcite:* Sweet Palamon

There is something soft about this; it is the equivalent, in poetry, of the action of a man who, having mortally offended his wife, thinks that he can make up to her by stroking her cheek.

But then Emilia, who is to be the cause of their dissension, appears below with the waiting woman, talking about flowers. Palamon sees her first and stands transfixed. Arcite tries to urge him on to further protestations of friendship, but he can get nothing out of him, so he too looks down at the garden, is hopelessly smitten, and a very deftly managed series of interwoven short speeches follows, in which Arcite and Palamon comment on the beauty of Emilia while she and her woman go on talking about flowers. When Emilia leaves it is all over with the friendship between Palamon and Arcite; they are both in love up to the ears, they can think of nothing but Emilia, and the scene comes to an end with their mutual recriminations, an ironic and successful contrast to their feelings toward each other at the beginning.

This smooth and accomplished action is almost the reverse of Shakespeare's static pageantry. And the way Fletcher describes his two heroes is very different from the way Shakespeare had described them earlier, the first time we see them, in Act I, scene ii. The words Shakespeare puts into their mouths are not the words of sentiment; Palamon and Arcite are not like two graceful saplings, swaying in unison in a sentimental moonlight. They are a pair of moralists, with a strong sense of evil and a strong sense of indignation at the corruption engendered in Thebes by their wicked uncle, Creon. What Fletcher tells us about them bears only on the immediate dramatic situation; they say no more than is necessary to put the particular scene across. But Shakespeare reveals their characters by their attitude to a general situation, and we are in a different, a wider world of perception. His Arcite and Palamon talk as follows:

Arcite: Dear Palamon, dearer in love than blood,
And our prime cousin, yet unhard'ned in
The crimes of nature—let us leave the city
Thebes and the temptings in't before we further
Sully our gloss of youth.
And here to keep in abstinence we shame
As in incontinence; for not to swim

I' th' aid o' th' current were almost to sink,
At least to frustrate striving; and to follow
The common stream, 'twould bring us to an eddy
Where we should turn or drown; if labor through,
Our gain but life and weakness.

Palamon: Your advice
Is cried up with example. What strange ruins,
Since first we went to school, may we perceive
Walking in Thebes!

He goes on to describe how the soldier, dedicated to Mars, receives nothing but scars and rags for his reward. Arcite widens the application: in Thebes there is nothing good; it is a place

where every evil
Hath a good color; where ev'ry seeming good's
A certain evil; where not to be ev'n jump
As they are here, were to be strangers, and
Such things to be mere monsters.

They talk in this style for some eighty lines, and it is only when they are told that they must fight for Thebes against Theseus that their sense of duty makes them cast off their bitter mood and find a solution in action.

Now this is a very extraordinary way of presenting a pair of romantic lovers to an audience. To be sure, it shows them as highly idealistic, but we have only to think of Romeo to realize that what they are being idealistic about has nothing to do with what is to be their predominant emotion in the action that follows. Romeo, when he is first presented to us, is an idealist; but he is a positive idealist in the sense that he is in a dream of illusion, and that his waking is the fulfillment of his dream. Palamon and Arcite are *dis*-illusioned; their view of the world they live in may be said to begin where the view of Shakespeare's tragic heroes leaves off: in an awareness of the evil which conditions their existence. Their speeches are haunted by the ghost of Timon. But Timon looks back at Athens and curses its vileness as a result of a disillusionment which has been led up to by the previous action.

Palamon and Arcite look back in disgust at Thebes before we have been given any satisfactory reason for their disgust. One cannot help wondering why Shakespeare should have presented them in so remarkable a fashion. Was he relying, in a fatigued or bored state of mind, on a means of arousing interest which he had found useful in the past, and was here repeating half automatically because he could not think of anything else? This explanation is borne out by the fact that Palamon and Arcite use, in their disgusted speeches, a rather stock set of images and comparisons. The hard lot of the unrewarded soldier is an Elizabethan commonplace; so is the foolishness, described by Palamon, of contemporary fashions in dress; and the shocking difference between what seems and what is, which Palamon emphasizes in the speech I have just quoted, is one of the main themes in all of Shakespeare's mature work. In other words, just as we find, in the first scene of the play, the almost ritualistic manipulation of the ghosts of dramatic action, so we find here the ghosts of familiar themes, used as convenient means for exposition, but lacking, in the long run, the reality of conviction. Shakespeare, we feel, is looking back on what once mattered, but which matters no longer, and his description of the emotions of Palamon and Arcite about the world they live in does not quite convince us because it no longer seems necessary to Shakespeare to have those emotions explained: they can, undramatically, be taken for granted.

V

Yet the composition of Shakespeare's opening scenes consists by no means merely of repetitions or echoes of his earlier emotional grooves and dramatic triumphs; these scenes emphasize a positive value of their own—the value of loyalty. The queens are passionately loyal to their dead husbands; Palamon and Arcite, "dearer in love than blood," share a common view of their debased country; the intimate friendship of Theseus and Pirithous is richly described (I, iii, 41):

Their knot of love
Tied, weav'd, entangled, with so true, so long,
And with a finger of so deep a cunning,
May be outworn, never undone—

and the first (if only) human, individualizing fact we learn about Emilia is that she once had an intimate friendship of a similar kind with a girl named Flavina who died at the age of eleven.[8] "You talk," says Emilia (I, iii, 55 ff.):

You talk of Pirithous' and Theseus' love.
Theirs has more ground, is more maturely season'd,
More buckled with strong judgment, and their needs
The one of th' other may be said to water
Their intertangled roots of love, but I
And she I sigh and spoke of, were things innocent,
Lov'd for we did, and like the elements
That know not what nor why, yet do effect
Rare issues by their operance, our souls
Did so to one another. What she lik'd
Was then of me approv'd; what not, condemn'd,
No more arraignment. The flow'r that I would pluck
And put between my breasts (then but beginning
To swell about the blossom) she would long
Till she had such another, and commit
To the like innocent cradle, where, phoenix-like,
They died in perfume. On my head no toy
But was her pattern; her affections (pretty,
Though happily her careless wear) I followed
For my most serious decking. Had mine ear
Stol'n some new air, or at adventure humm'd one
From musical coinage, why, it was a note
Whereon her spirits would sojourn (rather dwell on)
And sing it in her slumbers.

This charming, this delicious speech crowns the theme of friendship, already so clearly illustrated by Theseus and Pirithous and by Palamon and Arcite. But the theme is to be disrupted by the subsequent behavior of Palamon and Arcite; that is one reason why it is so strongly emphasized at the start. One of Shakespeare's favorite dramatic de-

[8] There is no hint of this in Chaucer.

vices in his mature work is to establish a set of values and then to show how it is violated by the individual action which follows. He does this in *Troilus and Cressida* through the speeches of Ulysses; he does it more indirectly in *Hamlet, Othello,* and *King Lear;* he clearly had it in mind when planning *The Two Noble Kinsmen.* But Fletcher, tied by temperament to the immediate and the obviously practical, was not concerned with such matters, and, when he took charge of the situation after the first act, the wider implication, the fundamental and general contrast which the story, in Shakespeare's eyes, could be seen to illustrate, disappeared. It was not appropriate to Fletcher's romantic and myopic vision.

That Shakespeare should have so strongly emphasized the theme of union through friendship is as characteristic of the tone of his final period as his habit of breaking the thought in the middle of a line is characteristic of his final metrical technique. It is not, to be sure, quite the same as the theme of reconciliation, which we find in all the plays from *Pericles* on. But it is the state of mind which occurs *after* reconciliation. And as the vile picture of Thebes given by Palamon and Arcite is different, not being the result of previous action, from the picture of Athens given by Timon, so Emilia's account of her friendship with Flavina is different from the reunion of Pericles with Marina or of Leontes with Hermione. The union of Emilia and Flavina did not come about as the result of a dramatic process. It just was. Such writing, as I have already observed, is the writing of a man who has been *through* experience, for whom process and movement are over, who does not care about how or why things happen, as long as they are. In such a state of mind one may plan dramatic action, in a routine, habitual way, but one cannot put one's heart into making it exciting. Another desire is much more important; the desire to contemplate—not turmoil, or contrast, or fraction—which are dreams—but the beauty of the individual life itself, in a garland of flowers.

O queen Emilia,

Fresher than May, sweeter
Than her gold buttons on the boughs or all
Th' enamel'd knacks o' th' mead or garden! Yea,
We challenge too the bank of any nymph,
That makes the stream seem flowers! Thou, O jewel
O' th' wood, o' the world, hast likewise bless'd a place
With thy sole presence.[9]

There is some uncertainty in the phrasing of Arcite's speech; it has not the perfection of Perdita's flower speeches in *The Winter's Tale;* but the caught breath, the broken wonder; the magical invocation are still here, trembling through a shattered rhythm into words.

VI

There is one episode in the story of Arcite and Palamon which, unlike the previous parts, definitely demands the tone of invocation; it is the episode where the two lovers pray respectively to Mars and Venus for success in their combat. The scene, as was to be expected, is obviously by Shakespeare; it was his meat exactly, and he does it handsomely, in a manner that repays close attention. The first speech (V, i, 49 ff.), that of Arcite before the altar of Mars, is a dignified and exalted piece of writing, and the familiar invocatory rhythms of Shakespeare's latest style are obvious throughout:

O great corrector of enormous times,
Shaker of o'er-rank states, thou grand decider
Of dusty and old titles, that heal'st with blood
The earth when it is sick, and cur'st the world
O' th' plurisy of people! I do take
Thy signs auspiciously, and in thy name
To my design march boldly.

This is more or less what we would expect in an address to Mars, and it is not unlike what we find in Chaucer. But when Arcite leaves the stage, and Palamon takes his place to pray to Venus, we have a very remarkable speech

9 III,i,4ff

indeed, so remarkable that it is odd that no one seems to have noticed its peculiarity. It is not in the least like the speech made by Chaucer's Palamon, who praises the goddess, and swears to serve her forever if she will give him Emily. Chaucer's Palamon is devoted and charming, his words are tender and youthful, full of graceful pleading. Shakespeare's Palamon addresses Venus in a different manner—I give the long speech entire:

> Hail, sovereign queen of secrets, who hast power
> To call the fiercest tyrant from his rage,
> And weep unto a girl; that hast the might,
> Even with an eye-glance, to choke Mars's drum
> And turn th' alarm to whispers; that canst make
> A cripple flourish with his crutch, and cure him
> Before Apollo; that mayst force the king
> To be his subject's vassal, and induce
> Stale gravity to dance; the polled bachelor—
> Whose youth, like wanton boys through bonfires,
> Have skipp'd thy flame—at seventy thou canst catch,
> And make him, to the scorn of his hoarse throat,
> Abuse young lays of love. What godlike power
> Hast thou not power upon? To Phoebus thou
> Add'st flames, hotter than his: the heavenly fires
> Did scorch his mortal son, thine him. The huntress
> All moist and cold, some say, began to throw
> Her bow away, and sigh. Take to thy grace
> Me thy vowed soldier, who do bear thy yoke
> As 'twere a wreath of roses, yet is heavier
> Than lead itself, stings more than nettles. I
> Have never been foul-mouth'd against thy law;
> Nev'r reveal'd secret, for I knew none—would not,
> Had I learn'd all that were. I never practic'd
> Upon man's wife, nor would the libels read
> Of liberal wits. I never at great feasts
> Sought to betray a beauty, but have blush'd
> At simp'ring sirs that did. I have been harsh
> To large confessors, and have hotly ask'd them
> If they had mothers. I had one, a woman,
> And women 'twere they wrong'd. I knew a man
> Of eighty winters—this I told them—who

A lass of fourteen brided. 'Twas thy power
To put life into dust. The aged cramp
Had screw'd his square foot round,
The gout had knit his fingers into knots,
Torturing convulsions from his globy eyes
Had almost drawn their spheres, that what was life
In him seem'd torture. This anatomy
Had by his young fair fere a boy, and I
Believ'd it was his, for she swore it was,
And who would not believe her? Brief, I am
To those that prate and have done, no companion;
To those that boast and have not, a defier;
To those that would and cannot, a rejoicer.
Yea, him I do not love that tells close offices
The foulest way, nor names concealments in
The boldest language. Such a one I am,
And vow that lover never yet made sigh
Truer than I. O, then, most soft-sweet goddess,
Give me the victory of this question, which
Is true love's merit, and bless me with a sign
Of thy great pleasure.

Here music is heard and doves are seen to flutter. They fall again upon their faces, then on their knees.

O thou that from eleven to ninety reign'st
In mortal bosoms, whose chase is this world,
And we in herds thy game, I give thee thanks
For this fair token; which being laid unto
Mine innocent true heart, arms in assurance
My body to this business.

I have quoted the whole of this speech because its peculiarity can only be fully seen if all of it is taken into account. It is divided into three main parts: the first describes the effects of Venus, the second describes the purity of Palamon, the third is a final invocation in (as usual) generalized terms, which unites the other two. But what extraordinary images, for a prayer to Venus, the speech contains! We are first told that love affects a man of seventy, then that it affects a man of eighty, and finally that it affects a man of ninety. The emphasis is, throughout, on old age, and the result is that what impresses us, after reading or hearing the speech, is not the power of love, but a series of images of decay. The speech accomplishes the reverse of what is intended; the negatives dominate the positives; it is, as it were, poetry inside out. The cripple and his crutch, the "polled bachelor" of seventy, his hoarse throat abusing "young lays of love," the gouty old man of eighty with his foot screwed around and his eyes convulsed—such are the vivid pictures that remain in the mind. And even if we think of these ancient wrecks as being rejuvenated by love, the process is not an agreeable one. The flames of love scorch more than the sun; the yoke of love, while it seems like a wreath of roses, is actually heavier than lead and stings more than nettles. And as Palamon goes on to describe his own purity, and his avoidance of the way society in general treats love, we notice, not his avoidance, but rather the things he avoids—the liberal wits, the simp'ring sirs, and the large confessors. So that when, toward the end of the speech, Palamon calls Venus a "soft-sweet goddess," we are surprised; hardly anything he has previously told us about her has prepared us for such a description.

This speech is interesting in yet another fashion. For it is a mixture, not quite fused, of the two moods which we have already seen as predominant in Shakespeare's part of the play: the invocatory mood of Arcite's speech in Act III to the imagined Emilia, and the satirical mood of Arcite's and Palamon's speeches about Thebes in Act I. As it begins we are once more caught by the echo of that indescribable slow magic, that rich exalted wonder of the final style:

> who hast power
> To call the fiercest tyrant from his rage,
> And weep unto a girl.

But it is not sustained, and Shakespeare calls back, with a good deal of inappropriateness, the ghost of his almost forgotten mood of disillusionment to fill out the remaining lines. He does not seem, in other words, to be interested in writing for Palamon the kind of speech which Palamon —eager and ardent with young love—should speak. Writing rapidly, as it is likely he did, to get a job finished, he relied on habitual tones and habitual rhythms, using the artifice of long practice without the intensity of the appropriately dramatic emotion.

But Emilia's speech to Diana, which follows Palamon's to Venus, is eminently appropriate, and it is significant that Emilia must pray "bride-habited, but maiden-hearted," and without passion to her "sacred, silver mistress." Hers is a prayer with which reality has nothing to do, for it cannot, under the circumstances, be granted. And here Shakespeare's words fit their occasion admirably:

> O sacred, shadowy, cold, and constant queen,
> Abandoner of revels, mute, contemplative,
> Sweet, solitary, white as chaste, and pure
> As wind-fann'd snow . . . .
> I here, thy priest,
> Am humbled fore thine altar.

VII

The rest of the play—the subplot of the jailer's daughter who goes mad for love of Palamon, the meeting of Palamon and Arcite in the forest, the entertainment given to Theseus by the yokels, and the denouement—all this moves competently and swiftly; situation rather than character is emphasized, the style is clear and easily understood, and it was doubtless entirely successful on the stage. Now and then we recognize Shakespeare's hand, as in the extremely vivid account, in the last scene, of the rearing horse that killed Arcite, but most of it is Fletcher's, and, for our present purposes, not worth careful analysis.

The Shakespearean parts of the play, however—as I hope I have shown—*are* worth careful analysis, for they illustrate what was happening to Shakespeare at the end of his career more clearly than anything in *The Tempest* or *Henry VIII*. The most striking fact that stands out is that Shakespeare seems no longer to be interested in process or in change and hence is no longer interested in the development of character. Whether he wrote the lines or not, what is apparently his state of mind is summed up in Theseus' address to the gods in the last speech of the play:

> Let us be thankful
> For that which is, and with you leave dispute
> That are above our question.

And in this acceptance of "that which is," there is a mingling—it is of course inevitable—of an awareness of good and an awareness of evil, the one felt almost ecstatically, though never, as in *The Winter's Tale,* entirely so; the other felt as being continually in the background, though never pressing into the immediate situation. The speeches of Theseus, of the queens, of Palamon and Arcite are contemplative, not active, and what change occurs in the main characters is very superficial. The story itself, to be sure, demands remoteness, a pageant-like treatment, and a slighting of differences in character, but though Shakespeare must obviously have seen this, his seeing it does not satisfactorily account for the almost unnecessary *stasis* of his presentation. Nor does it account for the incompleteness of much of the actual writing. Professor Tucker Brooke is right when he speaks of each act, scene, or verse falling "just short of what it should be." Professor Brooke thinks that this means that Shakespeare could not have written those acts or scenes, but that is not a necessary conclusion. It means more probably that he was no longer fully interested in what he was doing. The style of the Shakespearean parts of *The Two Noble Kinsmen,* as Palamon's address to Venus so clearly shows, is the style of an old man, a style that reveals, to be sure, an expert technique in handling words, and a mastery of incantation, but which has little concern for the tricks that would please an audience, and which is, in a sense, dramatically stagnant. After studying Shakespeare's part of the play, we feel that his return to Stratford and his abandonment of writing were almost inevitable. In fact, it is possible to wonder whether his retirement was entirely voluntary. The shareholders in the Globe knew what the public wanted; the differences between Shakespeare's slow pageantry—its faded, difficult magnificence, its elaborate remoteness—and Fletcher's easy, accomplished manipulation, were clear enough to anyone with an eye on the box office: Fletcher's style was obviously much better adapted to the increasing superficiality of the popular taste. One can even imagine a deputation calling on Shakespeare—it is not an agreeable thought—to suggest that, all things considered, it would be wise to go home and write no more.

PHILIP EDWARDS

On the Design of "The Two Noble Kinsmen"

I suspect that most readers of *The Two Noble Kinsmen* have at some time felt reluctant to acknowledge that Shakespeare had much to do with the play. No doubt they are put off because the work is so undramatic: the action, particularly in the "Shakespearian" first and last acts, is sluggish, and the whole plot, twice boiled down from Boccaccio's epic, remains essentially narrative; the characters lack the interest of real individuality, and, though a great deal happens to them, they do not grow, or alter, in a Shakespearian way. Yet we are prepared to accept much that is similarly "undramatic" as Shakespeare's, in the work of the five years or so between the time he engaged himself with *Pericles* and the writing of *The Two Noble Kinsmen,* probably in 1613. Again, the quality of the verse perplexes readers in search of Shakespeare; there is something wordy in those long speeches which fail to advance the action, something elaborate and self-conscious in the weighing of the rhythms, in the complex network of syntax, in the bold images; there seems a tendency to "write it up":

O, when
Her twining cherries shall their sweetness fall
Upon thy tasteful lips, what wilt thou think
Of rotten kings or blubber'd queens?
(I.i.177–80)

From *A Review of English Literature,* V (1964), 89–105. Reprinted by permission of the author and the editor.

When we come across a passage like that, we may feel some sympathy with Tucker Brooke: "Always there is the strong Shakespearian reminiscence, but nowhere quite the full and perfect reality that we could swear to."[1] But it is not really debatable that the verse of part of *The Two Noble Kinsmen* is Shakespeare's, the rest being Fletcher's. Theodore Spencer, Marco Mincoff and Kenneth Muir have all written excellent essays, approaching the verse along different paths, which strongly back up the old evidence of the metrical tests.[2] The arguments for Shakespeare do not need rehearsing here.

The reluctance to believe that *The Two Noble Kinsmen,* even in part, is a product of Shakespeare's mind and art really comes, not from the feeling that the play is undramatic or that the verse cannot be his, but from a conviction that the play is inane. It is worth quoting Tucker Brooke again: "It contains no spark of psychological insight or philosophy of life which can in sober moments be thought either worthy of the mature Shakespeare or even suggestive of him."[3] I am sure that it is the seeming want of "idea" in the play that makes readers find fault with verse and dramaturgy which they would be content to accept as Shakespeare's if the play were, to them, more intellectually respectable. That rich fund of suggestion which sets us on to our theories of what Shakespeare *meant* by the Romances certainly seems absent from the play. Even Spencer, acknowledging Shakespeare's hand, and admiring so much in the verse, saw the Shakespeare of this play as an old man who had been *through* experience, no longer interested in process or in change, not caring how or why things happen, but speaking of "that which is"; and, working rapidly to get a job finished, giving us tired writing, the muscles behind it slack and old. So re-

1 *The Shakespeare Apocrypha* (1908), p. xliii.

2 *Modern Philology,* xxxvi (1938–9), pp. 255–76; *English Studies,* xxxiii (1952), pp. 97–115; *Shakespeare as Collaborator* (1960), pp. 98–147. See also A. Hart, *Shakespeare and the Homilies* (1934), pp. 242–256. Putting aside some scenes about which there *could* be debate, the Shakespearian portions are I.i–iii, III.i, V.i, iii, iv.

3 *op. cit.*, p. xliii.

mote and so dramatically stagnant is the result, in Spencer's view, that he imagines a deputation calling on Shakespeare to suggest that "it would be wise to go home and write no more."

It seems to me that there is much more purposeful thought in the play than Brooke and Spencer saw; we really need not be ashamed of it. It is strange that the pensiveness of the play, in the first and last acts, has not aroused more interest: a pensiveness which, through those slow-moving scenes, hatches an "idea" bewildering enough but subtle (however unsubtle it seems in the simplifications of one's commentary). So far as I know, Clifford Leech has been the only critic to remark on the curious division of view which belittles the love in the play, and on the insistence that "mature" love means abandoning something more worthwhile.[4] Though Leech finds a contradiction where I find consistency, and though the "totality of its effect" speaks to him of Fletcher and to me of Shakespeare, it was from his remarks that this small exploration began.

Spencer noted the strangeness of Palamon's address to Venus (V.i.77–136) in the ceremonial scene of prayer to the gods for divine aid before the great tournament. As seen by Palamon, the power of Venus is a power that changes her victims' natures, overturns them rather, that grips them the more the older they get, making them more and more ludicrous and grotesque. As the apparently sincere tribute to the might of Venus continues, the operations of almighty love seem more and more disgusting. The invocation is fairly harmless:

> Hail, sovereign queen of secrets, who hast power
> To call the fiercest tyrant from his rage,
> And weep unto a girl . . .

But before we reach the parallel invocation, "that may'st force the king/To be his subject's vassal," we hear the words, "that canst make/A cripple flourish with his crutch"; it is in this manner the address goes on:

4 *The John Fletcher Plays* (1962), pp. 147–50.

the poll'd bachelor—
Whose youth, like wanton boys through bonfires,
Have skipt thy flame—at seventy thou canst catch,
And make him, to the scorn of his hoarse throat,
Abuse young lays of love.

The "tributes" grow more satirical as the man of eighty takes the place of the man of seventy:

I knew a man
Of eighty winters—this I told them—who
A lass of fourteen brided: 'twas thy power
To put life into dust; the aged cramp
Had screw'd his square foot round,
The gout had knit his fingers into knots,
Torturing convulsions from his globy eyes
Had almost drawn their spheres, that what was life
In him seem'd torture: this anatomy
Had by his young fair fere a boy, and I
Believ'd it was his, for she swore it was,
And who would not believe her?

This emblem of the power of love is used in the address as a defense of the chastity of wives! Eighty does not see the end of Venus' power:

O thou that from eleven to ninety reign'st
In mortal bosoms, whose chase is this world,
And we in herds thy game . . .

The long speech emphasizes not only the power of love to transform and to make the deformed more deformed, but also the surreptitious and clandestine. It is the close chamber work that is described, even if Palamon professes to reject it. As Muir mildly sums up, "The pleasanter side of love is not represented." Palamon, one of the victims of Venus, describes himself as:

Thy vow'd soldier, who do bear thy yoke
As 'twere a wreath of roses, yet is heavier
Than lead itself, stings more than nettles.

Of this strange speech, Muir says it is absurd to think that Shakespeare "was putting his own personal sentiments into Palamon's mouth," and remarks that "Shakespeare was in danger of shattering the conventions in which the play was written." Muir makes a good justification of the speech in terms of Palamon's disillusioned temperament, the suffering and loss he has undergone through his love for Emilia, and the pains he has still to undergo—either to win the tournament and so cause the death of his blood-brother, Arcite, or else to lose, and so be executed. But perhaps Palamon is not meant to recognize the drift of his own speech; the cynicism *may* be not his, but Shakespeare's; I think we must consider what the conventions of this play are, before we say that this speech risks shattering them.

Both Spencer and Muir say that this address to Venus does not at all resemble the corresponding speech in Chaucer's *The Knight's Tale* (the source of the play). True, but in Chaucer's poem the walls of Venus' temple are painted with all the miseries of love:

> First in the temple of Venus maystow se,
> Wroght on the wal, ful pitous to biholde,
> The broken slepes, and the sikes colde,
> The sacred teeris, and the waymentynge,
> The firy strokes of the desirynge
> That loves servantz in this lyf enduren . . .
> (1918–23)[5]

The famous victims of love are also there, Solomon, Hercules, Medea and so on:

> Thus may ye seen that wysdom ne richesse,
> Beautee ne sleighte, strengthe ne hardyesse,
> Ne may with Venus holde champartie,
> For as hir list the world than may she gye.
> Lo, alle thise folk so caught were in hir las,
> Til they for wo ful ofte seyde 'allas!'

5 Quotations from *The Knight's Tale* are taken from *The Works of Geoffrey Chaucer*, ed. F. N. Robinson, Cambridge, Mass. (1957).

Suffiseth heere ensamples oon or two,
And though I koude rekene a thousand mo.
(1947–54)

Chaucer's lines are an effective shortening of Boccaccio, and are central to his story. There is a corresponding mood in Theseus' derisive words as he finds the cousins, Arcite and Palamon, fighting to the death over a woman they have never spoken to, who knows nothing of their desire:

Se how they blede! be they noght wel arrayed?
Thus hath thir lord, the god of love, ypayed
Hir wages and hir fees for hir servyse! (1801–03)

The Knight's Tale is a magnificent study of human helplessness, of men and women floundering after happiness, but, being entirely at the mercy of love, of the mighty of this world, and of the gods—or destiny—or fortune, moving steadily into wretchedness. The image which comes out on top is the Boethian image of the drunken man: every step he takes toward his house is a step away from it.

Infinite harmes been in this mateere.
We witen nat what thing we preyen heere.
We faren as he that dronke is as a mouse.
A dronke man woot wel he hath an hous,
But he noot which the righte wey is thider;
And to a dronke man the wey is slider.
And certes, in this world so faren we;
We seken faste after felicitee,
But we goon wrong ful often, trewely. (1259–67)

In the Prologue to *The Two Noble Kinsmen* is a tribute to Chaucer, the seriousness of which is perhaps obscured by the facetious tone of the opening lines and the conventional humility of the plea for sympathy. Twenty of the thirty-two lines keep Chaucer in mind:

> Chaucer, of all admir'd, the story gives;
> There constant to eternity it lives . . .
> . . . to say truth, it were an endless thing,
> And too ambitious, to aspire to him,
> Weak as we are, and almost breathless swim
> In this deep water.

It seems to me that Shakespeare was fired by the dark Chaucerian vision of what happened to two men pursuing their desires, or being pursued by their desires. Emulation would be the wrong word—the Prologue discounts it—but he had his own dark vision to present of men moving into their future as through a thick fog, and so slight a play as *The Two Noble Kinsmen* is made much less slight when we understand this vision, and realize that Palamon's address to Venus is the center of the play. And what of Fletcher? According to Spencer, Fletcher was congenitally incapable of appreciating the significance of the Shakespearian scenes. Certainly, Shakespeare's grand design sags when Fletcher takes over; but that he knew the design and tried to fill it out is inescapable.

To take simple matters first, the address to Venus is at all times relevant to the subplot of the jailer's daughter. She falls in love with Palamon, who is quite unaware of her passion during the whole of its wretched course. She acts to bind him to her, secretly letting him out of prison, but her action has no effect. She goes mad, her mind filled with images of sexual pleasure, and in the end she is brought towards a cure by her former wooer's pretending to be Palamon and going to bed with her. "For all the genuineness of her love," says Leech, "it is not proof against substitution," and he notices here an important link with Emilia's acquiescence in either of the two cousins as a husband. This we must look at later: at the moment, it is enough to say that the story of the jailer's daughter gives a particularly unpleasant picture of what happens when sexual desire gets hold of one:

> What pushes are we wenches driven to
> When fifteen once has found us! (II.iv.6–7)

The idea of the play is very carefully worked into those first three slow-moving scenes which are unquestionably Shakespeare's. In the first scene, the solemn wedding of Theseus and Hippolyta is interrupted by the three widowed queens, who beseech Theseus to break off the wedding and go to war against Creon at Thebes; in the end he consents.

It is clear that Shakespeare is taking trouble to show us the marriage as a momentous change in Theseus' life. Before a word is spoken, there is the solemn ritual of the wedding procession, described in an elaborate stage direction. As the queens plead that he should turn aside, he insists on the magnitude of his resolution:

> This is a service, whereto I am going,
> Greater than any war;[6] it more imports me
> Than all the actions that I have foregone
> Or futurely can cope. (I.i.171–74)

More portentously, he calls his marriage

> This grand act of our life, this daring deed
> Of fate in wedlock. (I.i.164–65)

"This daring deed of fate" means, I think, "this deed which dares fate." Theseus sees himself as consciously bringing about, by marriage, an elemental change in his life. The sense of new life in marriage, of metempsychosis, almost, is seen more clearly in the appeal of one of the queens to Hippolyta:

> Honor'd Hippolyta,
> Most dreaded Amazonian, that hast slain
> The scythe-tusk'd boar; that, with thy arm as strong
> As it is white, wast near to make the male
> To thy sex captive, but that this thy lord—
> Born to uphold creation in that honor
> First Nature styl'd it in—shrunk thee into
> The bound thou wast o'erflowing, at once subduing
> Thy force and thy affection . . . (I.i.77–85)

6 'was' in the Quarto.

Here, marriage is more than a change in a manner of life, it is the shaping of a new identity for Hippolyta. The images for this change of personality are startling. In making the Amazonian warrior a bride, Theseus is confirming the order of nature, but it is constriction and not release: "*shrunk* thee into/The bound thou wast o'erflowing"; "*subduing*/Thy force and thy affection." There is no sense here, of course, of crude subjugation; Hippolyta is more than acquiescent in her "shrinking": "never yet," she says, "went I so willing way" (I.i.103–04). Like Theseus, she moves by resolve into a new continent of her life; she moves also into a state which nature demands; but she moves also out of freedom into restriction.

By itself, this passing reference to Hippolyta's past life is nothing, and the images of containment might point only to the commonplace idea of there being truer fulfillment and freedom in the service and subordination of self in marriage. But the reference looks forward to the third scene, which elaborates, disconcertingly, the comparison between the two stages of life, youth and the riper days of marriage. Hippolyta and Emilia mention the former life of Theseus as they discuss the depth of his friendship with Pirithous; Hippolyta appears to excuse herself from the charge of supplanting Pirithous:

> Their knot of love
> Tied, weav'd, entangled, with so true, so long,
> And with a finger of so deep a cunning,
> May be out-worn, never undone. I think
> Theseus cannot be umpire to himself,
> Cleaving his conscience into twain, and doing
> Each side like justice, which he loves best. (I.iii.41–47)

To this, Emilia, all politeness, replies

> Doubtless
> There is a best, and reason has no manners
> To say it is not you.

But her real reply follows at once in her very beautiful

story of her childhood love for Flavina, who died when she was—eleven ("O thou that from eleven to ninety reign'st"). Theirs was a love of absolute spontaneity and absolute Innocence:

> But I,
> And she I sigh and spoke of, were things innocent.
> Lov'd for we did, and like the elements
> That know not what nor why, yet do effect
> Rare issues by their operance, our souls
> Did so to one another: what she lik'd
> Was then of me approv'd; what not, condemn'd,
> No more arraignment; the flower that I would pluck
> And put between my breasts, O—then but beginning
> To swell about the blossom—she would long
> Till she had such another, and commit it
> To the like innocent cradle . . . (I.iii.59–70)

The evocation of a state of happiness and innocent impulse is wonderful, but Emilia calls it

> this rehearsal
> Which, every innocent wots well, comes in
> Like old importment's bastard.

This must mean (as Herford glimpsed) that words can give only the feeblest picture of what was once all-important. Finally, Emilia says she has told her story with this purpose, to show

> That the true love 'tween maid and maid may be
> More than in sex dividual.[7] (I.iii.81–82)

That Hippolyta is shaken by this firm belief that the second stage of life can yield nothing to compare with the spontaneous love of youth is clear from some asperity and assertiveness in her reply, which ends:

> But sure, my sister,

7 "Individual" in the Quarto.

If I were ripe for your persuasion, you
Have said enough to shake me from the arm
Of the all-noble Theseus; for whose fortunes
I will now in and kneel, with great assurance
That we, more than his Pirithous, possess
The high throne in his heart.

Emilia. I am not
Against your faith; yet I continue mine.
(I.iii.90–97)

In these two scenes, there is the clearest presentation of three people conscious of the two major "ways of life" it is necessary to tread, innocence and experience, the impulsive life of youth with its friendship, and the more contained life of marriage. The first stage of each of the three characters has been shown to us: Hippolyta the "o'erflowing" Amazon, Theseus the warrior in firm bands of mutually supporting friendship with Pirithous, and, most fully, Emilia in childish love with Flavina. Theseus and Hippolyta have willingly moved to the second stage which Emilia refuses; she is sure she will not "love any that's call'd man" (I.iii.85). The two ways of life have already been compared in value; the poetic weight is obviously with innocence and Flavina.

The second scene of the play, introducing us to the noble kinsmen and having nothing to do with marriage, can now be seen to interlock. Palamon and Arcite, disgusted by the corruption of Thebes, dedicated to each other and to honor, resolve to break with their past and begin a new life elsewhere; they are prevented by the interruption of the news that Theseus is moving against Thebes; they decide that they must fight for their city in spite of their contempt for Creon. The course of this scene is parallel with the course of the first scene. In that first scene, Theseus, resolved to enter a new life, has to alter his resolution when the queens burst in on his wedding. Both Theseus and the cousins must put a good face on their being diverted from their intentions, justifying themselves as following the only honorable course, but the fact of diversion is underlined very strongly: the *action* of each scene is basically the action of change of cherished purpose under the pressure of unexpected events. It is, I think, a Chaucerian view of the frailty of our determinations which comes across, accompanied by the Chaucerian irony that the protagonists, accepting the change of purpose as being the only honorable choice, usher in the misery which follows. By supporting the queens, Theseus brings war to Thebes; by staying to fight in that war, Palamon and Arcite are captured and so brought to their fatal sight of Emily.

Palamon is troubled by the exigence of things pulling us aside from what we purpose; he knows it is his duty to fight under a man he despises, but will it not damage his soul? he asks:

> Our hands advanc'd before our hearts, what will
> The fall o' the stroke do damage?

Arcite's dour reply is deeper than it looks:

> Let th' event,
> That never-erring arbitrator, tell us
> When we know all ourselves; and let us follow
> The becking of our chance. (I.ii.112–16)

In other words, we shall know enough to comment on the morality of actions only when we see what the actions have led to; from that point of view, Palamon's question is idle, for we cannot judge beforehand the advisability of an action. That his question is idle from a second point of view is implied by Arcite's closing words; which suggest that we have little choice but to follow where chance beckons us. Perhaps I overinterpret, but I set these remarks, comments on the ignorance and ineffectiveness of man, by Theseus' famous remarks at the end of the play:

> O you heavenly charmers,
> What things you make of us! For what we lack
> We laugh, for what we have are sorry; still
> Are children in some kind. Let us be thankful

> For that which is, and with you leave dispute
> That are above our question. (V.iv.131–36)

The first two scenes show the breaking of resolutions; the third scene stops short with a resolution—Emilia's, not to marry. Even if we did not know the story, we might guess the play would go on to tell us how she was proved wrong.

There is one more touch in these first three scenes which must be noted, Hippolyta's disbelief that Emilia will never "love any that's call'd man":

> I must no more believe thee in this point—
> Though in't I know thou dost believe thyself—
> *Than I will trust a sickly appetite,*
> *That loathes even as it longs.* (I.iii.87–90)

We are here introduced to that division of the self, one of Venus' tortures, which has been seen in Palamon's invocation, when he spoke of himself bearing Venus' yoke as though it were a wreath of roses, "yet is heavier than lead itself." We seek what we know destroys. When a resolution means resisting a stage of life on which nature insists, the life of sexual relations, there will be more than unexpected happenings to fight against it, there will be one's own desires. In essence, Emilia's resolve is to live in the past, in the age before puberty; if the rest of the play is to show how vain such a resolve is, it is also going to show good grounds for that nostalgia for innocence.

We move from the first act with the themes of the play set out in full: a simplified division of life into the two stages of innocence and experience, the uncertainty of feeling with which one moves from one to another, a sense of how fragile our determinations are. We may well wish that Shakespeare had gone on to develop the themes and not left so much to Fletcher. But obviously Fletcher was working to Shakespeare's design (I hardly suppose it was Fletcher's in the first place).

In Act II, scene ii, the imprisoned Palamon and Arcite

talk about their predicament. The pleasures of their youth are ended, the pleasures of the future are closed to them:

> Here the graces of our youth must wither,
> Like a too timely spring; here age must find us,
> And which is heaviest, Palamon, unmarried.
> (II.ii.27–29)

Arcite expatiates (it is too feeble to quote) on the pleasures of marriage and having children. He is thinking conventionally of the two stages of life, one kind of happiness following another in due season. But as the kinsmen try to rouse themselves from their dejection, they realize that the one thing which they can keep while they are in prison, their friendship and brotherhood, is in fact something finer than what marriage would bring:

> Here being thus together
> We are an endless mine to one another;
> We're one another's wife, ever begetting
> New births of love . . .
> Were we at liberty,
> A wife might part us lawfully, or business.
> (II.ii.78–81; 88–89)

But almost at once they catch sight of Emilia, and, in wrangling over their "rights" to her love, their vaunted friendship and their vaunted superiority to the claims of women are alike shattered; the long and bitter rivalry begins.

Before Emilia walks in the garden, Arcite shows both a longing for marriage and an intenser clinging to a friendship which is above marriage. He is both the Theseus and the Emilia of the first act. But what are his divided sentiments worth? "Let us follow the becking of our chance"—even in prison. Once Emilia has walked beneath the window of their cell, there is no more basking in youthful friendship. They must take their future in the way in which chance and Venus insist upon it. It is a horrible enough future, because the Venus who debases them as they struggle with each other for Emilia is of course their own sexual nature.

It is interesting that Shakespeare and Fletcher, in handling the story, from the duel in the wood onwards, insist as Chaucer does not that whichever of the two cousins does *not* get Emily shall die. An extra incident is brought in (III.vi.273–82) in which Emilia is given her choice of the two lovers, and the one not chosen is to die. In the deciding tournament, the dramatists leave out the ban on slaughter which Chaucer's Theseus pronounces. Not only do they leave it out, but they put in an extra scene of preparation for the execution of the loser, Palamon. One reason for this emphasis is, no doubt, to increase the painfulness of Emilia's position. But it is also a very strong way of indicating that to gain the new love is to destroy the old; it is the development of the theme played quietly in the first act, on the "rivalry" between Pirithous and Hippolyta for Theseus' affection. When Arcite is the victor in the lists, he says:

> Emily,
> To buy you I have lost what's dearest to me,
> Save what is bought. (V.iii.111–13)

When Arcite has met with his fatal accident and Palamon is in turn received as husband, Palamon speaks to the dying man:

> O cousin,
> That we should things desire, which do cost us
> The loss of our desire! That naught could buy
> Dear love but loss of dear love. (V.iv.109–12)

Emilia's role in both the old tale and in the play is central to the author's exhibition of the pains of love. In Chaucer, it is managed mainly by silence: Emily's passiveness and aloofness add much to the sense of the absurdity of the strife of the two cousins, and to the whole comment on human helplessness. Her prayer to Diana is that she be left alone:

> Chaste goddesse, wel wostow that I
> Desire to been a maiden al my lif,
> Ne nevere wol I be no love ne wif. (2304–06)

There is too little in this figure of silence and withdrawal to make a character in a play; but up to the time of the tournament, her role is amplified rather than changed. Her reasons for wishing to remain a maiden are magnificently filled out in the Flavina scene and though she plays a more active part in the scene in which the cousins are discovered fighting in the wood, her answers are strictly neutral; she is moved by pity that these young men should miscarry, not by affection or any desire for a husband. But, from Act IV onwards, Chaucer's Emily is completely altered and, in Fletcher's hands, immensely cheapened. There is something missing in the play; we do not see her moving towards accepting her role as a wife; she is suddenly there, trying to make up her mind which one of the cousins she likes best. The design of the play has only temporarily disappeared. When Shakespeare resumes with Emilia in Act V, we can see what was meant to happen; to romance a little, that Emilia should move, listlessly and as in a dream, to abandon her old resolution and accept "the becking of her chance":

> This is my last
> Of vestal office: I'm bride-habited,
> But maiden-hearted: a husband I have 'pointed
> But do not know him; out of two I should
> Choose one, and pray for his success, but I
> Am guiltless of election. (V.i.149–54)

With the phrase, "I am guiltless of election," Emilia's indecision over the merits of Palamon and Arcite, of which so much is made, falls into place as a contrast with her relations with Flavina— "Lov'd for we did." If we take Clifford Leech's hint, and link her indecision with the willingness of the jailer's daughter to accept a pseudo-Palamon as a lover, we can see more sharply the distinction between the two stages of love: the first all impulse and spontaneity, the second a forced movement into a love so half-hearted that the object might be either of two cousins, a love so uncentered that a substitute will do as well as the real thing. The absurdity of the ending of the story—that Emilia should accept Arcite because he wins a fight, and then, when Arcite is killed, accept with equal readiness his cousin—is not "got round" by Shakespeare; it is the clinching of the case against Venus and the poverty of the relationships which she provides.

In this play, shared between two authors, the central idea is again and again approached from a different point; the idea is built up cumulatively by a series of comments and speeches which lie about the hub of the plot; the plot gets its true meaning by the reflected light of the surrounding meditations. We are given, clearly enough, a life in two stages: youth, in which the passion of spontaneous friendship is dominant, and the riper age in which there is a dominant sexual passion, leading to marriage where it can. The movement from one stage to the next, the unavoidable process of growth, is a movement away from innocence, away from joy. Theseus and Hippolyta apparently succeed in avoiding misery (are we meant to recall any of the tragic stories of love associated with the Theseus legend?), but the backward look to a fuller, richer youth is there for both; indeed, the lack of misery in Theseus and Hippolyta gives strength to a thesis of the loss of innocence which otherwise becomes too lurid.

The growth into experience I described as walking into the future as through a fog. Theseus goes forward boldly enough, but the postponement of the wedding by the three queens is an omen of the weakness of our powers. It is not our contriving that sends us steadily forward; we have to do what chance and circumstance and our own sexuality drives us to. The ingredients will differ. But, in the range between Emilia, with hardly any sexuality, and the jailer's daughter, all sexuality, there is not much free choice evident; the example of Palamon and Arcite is obviously meant to be the most striking. The irony of the way in which their course is shaped by chance and coincidence is harped on more by Chaucer than by Shakespeare, but it is in *The Two Noble Kinsmen*; what is most impressive is that every step, whether forced or free, in the course of that love which is the strongest thing in their lives, further disrupts the friendship which they know to be the finest thing in their lives. They are like men enchanted, gladly accepting what they are forced to do, yet knowing it to be ruin. The only arbitrator is "th' event."

If I see Shakespeare looking dim-eyed at innocence and seeing salvation disappear with puberty, I have to ask what relevance this "attack" on maturer life and love has to the portrayal of innocence in the earlier romances. There, sexual love may seem the natural and beautiful fulfillment of an otherwise immature innocence, particularly in Perdita and Miranda. But the idea of the deforming power of sexuality does exist in the romances; it is there in *Pericles,* when the youthful Pericles meets Antiochus' daughter and when Marina is in the brothel. It is there in *The Winter's Tale*; Clifford Leech most aptly cites (*op. cit.,* p. 149) Polixenes' recollection of his idyllic youth in friendship with Leontes:

> We were as twinn'd lambs that did frisk i' the sun,
> And bleat the one at the other: what we changed
> Was innocence for innocence; we knew not
> The doctrine of ill-doing, nor dream'd
> That any did. Had we pursued that life,
> And our weak spirits ne'er been higher rear'd
> With stronger blood, we should have answer'd heaven
> Boldly "not guilty"; the imposition clear'd,
> Hereditary ours. (I.ii.67–75)

There is no holding Shakespeare to one set of ideas; always, a new play releases a new evaluation; if we sense inconsistency it is generally because our vision is too myopic; we cannot hold such a range of focus as Shakespeare could. *The Two Noble Kinsmen* seems to me to give the most cynical assessment of the progress of life since the writing of *Troilus and Cressida.* It is a pity that Shakespeare did not write the whole of the play, but there is real intellectual substance in the work even as it is. Perhaps the flavor is unpalatable, still not the sort of thing one wants to associate Shakespeare with. Certainly, the vision is rather sweeping and careless of detail, but I believe it is Shakespearian.

Suggested References

The number of possible references is vast and grows alarmingly. (The *Shakespeare Quarterly* devotes a substantial part of one issue each year to a list of the previous year's work, and *Shakespeare Survey*—an annual publication—includes a substantial review of recent scholarship, as well as an occasional essay surveying a few decades of scholarship on a chosen topic.) Though no works are indispensable, those listed below have been found helpful.

1. Shakespeare's Times

Byrne, M. St. Clare. *Elizabethan Life in Town and Country*. Rev. ed. New York: Barnes & Noble, Inc., 1961. Chapters on manners, beliefs, education, etc., with illustrations.

Craig, Hardin. *The Enchanted Glass: the Elizabethan Mind in Literature*. New York and London: Oxford University Press, 1936. The Elizabethan intellectual climate.

Nicoll, Allardyce (ed.). *The Elizabethans*. London: Cambridge University Press, 1957. An anthology of Elizabethan writings, especially valuable for its illustrations from paintings, title pages, etc.

Shakespeare's England. 2 vols. Oxford: The Clarendon Press, 1916. A large collection of scholarly essays on a wide variety of topics (e.g., astrology, costume, gardening, horsemanship), with special attention to Shakespeare's references to these topics.

Tillyard, E. M. W. *The Elizabethan World Picture*. London: Chatto & Windus, 1943; New York: The Macmillan Company, 1944. A brief account of some Elizabethan ideas of the universe.

Wilson, John Dover (ed.). *Life in Shakespeare's England.* 2nd ed. New York: The Macmillan Company, 1913. An anthology of Elizabethan writings on the countryside, superstition, education, the court, etc.

2. Shakespeare

Bentley, Gerald E. *Shakespeare: A Biographical Handbook.* New Haven, Conn.: Yale University Press, 1961. The facts about Shakespeare, with virtually no conjecture intermingled.

Bradby, Anne (ed.). *Shakespeare Criticism, 1919–1935.* London: Oxford University Press, 1936. A small anthology of excellent essays on the plays.

Bush, Geoffrey Douglas. *Shakespeare and the Natural Condition.* Cambridge, Mass.: Harvard University Press; London: Oxford University Press, 1956. A short, sensitive account of Shakespeare's view of "Nature," touching most of the works.

Chambers, E. K. *William Shakespeare: A Study of Facts and Problems.* 2 vols. London: Oxford University Press, 1930. An invaluable, detailed reference work; not for the casual reader.

Chute, Marchette. *Shakespeare of London.* New York: E. P. Dutton & Co., Inc., 1949. A readable biography fused with portraits of Stratford and London life.

Clemen, Wolfgang H. *The Development of Shakespeare's Imagery.* Cambridge, Mass.: Harvard University Press, 1951. (Originally published in German, 1936.) A temperate account of a subject often abused.

Craig, Hardin. *An Interpretation of Shakespeare.* Columbia, Missouri: Lucas Brothers, 1948. A scholar's book designed for the layman. Comments on all the works.

Dean, Leonard F. (ed.). *Shakespeare: Modern Essays in Criticism.* New York: Oxford University Press, 1957. Mostly mid-twentieth-century critical studies, covering Shakespeare's artistry.

Granville-Barker, Harley. *Prefaces to Shakespeare.* 2 vols. Princeton, N.J.: Princeton University Press, 1946–47. Essays on ten plays by a scholarly man of the theater.

Harbage, Alfred. *As They Liked It*. New York: The Macmillan Company, 1947. A sensitive, long essay on Shakespeare, morality, and the audience's expectations.

Ridler, Anne Bradby (ed.). *Shakespeare Criticism, 1935–1960*. New York and London: Oxford University Press, 1963. An excellent continuation of the anthology edited earlier by Miss Bradby (see above).

Smith, D. Nichol (ed.). *Shakespeare Criticism*. New York: Oxford University Press, 1916. A selection of criticism from 1623 to 1840, ranging from Ben Jonson to Thomas Carlyle.

Spencer, Theodore. *Shakespeare and the Nature of Man*. New York: The Macmillan Company, 1942. Shakespeare's plays in relation to Elizabethan thought.

Stoll, Elmer Edgar. *Shakespeare and Other Masters*. Cambridge, Mass.: Harvard University Press; London: Oxford University Press, 1940. Essays on tragedy, comedy, and aspects of dramaturgy, with special reference to some of Shakespeare's plays.

Traversi, D. A. *An Approach to Shakespeare*. Rev. ed. New York: Doubleday & Co., Inc., 1956. An analysis of the plays, beginning with words, images, and themes, rather than with characters.

Van Doren, Mark. *Shakespeare*. New York: Henry Holt & Company, Inc., 1939. Brief, perceptive readings of all of the plays.

Whitaker, Virgil K. *Shakespeare's Use of Learning*. San Marino, Calif.: Huntington Library, 1953. A study of the relation of Shakespeare's reading to his development as a dramatist.

3. Shakespeare's Theater

Adams, John Cranford. *The Globe Playhouse*. Rev. ed. New York: Barnes & Noble, Inc., 1961. A detailed conjecture about the physical characteristics of the theater Shakespeare often wrote for.

Beckerman, Bernard. *Shakespeare at the Globe, 1599–1609*. New York: The Macmillan Company, 1962. On the playhouse and on Elizabethan dramaturgy, acting, and staging.

Chambers, E. K. *The Elizabethan Stage.* 4 vols. New York: Oxford University Press, 1923. Reprinted with corrections, 1945. An invaluable reference work on theaters, theatrical companies, and staging at court.

Harbage, Alfred. *Shakespeare's Audience.* New York: Columbia University Press; London: Oxford University Press, 1941. A study of the size and nature of the theatrical public.

Hodges, C. Walter. *The Globe Restored.* London: Ernest Benn, Ltd., 1953; New York: Coward-McCann, Inc., 1954. A well-illustrated and readable attempt to reconstruct the Globe Theatre.

Kernodle, George R. *From Art to Theatre: Form and Convention in the Renaissance.* Chicago: University of Chicago Press, 1944. Pioneering and stimulating work on the symbolic and cultural meanings of theater construction.

Nagler, A. M. *Shakespeare's Stage.* Tr. by Ralph Manheim. New Haven, Conn.: Yale University Press, 1958. An excellent brief introduction to the physical aspect of the playhouse.

Smith, Irwin. *Shakespeare's Globe Playhouse.* New York: Charles Scribner's Sons, 1957. Chiefly indebted to J. C. Adams' controversial book, with additional material and scale drawings for model-builders.

Venezky, Alice S. *Pageantry on the Shakespearean Stage.* New York: Twayne Publishers, Inc., 1951. An examination of spectacle in Elizabethan drama.

4. Miscellaneous Reference Works

Abbott, E. A. *A Shakespearean Grammar.* New edition. New York: The Macmillan Company, 1877. An examination of differences between Elizabethan and modern grammar.

Bartlett, John. *A New and Complete Concordance . . . to . . . Shakespeare.* New York: The Macmillan Company, 1894. An index to most of Shakespeare's words.

Berman, Ronald. *A Reader's Guide to Shakespeare's Plays*. Chicago: Scott, Foresman and Company, 1965. A short bibliography of the chief articles and books on each play.

Bullough, Geoffrey. *Narrative and Dramatic Sources of Shakespeare*. 5 vols. Vols. 6 and 7 in preparation. New York: Columbia University Press; London: Routledge & Kegan Paul, Ltd., 1957–. A collection of many of the books Shakespeare drew upon.

Greg, W. W. *The Shakespeare First Folio*. New York and London: Oxford University Press, 1955. A detailed yet readable history of the first collection (1623) of Shakespeare's plays.

Kökeritz, Helge. *Shakespeare's Names*. New Haven, Conn.: Yale University Press, 1959; London: Oxford University Press, 1960. A guide to the pronunciation of some 1,800 names appearing in Shakespeare.

———. *Shakespeare's Pronunciation*. New Haven, Conn.: Yale University Press; London: Oxford University Press, 1953. Contains much information about puns and rhymes.

Linthicum, Marie C. *Costume in the Drama of Shakespeare and His Contemporaries*. New York and London: Oxford University Press, 1936. On the fabrics and dress of the age, and references to them in the plays.

Muir, Kenneth. *Shakespeare's Sources*. London: Methuen & Co., Ltd., 1957. Vol. 2 in preparation. The first volume, on the comedies and tragedies, attempts to ascertain what books were Shakespeare's sources, and what use he made of them.

Onions, C. T. *A Shakespeare Glossary*. London: Oxford University Press, 1911; 2nd ed., rev., with enlarged addenda, 1953. Definitions of words (or senses of words) now obsolete.

Partridge, Eric. *Shakespeare's Bawdy*. Rev. ed. New York: E. P. Dutton & Co., Inc.; London: Routledge & Kegan Paul, Ltd., 1955. A glossary of bawdy words and phrases.

Shakespeare Quarterly. See headnote to Suggested References.

Shakespeare Survey. See headnote to Suggested References.

Smith, Gordon Ross. *A Classified Shakespeare Bibliography 1936–1958*. University Park, Pa.: Pennsylvania State University Press, 1963. A list of some 20,000 items on Shakespeare.

5. *The Two Noble Kinsmen*

Agate, James. *Brief Chronicles, a Survey of the Plays of Shakespeare and the Elizabethans in Actual Performance*. London: Jonathan Cape, 1943. [Contains a review of the 1928 Old Vic performance, pp. 153–56.]

Bertram, Paul. "The Date of *The Two Noble Kinsmen*," *Shakespeare Quarterly*, XII (Winter 1961), 21–32. [Reprinted in the next item.]

———. *Shakespeare and The Two Noble Kinsmen*. New Brunswick: Rutgers University Press, 1965.

Hart, Alfred. "Shakespeare and the Vocabulary of *The Two Noble Kinsmen*," *The Review of English Studies*, X (July 1934), 274–87. [Reprinted in Alfred Hart, *Shakespeare and the Homilies*. Melbourne: Melbourne University Press, 1935.]

Kermode, Frank. *William Shakespeare: The Final Plays*. (Writers and their Work, No. 155.) London: Longmans Green and Co., 1963. [Reprinted in Bonamy Dobrée (ed.), *Shakespeare: The Writer and his Work*. London: Longmans, 1964.]

Leech, Clifford. *The John Fletcher Plays*. London: Chatto & Windus; Cambridge, Mass.: Harvard University Press, 1962. [Contains a chapter on "Fletcher and Shakespeare."]

Littledale, Harold (ed.). *The Two Noble Kinsmen*. (The New Shakspere Society.) London: N. Trübner and Co., 1876–85.

Mincoff, Marco. "The Authorship of *The Two Noble Kinsmen*," *English Studies*, XXXIII (1952), 97–115.

Muir, Kenneth. *Shakespeare as Collaborator*. London: Methuen and Co., 1960. [Contains two chapters on *The Two Noble Kinsmen.*]

Spalding, W. *A Letter on Shakspere's Authorship of The Two Noble Kinsmen.* Edinburgh, 1838. [Reprinted in *Transactions of the New Shakspere Society,* 1876.]

Waller, Frederick O. "Printer's Copy for *The Two Noble Kinsmen,*" *Studies in Bibliography,* XI (1958), 61–84.

LOVE'S LABOR'S LOST. EDITED BY JOHN ARTHOS (#CD306)

MACBETH. EDITED BY SYLVAN BARNET (#CD161)

MEASURE FOR MEASURE. EDITED BY S. NAGARAJAN (#CD233)

THE MERCHANT OF VENICE. EDITED BY KENNETH O. MYRICK (#CD277)

THE MERRY WIVES OF WINDSOR. EDITED BY WILLIAM GREEN (#CD318)

A MIDSUMMER NIGHT'S DREAM. EDITED BY WOLFGANG CLEMEN (#CD171)

MUCH ADO ABOUT NOTHING. EDITED BY DAVID L. STEVENSON (#CD173)

OTHELLO. EDITED BY ALVIN KERNAN (#CD162)

PERICLES. EDITED BY ERNEST SCHANZER (#CD294)

RICHARD II. EDITED BY KENNETH MUIR (#CD163)

RICHARD III. EDITED BY MARK ECCLES (#CD175)

ROMEO AND JULIET. EDITED BY JOSEPH BRYANT (#CD270)

THE TAMING OF THE SHREW. EDITED BY ROBERT HEILMAN (#CD331¢

THE TEMPEST. EDITED BY ROBERT LANGBAUM (#CD174)